RAVE REVIEWS FOR VIRGINIA FARMER!

SPENCEWORTH BRIDE

"Virginia Farmer shatters the barriers of time with warmth, wit and tenderness to prove love really does conquer all. *Spenceworth Bride* is a treasure!"

—Award-winning author Deb Stover

SIXPENCE BRIDE

"A delightful romp of a book! Farmer fully exploits her time-travel theme to maximize the fun."

—*The Romance Reader*

"Ms. Farmer's characters make this an enjoyable read."

—*Romantic Times*

TENDING TO AN INJURY

Nelwina returned the kettle to the fire and sat down beside Adam. Dampening the towel, she took his injured hand in hers and dabbed at the blood pooling in his palm.

He sat mute under her ministrations, admiring the smoothness of her skin, the dark fan of lashes against her cheeks as she wiped his cut. His gaze clamped on the tip of her tongue as it made a circuitous route, moistening her lips. He closed his eyes, swallowing a groan as his body reacted to her.

"You're not going to faint, are you?"

Adam opened his eyes at the sound of Nelwina's concerned voice and found himself leaning toward her. His gaze met hers and he leaned closer, drawn by the warmth in her eyes. He brought his right hand up and palmed her cheek. Her skin was warm and she stilled under his touch.

"No, I'm not goint to faint, Nelwina." He ran his thumb over her moist lips and his nerve endings hummed. "But I am going to kiss you."

Spenceworth
BRIDE

Virginia Farmer

LOVE SPELL NEW YORK CITY

LOVE SPELL®

September 2003

Published by

Dorchester Publishing Co., Inc.
200 Madison Avenue
New York, NY 10016

ISBN 0-505-52560-7

The name "Love Spell" and its logo are trademarks of Dorchester Publishing Co., Inc.

Printed in the United States of America.

Visit us on the web at www.dorchesterpub.com.

For my critique partners, Leah Marie Brown and Cindy Homberger. You kept me sane, motivated, inspired, on task and grounded. Thank you for the laughter, the shopping, the crazy cards, the chocolates, the emails, the phone calls and the chats. But mostly, thank you for the deep, abiding friendship we share. I'm a better person and writer because of you both.

Spenceworth
BRIDE

Prologue

England, 1799

"You puzzle-headed fool!" Nelwina Ham shouted as she tripped along behind the cart, her wrists bound and tied to the back of the wagon. "You think to *sell* me?"

"Exactly," Haslett, her husband, nodded. " 'Twas a stroke of genius, wasn't it? I can't be spending every waking minute chasing ye down and dragging ye home again." He glanced over his shoulder. "And with ye taking to thievery—well, a man can't very well hold his head up in the tavern when his wife steals money from him, now can he?"

"I've never stolen a thing in my life. The money was mine, Haslett." She tugged at the rope in frustration. " 'Twas honestly earned."

"Hah. Then where's the sixpence ye pocketed from the sale of the pig?" He snapped the reins and the nag ambled along, its pace never changing.

"You expected three shillings." Nelwina blinked

1

back tears. "And 'tis exactly what you received." She refused to feel guilty over the extra sixpence she'd been paid. She'd earned it caring for the pig *and* Haslett. "How was I to know Mistress Dray wouldn't haggle over the price?"

She'd planned and saved for the day she could leave him. She was sick unto death of doing the work of two. Haslett couldn't be bothered with physical labor, so it was left to her to see that food found its way to their table. And her reward for these efforts was a slovenly husband who spent his days and coin at the tavern, taking time to mete out frequent beatings.

As a young girl, Nelwina had imagined having a husband as devoted and loyal as the old earl of Spenceworth. He always smelled of soap and mint and his deep jovial voice had made her feel welcome, even when he wasn't speaking to her. He had treated her kindly—and she but the daughter of the manor seamstress and hardly worth his notice.

She gazed at the back of Haslett's greasy head, pushing her memories aside.

She'd been so close to freedom. Had Farmer Dray not met her husband at the tavern and mentioned the price of the pig, she would be free of Haslett now.

But he had caught her on the road and taken her coins. Tears of frustration burned her eyes. She'd been so very close.

"Ye've become more trouble than ye're worth. Let another 'un take ye off my hands."

"And who'll fetch and carry for you when I'm

2

gone?" Nelwina's question was lost in the rattle of the cart.

She stumbled. By now, her dull yellow skirt was streaked with dirt. The length of twine holding her hair was gone, allowing her long blond locks to fall over her shoulders.

"Well, certainly I can do better than you." Couldn't she? Or could she do worse?

But how much worse could it be? Haslett had taken to using a strap on her each time he thought she'd taken a misstep. Though of late, he'd spent more time drinking and less time at home, so the beatings had become fewer.

"Hah. Let's just hope there's enough men from Ramsgil and beyond who have no knowledge of yer ways."

"And who in Ramsgil has such knowledge?" She'd been to Ramsgil all of three times in the last five years. She doubted anyone would even recognize her. The women she sewed for seldom went to town and never came around when Haslett was home.

Haslett pulled the cart to a halt at the side of the tavern in Ramsgil.

"You've the money, Haslett." Nelwina grasped the back of the cart, her shoulders slumped as she caught her breath. "Don't humiliate us both with this sale. We don't suit. Can't you simply let me be?"

Haslett climbed off the cart and came to stand beside her.

"We don't suit, do we?" He mimicked her. "Ye had no problem five years ago when ye needed me. Do ye think ye don't need me now?" He glared at her.

" 'Twas a mistake on my part to marry a nobleman's bastard." He gave a negligent shrug. "But what's done is done."

"A mistake?" Nelwina felt her eyes round in shock and she straightened her shoulders. " 'Twas that very happenstance that brought you to our door. The money my grandfather paid my mother." Haslett's nostrils flared in anger, but Nelwina ignored him. "You thought you'd come upon the easy life when you found out." Her laughter sounded harsh even to her ear.

"What a disappointment to find out that but a month after my mother died, my grandfather passed on as well. And the money you expected to get your hands on disappeared." Nelwina shook her head. "You're a sorry excuse for a man, Haslett."

"Aye, well ye might think so, but look ye there." He pointed to a handbill posted to the wall.

To be sold, on the morrow at market, my wife, Nelwina Ham. She is stout of body, standing firm on her posterns. She is strong and can sow and reap. She stitches a fine seam and can read and do sums. She is headstrong, but, if managed properly, will meekly follow any man's lead.

Nelwina gasped. Did Haslett actually understand the words printed on the page? Surely no man would want a wife of that description. And what was that about her posterns?

She raised her gaze to Haslett. He flashed her a

4

confident grin and she groaned. The fool would humiliate the both of them.

He untied the rope from the cart. "A right fine job we did, eh?" He nodded toward the handbill. "Aye, today will see me free of ye and yer high and mighty ways, and with a little coin in my pocket for my trouble."

Nelwina simply stared at him, picturing the man who'd come to her mother's door more than five years ago. Oh, his hair had been thinning even then, but he hadn't the paunch that now stretched his shirt. And his teeth had since blackened with decay. Mayhap he hadn't bathed as often as she, but certainly he hadn't smelled of slop jars as he did now. Nay, he wasn't the man he was when first they met.

"And I'll be free of your slovenly ways." Well, mayhap she'd be that lucky, but the way things were working out, she could be going from the kettle to the fire.

Haslett gave the rope a jerk, hauling Nelwina behind him to the center of the market of Ramsgil. She followed along, clumps of tamped-down weeds catching at her feet, making it difficult to keep herself from falling as she dodged the dogs and children running about.

Ramsgil was a bustling village. The early morning sunshine glinted off the windows of the prosperous shops. Pink and yellow flowers filled the window boxes of some of the buildings. Carts piled with an assortment of goods lined the perimeter of the green. Nelwina's stomach grumbled as the smell of meat pies wafted to her on the breeze. Her gaze roamed the carts and she longed to wander around, to test the softness of the material one vendor displayed or check the quality of the pots of another. And had she the money, she would have purchased one of those pies.

Despite the loveliness of the village, Nelwina muttered, "Lord, I wish I was anywhere but here, with anyone but Haslett." She bumped into an old woman wearing a brightly colored skirt and a scarf tied around her head.

"Wishes be powerful things. A heart's desire isn't always as easy as ye think." The woman shook her head. "Careful what ye wish fer, girl. Things are goin' to change, and ye'll wonder if ye've gone from bad to worse." She cackled at Nelwina's surprise. "Aye, things are goin' to change. Best to accept 'em." The multitude of bracelets circling her wrist jangled as she waved and wandered off.

"Crazy old Gypsy." A shiver of apprehension traveled down Nelwina's spine nonetheless.

Dismissing the woman's rantings, Nelwina gazed at a group of women standing together laughing and talking, their children running around them. The women met her gaze and she read pity from some and condemnation from others. The loneliness and isolation of the past five years swept over her and she choked back the moan rising in her throat.

The late-morning sun beat down on her head as Haslett removed the rope from her wrists and pushed her toward the block. She looked down at her scuffed brown boots, her cheeks heated in embarrassment. Rebellion bubbled within her.

Humiliated she may be, but she'd show it to no

one. She squared her shoulders and brought her gaze up. Up past the gawking stares of the crowd on the green. Up past the rooftops of the buildings in town. Up to the bright blue sky and the silver-white sun burning down. She stared at the sun, blocking out the sounds around her. One wish beat a tattoo in her mind.

Take me away, far away from all of this.

Haslett pushed her down to sit on the block and she glanced to the side. Spots danced before her eyes, and the moment she made contact with the wood, a tingling raced through her body, setting her nerves on edge. And then a wave of dizziness and nausea swept over her.

Nelwina closed her eyes, as much to clear the spots as to control the sick feeling in her stomach. Weakness washed over her and a ringing began in her head.

Chapter One

Ramsgil, England, present day

"So who's the lucky lady? Where's my *wife?*" Adam Warrick glanced to the front of the tour bus where a balding, overweight American man stood, waving his brochure.

"Congratulations, Mr. Owens." The tour guide placed a hand on Mr. Owens's arm and turned to the rest of the passengers. "Please, ladies, check your brochures. One of you will find the pink star."

Adam scanned the occupants. The brochure had touted the re-enactment of an eighteenth-century wife sale as the only one of its kind. He'd learned that several tour groups stopped in Ramsgil to watch the mock sale, and he'd joined out of curiosity.

It was a good idea. And to involve the tourists in it was a stroke of genius. No two re-enactments would ever be the same. It wouldn't appear staged and common. Yes, it was a good idea. He just hoped the tourist trade would support another attraction—Spenceworth.

Inheriting the title and lands of Spenceworth had never been part of his plans. After gaining his degree in architecture, Adam had taken a job in the United States. It was on one of his frequent trips home to visit his mother that his father's older brother had died.

Spenceworth and the earldom had been passed to Adam, the last living male, along with the financial difficulties. It didn't help that he'd had to leave his job in Chicago in order to administer the estate. Now the only income he had was from the investments tied to the manor. Until he could get his fledgling architecture firm established, there had to be a way to make the manor support itself.

The brunette sitting across and one row in front of him drew his attention as she opened her brochure. Sunlight reflected off the pink foil star. She glanced up at Mr. Owens and Adam thought he heard her groan.

He grinned. Glancing from her to Mr. Owens, Adam didn't blame her.

He'd noticed her waiting with the other tourists for the tour bus. She was without a travel mate, but didn't seem to mind. She smiled as she chatted with two blue-haired, elderly women. Her soft Southern accent floated to him, gifting him with her name: Jocelyn Tanner.

As she moved off, one of the ladies commented, "I can't imagine any man abandoning such a sweet girl."

"Well, what can you expect from a man with two first names?"

"Silly, James is his last name. Philip is his first."

Abandoned. Adam shrugged. She seemed like a nice person. She was definitely pleasant to look at; tall, long-legged and trim. She took care of herself, from her tidy white shoes to the satiny shine of her fingernails. Her hair shone with warm golden highlights and Adam wondered if it would be warm to the touch. He entertained the idea for a moment. She was certainly attractive. I've got enough on my plate; I shouldn't even entertain a romantic relationship now, he reminded himself. He wasn't here to socialize.

Jocelyn bent down, and Adam watched as she dropped her brochure on the floor and shoved it beneath her seat with her foot. He was surprised at the disappointment he felt at her actions. Everyone on the bus knew before boarding that a few of them would be called upon to participate in the re-enactment. If she had a problem with it, she should have chosen a different tour.

He reached down and retrieved the paper.

"I believe you dropped this." Adam handed the brochure to her, smiling at her frown.

"Thank you." The insincerity of her words made him chuckle.

"My pleasure." He sat back in his seat as the tour guide directed the participants to the company office to pick up their costumes.

Adam was the last one off the bus, save Jocelyn, who'd sunk so low in her seat he wondered if she'd fall to the floor.

The tour guide stopped him. "Sir, may I take a look at your brochure?"

"Excuse me?" Adam glanced at the young guide, surprised, but gave her his brochure.

She opened it and gave him a bright smile. "You've drawn the lot to play the man who buys Miss Tanner in the re-enactment."

Adam opened his mouth to object and then snapped it shut. He'd just been berating Miss Tanner for trying to back out and here he was, thinking of doing the exact same thing.

The guide handed his brochure back to him and, touching his shoulder, said, "You'll find your costume at the tour office. If you wouldn't mind heading over there straightaway, we try to keep the identity of this part a secret from the others. Lends more authenticity to the sale, you see."

Adam nodded and followed her directions to the office, only too aware of what Jocelyn Tanner must be feeling about now. The bell tinkled when he entered, and a middle-aged woman looked up.

"Are you the buyer or the seller?" She looked him up and down over the narrow glasses resting near the end of her nose.

"The buyer."

"Hmm, lucky lady," she murmured, giving Adam another once-over. His cheeks heated.

Why the bloody hell was he blushing? He was thirty-three years old, well past such an adolescent reaction to a flirty woman.

"Excellent. You'll look smashing in the costume." She wiggled her brows and grinned. "There're several

11

different sizes in there." She pointed to a door across the hall.

"But—"

She held up a hand. "Rest assured. I make certain that the clothing is clean and the shoes disinfected." She gave him a stern look. "I'd say the brown coat and buff breeches would suit your coloring and are about the right size."

Adam hesitated.

"Go." She flicked her wrist. "We don't want the lady to see you and ruin the surprise."

A few minutes later, Adam shrugged on the coat that completed his eighteenth-century costume and looked into the mirror.

"Bloody uncomfortable clothing my forefathers wore," he mumbled to his reflection, loosening the cravat at his throat and adjusting the dark brown coat again. The buff-colored trousers were stuffed into high black boots that were surprisingly comfortable.

He plopped the tricorn hat on his head and nearly laughed aloud. He looked positively silly. With one last glance in the mirror, he left the dressing room.

"I knew the brown would suit," the woman with the glasses commented as Adam walked toward the front door of the office. He gave her a grim smile.

"Now, be sure to mingle with the others in costume. You'll blend in with them and the surprise will be genuine." She turned back to her desk. "Oh, sir, here's the coin you'll use to purchase your bride."

He retraced his steps, taking the gold coin from her hand.

"The bid is a pound. That'll ensure that you are the highest bidder." She smiled up at him.

Adam nodded and he left. Bloody pain, he thought grumpily, wishing he hadn't been so condemning of Miss Tanner's actions.

Maybe he should find her and together they could escape to Spenceworth. He grinned as he pictured them sneaking off to the manor, sharing an intimate meal and then—Adam blew out a breath of air and shook his head. That wasn't why he was here, he reminded himself again.

Crossing the street, he mixed with the crowd of spectators and the costumed locals. He milled around, searching for the best spot to view the re-enactment without being seen by Jocelyn. During the short walk to the green, he'd resigned himself to his fate and joined in the festive atmosphere, determined to give it his best effort.

Perhaps he and Jocelyn could have lunch together after the sale, a kind of reward for their suffering.

He smiled, recognizing his excuse as just that. He found her attractive and could now understand her desire to avoid the wife sale. He felt the thread of a bond forming between them, their shared experience its source.

A tendril of guilt snaked into his conscience. He was here on business, not romance.

Mentally putting the wife sale aside, he glanced around and noted a second tour bus pulling in, some twenty passengers disembarking. The tourists were greeted by a town that looked much like it must have two hundred years ago, from the cobblestone streets to the immaculate gardens, and old-fashioned carts lining the green.

The shops did a brisk business and the vendors on the green sold a nice variety of trinkets. The tourist trade was thriving; it was this trade he hoped to draw to Spenceworth.

"Have you ever seen so many flowers?" a woman said to her companion as they passed by Adam. "It seems like everyone here is obsessed with gardening."

Adam smiled. Yes, and at the moment, Adam was one of them. Renovating Spenceworth's grounds and offering garden tours was the only way he'd found to sidestep his uncle's will and perhaps make the manor less of a financial burden.

"Ah, so you're the lucky bloke who gets to buy the lady?"

Adam turned his back to the green and nodded to the older man. "Yes. Never done this sort of thing before."

"Aye, well, we do appreciate the participation." The man raised his eyebrows. "You're English, then?"

"Yes."

"Ah." The man nodded. "Niles Jefferson." He extended his hand.

Adam shook the gentleman's hand. "Adam Warrick."

The man squinted up at him. "You related to the Warricks of Spenceworth?"

"Yes, I am."

Jefferson rubbed his chin. "The heir, then." Adam

nodded. "My condolences on the death of your uncle."

"Thank you."

"Welcome home, my lord." And then he disappeared into the crowd.

"Oh dear, do you suppose she's sick?"

Adam glanced at the woman beside him.

"She doesn't look too well, does she?" The man beside her frowned.

Turning around, Adam followed their gazes to the block at the center of the green and almost didn't recognize Miss Tanner. She sat on the block, her short brown hair hidden by a long blond wig. Her face paled and she closed her eyes, bringing her hand up to her forehead. She swayed and Adam took a step forward to help her.

Mr. Owens appeared beside her and gave her hand a brief pat before stepping up on the block, pulling her with him. Owens took his place in the middle, crowding Jocelyn to one side. The block wobbled as she stepped up, but she kept her eyes closed.

Adam glanced over her costume and frowned. The dull yellow skirt of her gown barely reached her ankles, exposing the sturdy brown boots on her feet. His gaze traveled up to the vest-like garment she wore. Instead of fitting tightly, it hung loose about her trim frame. She looked better in modern clothes, he decided. He glanced at her pale face, and worry edged in.

Should he try to stop this? She didn't look well at all. Did she have some sort of problem standing before people? Was that why she had been so hesitant to play her part? And he'd practically forced her to do this. He pinched the bridge of his nose as guilt crowded the worry in his mind.

As Adam stood in indecision, Mr. Owens began the sale in an almost comical imitation of an English accent.

"Ye see before ye a nice little lady. Don't know why I have to sell her, but I do." Mr. Owens grinned at the crowd. "So, what do I hear as an opening bid?"

Nelwina opened her eyes and gazed around, frowning in confusion.

"I'll give ye a penny fer her," a man in the crowd in front of her shouted.

She glanced at the bidder, and her cheeks heated in humiliation.

"A penny? Hell, that's an insult to the little lady here." She looked down at the hand gripping her shoulder and then to the man beside her.

"Who are you?" Nelwina shrugged off his arm. "Where's Haslett?" She glanced around. " 'Tis just like him to hie himself off to the tavern and leave me to suffer the humiliation alone. So he trusted you to take care of the matter, did he?" She slapped her hands over her mouth, shock widening her eyes.

What was wrong with her voice?

The stranger beside her stepped away, nearly falling off the block. "Ah ... mm, well, ye see, he ..." Nelwina leaned back to avoid his flailing arms as he regained his balance. The block beneath her feet shifted and she inched away from the edge. "He had

16

some business to attend to and left me in charge." He gave Nelwina a crooked smile.

Why does the man act like we've met? she wondered.

"So, getting a commission on the sale, are ye? No wonder ye're going fer a higher price," a man shouted from the audience.

"I'll give ye a shilling."

"And what will yer missus say when ye bring home another wife, eh Morgan?" Laughter rumbled through the crowd. Nelwina looked at the people around the block, grateful the women from earlier weren't among them.

But no one looked familiar. She frowned. Nothing seemed right. She glanced beyond the strangers, wondering what was wrong.

"A shilling and two pence." The young male voice cracked and the audience roared. Nelwina brought her gaze down and saw the youth blush scarlet.

She turned on the boy, her hands on her hips. "And where's your mother, young sir? You've no business here." She shooed him away. "Now be gone."

She put her hand to her throat. 'Twas not sore, so why then was her voice so soft?

"Are ye taking my bid of a shilling?" the second bidder shouted.

"Do I hear two shillings?" The man beside her laughed as if he found great humor in her situation. "Come on, gentlemen, she's a fine looking filly." Nelwina shot him a scathing glare.

"Two shillings."

She turned that glare on the new bidder. "I sold a

17

swine for three and a half shillings just yesterday. 'Tis as insulting as a penny." She pressed her lips together, still confused about the voice, but if she must be sold, at least she could be valued above a pig.

"I have two shillings. Do I hear three?"

"No?" He looked over the crowd. "Going once." He paused. "Going twice."

Adam recalled himself and the part he was to play.

"One pound," he called out. Both Mr. Owens and Jocelyn searched the crowd for him. The audience parted and Adam stepped forward. Mr. Owens grinned while Jocelyn simply gaped at him as if she'd never seen him before.

"Sold." Mr. Owens laughed, giving Adam a broad wink.

Adam took the money from his pocket and flipped it to Mr. Owens. The coin flew high into the air and Owens made a jump for it, snatching it. Coming down, the block shifted and his forearm crashed into Jocelyn's shoulder. She toppled from the block and with a sickening thump, her head hit the wood and her body went still.

Adam rushed forward. Kneeling down, he gathered her limp form in his arms. Brushing the blond strands of her wig away, he found a large lump on her forehead.

"Oh, dear." The words came out in a gasp as the tour guide tried to catch her breath. "Is she badly hurt?"

Adam looked up. "I don't know. Is there a doctor nearby?"

18

"Dr. Seabrook is at a symposium in London." Niles Jefferson appeared beside the guide, a concerned frown wrinkling his brow. "There's a first-aid office over there across the square." He indicated the direction with a nod of his head. "But I can't vouch for the attendant. Never seen her here before."

"Can you manage to get Miss Tanner there? Or should I have a stretcher brought?" The guide touched Adam's shoulder, her eyes huge in her pale face.

"No, I'll take her." He shifted the unconscious woman's weight and, standing up, he followed the guide.

He never should have tossed that coin. What had he been thinking? The block wasn't that stable or large, and Mr. Owens took up most of it.

Stupid move, Adam old boy. It was his fault she was even up there. She hadn't wanted to participate, but he'd pretty much forced the matter.

He stepped into the confines of the office and placed his burden on a cot.

"What happened?"

Adam looked up as an elderly woman in a white jacket stepped to the cot. Her wiry gray hair was tucked into an untidy bun at the nape of her wrinkled neck. Adam met her frown.

"She fell off the block on the green and hit her head."

The attendant placed a wrinkled hand on Jocelyn's brow, a wealth of bangle bracelets jingling with the action. "She's unconscious."

Adam rolled his eyes. Bright woman, he thought, unease coupling with his concern.

She glanced at Adam. "But don't you worry. Hilda knows how to care for her."

The young guide spoke from the doorway. "Will she be okay?" Adam noticed the poor girl's hand shaking as she gripped her clipboard.

"Aye, she'll be fine." Hilda toddled over to a basin, wrung out a cloth, and handed it to Adam. "Put that on the lump, there."

Adam gently placed the cloth on Jocelyn's forehead, his guilt doubling when he noticed the blue bruise already forming on her pale skin.

"How long before she comes around?" The guide's voice quivered.

"Could be a few minutes or an hour." Hilda shrugged. "Hard to tell."

Adam cast a dubious glance at Hilda. Where had the woman acquired her medical instruction? he wondered. She certainly didn't show much concern for her patient.

"I'm not sure what to do. This sort of thing has never happened before." The guide fussed with the clipboard and glanced out at the green. "I have to get the other tourists back to their hotel." She glanced between Hilda and Adam. "Would you see that she gets in touch with Dr. Seabrook? He should check her out and complete the paperwork."

Hilda gave a cackle. "Oh, dearie, don't you worry about it. She don't need a doctor. I'll tend her. You just go on and take care of them others."

"But—"

"Shoo, now. She'll come awake and be right as rain." Hilda bustled over to the young girl and nearly pushed her out the door. "I'll see she gets where she needs to be." She closed the door and turned around. Adam shot her a furious glare.

He turned at a groan from Jocelyn. Her eyelids fluttered and then opened. She groaned again and closed them.

"What happened?" she mumbled in a definite English accent. Still in character, Adam noted.

"You took a tumble off the block and hit your head."

Hilda approached, bracelets clattering, and leaned over, staring intently down at Jocelyn. "How do you feel?"

"My head hurts." Jocelyn shifted and grimaced. "And my neck."

"And well it should. You've a lump the size of an egg on your head."

Jocelyn gave the woman a confused look. "You!"

The woman nodded. "Told you wishes were powerful things, didn't I?"

What wish? Did these two know each other? Adam wondered, untying the cravat at his throat. But Niles had said—

"So, you're to be my husband now?" Jocelyn broke into his thoughts and he gazed down as she squinted up at him.

"Excuse me?" He shook his head. "No . . ." Was she flirting with him? He smiled. Well, why not? He wouldn't mind getting to know her better. Giving her a wink, he amended, "Well, yes, I suppose that's how it would go." He smiled. "Adam Warrick, your husband-to-be."

She brought her hand up, cautiously touching the compress on her forehead. A frown wrinkled her brow and she gave him a perplexed look.

"Haslett is no doubt enjoying an ale or two at the tavern, courtesy of your coin."

"She's a little confused." Hilda edged between her patient and Adam. "The result of the lump on the head, you see."

Jocelyn pushed to her elbows and the compress fell to the floor. "Where am I?"

"Where you wanted to be. Far, far away." Hilda chuckled.

Adam glared at Hilda. The strange old woman didn't need to speak in riddles. Jocelyn was confused enough. Offering her a reassuring smile, he said, "You're in Ramsgil, Miss Tanner. I'm terribly sorry, I never should have tossed the coin."

Jocelyn looked from Adam to the old woman. "Ramsgil? That's hardly far, far away."

The old woman chuckled. "Aye, it is. Just you wait." She leaned down and whispered something in Jocelyn's ear. Whatever she said made Jocelyn's green eyes widen in confusion.

Hilda stepped away, giving Adam a calculating glance. "Well, now, I think you should be off." She tugged at Adam's arm. "Just leave her to me."

Adam glared at the woman. What was wrong with her? Jocelyn had just regained consciousness and this woman, purported to be a medical professional, hadn't even examined her patient.

There were certain precautions Hilda should be taking. He searched his memory for the advice the doctor had given him when he'd suffered a concussion at fifteen. He'd cracked his head playing rugby and had a devilish headache as well as a twisted ankle. The worst of it had been the nurses continually waking him throughout the night he spent in the hospital.

"Are you sure she's okay?"

Hilda gave Adam a negligent flick of her wrist. "Aye, she's fine. Nothing wrong with her that a little peace and quiet won't fix."

"Shouldn't you at least check her pupils?"

Hilda harrumphed. "If it'll make you happy." She leaned over her patient and peered into Jocelyn's eyes.

"Won't you need this?" Adam picked up a penlight from the nearby table, sure this woman knew nothing of medicine. And also sure he wasn't leaving Jocelyn in her care.

"Hmm? Oh, yes, I suppose so." She took the light and fussed with it a moment, then seemed surprised when the bright beam of light appeared. "Imagine that," she mumbled.

Jocelyn's eyes rounded in shock, and as Hilda flashed the light in her eyes, Jocelyn's arm shot out, knocking the light away. A bloodcurdling scream filled the tiny room.

Hilda gave Adam an apologetic look as her patient continued to scream, struggling to sit up. Adam reached over, gently pushing Jocelyn down. "Hush, Miss Tanner. Everything's going to be fine. Just relax."

Bright green eyes peered at him. "What's . . . what's wrong with me?" Her chin wobbled. She

23

brought a shaky hand up to wipe at a tear that streaked her cheek, her entire body trembling.

"You'll be fine. You just need to lie back, relax and stay calm." He gave her hand a gentle pat.

Hilda bustled over with a paper cup and handed it to Jocelyn.

"Here, dearie. This'll help calm you down and help the pain in your head."

Jocelyn took the cup and drank, grimacing as she swallowed the last of it. She stared at the cup. " 'Tis made of paper." She looked at Hilda, then back to the cup.

Hilda patted Jocelyn's shoulder, taking the empty cup from her hand. "You'll get used to things around here, dearie. Not to worry."

Adam looked at both women, blinked, and shook his head. The conversation between the two was odd, to say the least. He got the impression that they'd met before. Had Jocelyn been on this tour before? It didn't seem likely. And what of Niles's comment that he hadn't seen Hilda before?

"What the bloody hell did you give her?" He pinned the woman with an angry glare as Hilda's words sank in.

She backed away from him. "Just a little something to calm her and ease the pain."

"Don't you know you're not supposed to medicate a concussion? You don't know what damage has been done in the fall." Adam's heart pounded in his chest and heat flooded his face. "You have to keep her awake for a while, just to be certain she's all right. Surely you know that?"

"Well, I never." Hilda huffed and crumpled the paper cup.

"No, I don't imagine you have." He glanced over to Jocelyn and noticed she wasn't shaking quite as badly. Her eyes drifted closed and a deep fear clutched his heart.

He had to get her away from this woman and get some real medical help. Thank God he'd decided to take the train from Ramsgil to London on Wednesday and had left his car in the station lot. He doubted there was a cabby to be had in this little town. He moved past Hilda to the side of the cot and bent down, gathering Jocelyn in his arms.

"Here now, what do you think you're doing?" Hilda snagged his elbow. "Where are you taking my patient?"

Adam shrugged off the woman's grasp. "Away from you. I'll find a doctor to tend her."

He strode to the door, Jocelyn limp in his arms. He struggled with the door and glanced back at Hilda as he stepped over the threshold. The old woman stood there watching him, her arms akimbo, a strange glint in her eyes and a half smile on her lips.

Chapter Two

"Well, yes, she's regained consciousness. At least for a few moments, anyway." Adam ran his free hand through his hair, the phone pressed against his ear as he spoke with the ER nurse.

"That's a good sign, sir. Was her vision clear?"

How the bloody hell was he to know? Jocelyn had come to three times on the drive. Each time her gaze traveled around the interior of the car, panic clouded her eyes and she struggled frantically. It was impossible to drive and try to quiet her. He'd stopped in Castleside, but the doctor wasn't in. With no other choice, Adam had taken her to Spenceworth and was trying to find proper medical help by phone.

"I'm not sure. She was confused. You see, someone at the aid station gave her something to calm her and I don't think it worked well."

"Hm." The nurse was silent for a moment, and Adam heard the background noise of the hospital emergency room. "You could bring her in, sir, but it might be hours before anyone is able to see her."

Adam groaned silently. The idea of sitting with Jocelyn for hours in a hospital waiting room was anything but pleasant. He shook his head. "What do I need to do if I elect to keep her here?" Resignation filled his words.

"Just wake her every hour or so for the next twenty-four. And keep her calm." Adam heard the relief in her voice. "If she complains of head pain you can give her aspirin, but I'd wait until morning to do so, if you can."

"Fine." The one word lacked enthusiasm. "Thank you." Adam hung up.

With a deep sigh, he climbed the stairs to the room occupied by his guest.

"Miss Tanner?" He touched her shoulder. "Jocelyn, wake up."

Nelwina opened her eyes and peered up at her tormentor, Adam Warrick. She'd lost count of the number of times he'd awakened her, only to tell her to rest. It was passing strange, if you asked her.

"Aye, I'm awake." The voice sounded foreign to her. She started to rise, only to have him put up a hand.

"No, don't get up, just rest."

"Why then do you keep . . ." What was wrong with her voice? She gave Adam a confused glance and, lowering her voice, finished, "waking me if you want me to rest?" Frustration edged into her words. "Don't you think I'll rest better uninterrupted?"

"I see you're feeling better then." He raised a brow.

Nelwina took a deep breath. This was not Haslett.

Adam had saved her from her husband. She must remember that and curb her tongue. "What happened to my voice?"

"Your voice?" He shook his head, then smiled. "Nothing. It's wonderful."

Nelwina stared transfixed at the sight of his smile. His teeth shone a pearly white against his tanned skin. His lips would have been considered feminine had his chin been soft instead of a strong square line with a dimple in the center. Her gaze traveled up to meet his. Thick dark eyelashes lent a strong contrast to his light gray eyes, sparkling with humor at the moment. He took a step back and her gaze fell to his broad chest. White material clung to his form, molding to the hills and valleys of his muscles.

My stars, Nelwina thought as her gaze followed the white expanse until it disappeared into dark blue breeches. The garment fitted close, the material faded to nearly white at the seams and in the front.

Oh, my stars!

Her gaze froze on the front of his breeches and the faded area there. Her cheeks heated and she forced herself to look away, hoping he hadn't noticed what had snagged her attention.

Her betrothed was quite a specimen—the complete opposite of Haslett. She *had* done better. "Thank heavens," she sighed.

Glancing up at Adam, she forced herself to focus on the conversation.

She couldn't pull her gaze from his eyes. She leaned forward. "Your eyes . . ."

He moved closer, one brow arched. "Yes?"

She saw the ring of charcoal around the outer edge of his iris. "Seem so familiar." A shiver rattled up her spine and the fine hair on her arms rose. Indeed, something about his face tugged at her memory.

"You don't recall? We met on the bus. I sat behind you."

"Bus?" She tried to understand what he was saying.

"Yes. You know, the tour bus?"

She shook her head and then grimaced at the pain the action caused her head.

Adam frowned. "The tour. Don't you remember boarding the bus and going to Ramsgil to see the re-enactment?"

"Nay. I don't know of what you speak. I went to Ramsgil with Haslett." She clenched the bed linens. "And you paid him a pound." She focused her gaze on his face, willing him to understand her. "And now we're betrothed. I'm to be your wife."

Dear God, her injury was worse than he thought. He watched her fingers knead the coverlet on the bed. Distress darkened her eyes and the tautness around her mouth gave evidence of her agitated state.

He opened his mouth to speak, then closed it. Maybe it would be better just to go along with her for now. Surely she'll be better by morning, he thought.

He gave her a smile, one he hoped was reassuring, though he didn't feel at all assured at the moment.

"I wish I could give you something for the head-ache, but the hospital said it would be best if I didn't until morning." He took a few steps backward.

"Would you like a little something to eat?"

She just stared at him, her large green eyes reflecting her confusion.

"Are you hungry, Miss Tanner?"

"Why do you call me Miss Tanner?"

He frowned. "That's your name, isn't it? The one you gave the tour guide."

She moved her head carefully from side to side. "Nay, my name is Nelwina H . . . Honeycutt."

This was getting more and more confusing. He was certain he'd heard her say her name was Jocelyn Tanner. Oh, this wasn't good. No, not good at all. But rather than upset her by questioning her further, he just nodded. "Yes, of course."

He backed to the door. "Are you hungry?"

"Nay," she answered. "I'm just tired."

"Well, then, I'll leave you to rest. The loo is through that door." He pointed to the door across from the foot of the bed. "I'm sure things will be clearer by morning."

He turned, pulling the door closed behind him.

"Wait." Her voice held a note of panic and he pushed the door back open. "Where am I?"

He smiled. "Spenceworth."

And he closed the door, praying her confusion would be gone after she rested a while longer.

Nelwina sat there staring at the carved panel.

Was he then Lord Spenceworth? Had the old earl died? Her throat closed against the sadness that filled her.

She focused again on the door and the man on the

other side of it. No. She shook her head. He couldn't be, for no titled gentleman would purchase a commoner for a wife. Mayhap he was the second son. Aye, that must be it. It still didn't make sense to her, but as she stared at the door the manor's name played over and over again in her mind.

"Spenceworth." The word whispered past Nelwina's lips, and warmth radiated from her heart. Scooting across the bed, she swung her legs over the side near the window and waited for the wave of dizziness to pass. She pushed to her feet, curling her toes into the thick, soft, green carpet. She nodded, glancing down.

So that was why she'd never heard Adam's footsteps when he'd come in to wake her. 'Twas the thickest, softest carpet she'd ever felt.

She stepped over to the window, anxious to reacquaint herself with the manor. Moving the drapes aside, she glanced out at the forest beyond, where low-hanging gray clouds wrapped around the high treetops and vegetation blanketed the ground beneath. Grass butted up against the edge of the woods and stray flowers added spots of color here and there.

She didn't remember any rooms that looked out on the woods like this. But then she hadn't lived at Spenceworth since she was a child. Mayhap there had been an addition in those years. She sat in the chair beside the window, allowing her mind to go back to happier days.

Her mother sewed for Lady Spenceworth and the household staff back then, while Nelwina helped out in the kitchen gardens.

The old earl insisted that his servants be taught to read, write and cipher and Nelwina enjoyed her lessons immensely. She learned quickly, practicing her sums in the gardens, counting and recording the rows, the number of plants and the amount of produce from each.

The old earl discovered her in the garden one day, entering her findings in a small ledger her mother had given her. He had been pleased as he read each page.

" 'Tis well done, Nelwina." He smiled at her. "And now I know why there is an abundance of turnips at my table."

"Aye, my lord. I've told Cook we should plant only half the amount of them, but he says four rows of turnips have always been planted." She giggled. "And see, my lord, I've planted four rows." She edged closer and whispered, "But I've only planted half as many seeds. You'll not be enjoying quite so many this year."

"Ah, clever girl." The old earl chuckled and tousled her hair. "You've my thanks for that."

Those were wonderful days. Mama was healthy and happy, sewing for the lady of the house and teaching Nelwina how to stitch a fine seam and fit a bodice.

But then Lady Spenceworth had died and Nelwina and her mother had left. They'd found a little cottage to rent and her mother continued sewing for the ladies of the area. Nelwina tended the garden and small animals and helped her mother with the stitching. Life was simple yet comfortable for the next ten years. But then her mother had fallen ill and . . .

Nelwina shook her head. *No, I won't think on that. 'Twill only make me weep.*

She turned from the window and focused her gaze on the room.

'Twas an odd little room, but she couldn't put her finger on what made it so strange. Several nice land-scapes relieved the stark white walls. There was a large wardrobe on the wall opposite the end of the bed, and beside it was the white door to the "loo." What *was* a loo? she wondered.

A long, low chest with many drawers sat against the wall across from the bed. Beside it was the door Adam had used to leave. This one was carved, the wood panels polished to a satin sheen. There was just something out of place here.

She brushed her hands over the rose-print fabric covering the chair she sat in. Beside the bed stood a small table covered with the same material as the chair. Nelwina squinted at the shiny gold pole topped with a smooth, green, cone-like hat sitting on the ta-ble. She cocked her head to the side. What was it for? she wondered.

She walked around the end of the bed, intent on investigating the intriguing item, and caught a move-ment out of the corner of her eye. She froze.

Cautiously, she turned toward the movement and gasped. When had the woman entered the room? Had she always been there?

"Excuse me," Nelwina stammered.

The woman remained silent and Nelwina stared hard at her. Taking a few tentative steps toward the stranger, Nelwina stopped. The stranger stopped. Nelwina cocked her head. The stranger cocked her head.

Closing the distance between them, Nelwina put her hand out, her fingers making contact with the smooth, cool surface.

"Sweet Jesus!" Her skin turned clammy and her vision blurred as she leaned her head against the mirror. Fighting off the dizziness clawing its way over her, Nelwina met the gaze of the stranger in the mirror. "What has happened? Who are you?" She shook her head. "Who am I?"

She touched the short dark hair and gazed into unfamiliar green eyes. *Who is this woman looking back at me?* Tears welled within her eyes, blurring the image. She wiped the moisture away and stared at the hands of a stranger. Long tapered fingers, the skin smooth, the nails neatly filed and buffed to a soft shine. These weren't her work-worn, red hands.

She stepped back, studying the body. Where was her real body? What had happened to it?

This body was nothing like her own. No, this body was thin, painfully thin, by her mind. Breasts that could hardly be given the name did little to fill the bodice of her dress. She ran her hands over the narrow hips beneath the skirt. 'Twas more the shape of a boy.

The old Gypsy's words echoed in her mind as she stared at the stranger.

Ye made yer wish. And now 'tis time to live it. 'Tis yer lot to have a more difficult time than the one what's took yer place.

Mayhap she'd wished to be anywhere but in Ramsgil and with anyone but Haslett, but she never wished to *be* someone else.

34

What was she thinking? Nelwina spun away from the reflection. 'Twas impossible, this body-switching idea. If Hilda was to be believed, then she'd exchanged bodies with another woman. Nelwina gave an indelicate snort at that.

But why? How? And how could she get her own back?

Had Hilda cast a spell on her? Was it magic?

Her head started pounding and her eyes burned with frustrated tears. Nothing made any sense. What had happened to her?

Nelwina rubbed at her temples, blinking back her tears. She sat on the bed. "Am I crazed?"

She realized then what was out of place in the room—it was her. Unable to hold back the fear and confusion, she dropped onto the bed and sobbed into her pillow.

First thing in the morning she would find Hilda. Instinct told her that the old Gypsy woman was the root of her problems. If 'twas a spell cast by the Gypsy, then 'twould be the Gypsy who fixed it.

Chapter Three

"The severance package is a generous one, I'm sure you'll agree."

Philip James stared at a spot to the left of his boss. Or rather, his ex-boss.

"You do understand? We laid off according to seniority." Dempsey shrugged. "You were one of the last hired."

Philip shifted his gaze to the man sitting behind the desk and nodded. What else could he do? He certainly wouldn't beg. He might be unemployed now, but he still had his pride.

"Thank you, Mr. Dempsey." Philip turned to go.

"I'm sorry, Philip. I hate to see anyone leave the firm, but it's necessary to downsize, especially after the merger."

"Yes, sir. I understand." Philip walked the short distance to the door. "You mentioned a letter of recommendation?"

Mr. Dempsey stood. "Yes. I'll have my secretary forward it to you."

He walked around the desk. "Good luck, Philip."

Philip nodded, his hand on the doorknob. "Thanks."

He left Dempsey, walking down the hall to his own office at the very end. Dempsey, Daniel and Finch assigned offices to their accountants in order of seniority, just like they fired them, he thought. Last in, last office, and first out. He passed by Jocelyn's door. The lights were off. She'd taken her vacation to England. He still had the other half of their honeymoon ticket. Maybe he could cash it in.

Morning brought an urgent need and Nelwina scrambled out of bed. Looking beneath it, she didn't find the much-needed chamberpot. Oh dear, she thought, frantically glancing around the room. Her gaze lit on the white door.

She rushed over and pushed it open to behold the strangest room ever. She curled her stocking-clad toes away from the cold tile floor and gazed at the small room. The basin hung from a wall, a silver spigot arched over it with matching silver handles on either side. Above the basin, a fine looking glass reflected the opposite wall.

"Nay," she muttered. "I'll not look into the mirror just yet."

The chill from the floor stole up her feet to her legs and all thought of the mirror was replaced by immediate need.

Nelwina stepped on the cream-colored oval rug lying before a large window of glass. She touched the cool surface, wondering at the poor quality of it. I hope the glazier didn't charge much for such shoddy work, she thought, noting the bumpy glass, dull and opaque.

She turned from the glass and found a very strange chair. Stepping up to it, she ran her hand over the smooth cool surface of the seat.

Oh, where was that chamberpot? she wondered. All this coolness was making a bad situation even worse. Her fingers curled around the edge of the seat and with a start, she realized that it lifted up.

Staring down at the trough of water, she wondered what in the world the contraption was. A little lever on the back of the chair drew her attention and she pulled it down.

The gurgling of water startled Nelwina and she stepped back and gritted her teeth against the cold discomfort of the floor. If she didn't find that chamberpot quickly, she'd disgrace herself right here. She looked down into the trough and watched as the water disappeared.

She bent down and looked at the floor. Where had the water gone? As she came up, she noticed something hanging from the wall near the chair. Cautiously, she touched it. 'Twas the softest paper she'd ever felt.

And then it dawned on her. A room, a chair and paper nearby. A loo was a privy. She smiled in relief.

With her immediate needs taken care of, Nelwina left the little room. She retrieved her shoes and put them on. Crossing to the bed, she quickly smoothed the linens and plumped the pillows, her fingers lingering over the finely woven material.

Her gaze snagged on the unfamiliar hands doing her bidding and she spun around. She left the room quickly, with renewed determination to find Hilda and have the woman remove whatever spell or curse she'd cast.

Nelwina stood a moment in the narrow hall. At one end was a door; at the other a long window allowed in the early morning light.

Nay, she could not be at Spenceworth. Never had she been in this narrow hall. Adam must be mistaken, she thought. Or was there another Spenceworth, perhaps?

She'd not stay around to find out the answer.

With quick steps she went to the door and found herself in yet another hall, this one much wider and vaguely familiar. A red patterned rug ran the length of the hall, exposing only the edges of gleaming wood floors.

She traversed the hall and descended the stairs. Standing in the foyer, Nelwina turned in a slow circle, her gaze touching on the familiar proportions of the entry. 'Twas Spenceworth. She turned in another circle, her head tilted back to look at the chandelier and the molding on the high ceiling.

Aye, 'twas the same, she thought as she focused on the crystals dripping from the chandelier. *What strange-looking candles.* She squinted. Where were the wicks? How did one light them?

Frowning, she straightened, looking around the foyer again. Something wasn't right. Though it looked like the Spenceworth of her childhood, there were things out of place.

Like the large leather chair against the back wall. And the table beside the front door certainly didn't belong there.

She frowned. Nay, that table had always been in Lady Spenceworth's salon.

" 'Tis all part of the spell," Nelwina muttered. And she'd best be off to find the gypsy.

Striding to the front door, Nelwina fumbled with the locks, finally opening the door and stepping out. Taking a set of stairs to her right, she made it down to the drive.

She gazed out over the property and the strange black road bisecting it. Gravel crunched beneath her feet as she walked toward the road. Standing beside it, she gingerly stuck her foot out and quickly tapped it on the black surface. Then she knelt down and ran her hand over it.

'Twas the smoothest road she'd ever seen, nothing like the rutted tracks that led from her cottage to Ramsgil. Standing up again, Nelwina gave the road another tap with her foot and set out for Ramsgil. She had no idea the distance to Ramsgil, but she must find Hilda. Mayhap she could get a ride in the back of a farmer's wagon as he made his way to market.

Glancing behind her, she slowed her steps. This really was Spenceworth. She stopped and turned to look at the manor. The graceful twin staircases sweeping up to the large double doors remained as she remembered. But the well-tended bed of plants and flowers between them was now choked with weeds and the shrubs were scraggly and in need of attention.

Nelwina breathed in the morning air, heavy with

dampness, and turned back to the road. 'Twas a confusing place. And though some things seemed familiar, Nelwina didn't like this strange world she found herself in. She wanted to go home. How she would find Hilda was a problem she hadn't yet solved, but since Ramsgil was the last place she'd seen the woman, she'd start there.

As for the handsome Adam Warrick, well . . . she pushed Adam's image from her mind. He was simply one of Hilda's illusions.

Nelwina didn't know how far she'd traveled, but Spenceworth was out of sight when she spotted Hilda, perched on a low stone fence and munching on a green apple. Nelwina increased her pace, determination lending purpose to the movements of her body.

"Ah, so there you are," Hilda called out to her.

"What spell have you cast on me?" Nelwina glared at the older woman.

"I know no spells, girl."

"You must undo it."

"I tell you 'tis no spell. You made a wish and 'twas granted." She bit into the apple and watched Nelwina.

"Nay." Nelwina shook her head. "Many a time I wished for things, but never did I get them."

Hilda chewed her bite of fruit and swallowed noisily. "Mayhap you wished for the wrong things."

"What? Wrong wishes?"

Hilda opened her mouth, but Nelwina shook her head. "Nay, do not tell me. I wish to return from whence I came."

"You cannot." Hilda took another bite from the apple.

Nelwina gasped. "What do you mean, I cannot?"

The woman examined the apple core a moment, then tossed it over her shoulder. "I mean, you'll be staying here. For now, at least." She shrugged.

"What do you mean, staying here for now?"

" 'Tis all I know."

"But what am I supposed to *do* here?"

"Adapt."

Nelwina glanced around, her gaze going from the smooth black road to the line of poles placed alongside it. A dark line connected the poles to one another.

A little farther down the road, leading away from Spenceworth, another black road intersected the one she was on. Low stone fences like the one Hilda sat upon bisected the rolling green fields on either side of the road.

A low-pitched rumbling sounded ahead and, curious, Nelwina searched for the source. A moment later a black box-like thing appeared on the road.

"What is that?" She watched as it turned somehow and disappeared.

"A car."

Nelwina turned to Hilda. "A car?"

"Aye, 'tis what's used for travel here."

Nelwina stared at the Gypsy, waiting for more information.

Hilda sighed. "Instead of horses or carts, they use these motorized vehicles called cars or autos." Hilda slid off the wall. "They're quite safe."

Nelwina was still trying to understand what the woman had said when a thunderous noise sounded overhead. Nelwina glanced up and screeched. Dropping to the ground, she covered her head, and gasped as she peeked up. Never had she seen such a huge bird. And never one that sounded like that.

The sound faded and Hilda's cackle reached her.

"By the saints, that was funny." Nelwina glanced up at Hilda, who held her stomach, tears streaking down her cheeks. "Lawd, girl, 'tis too amusing."

Nelwina pushed to her feet and, dusting off her skirt, she stared up at the sky. "I don't find anything of humor in a giant bird whose call is near deafening."

" 'Twasn't a bird. 'Twas an airplane," Hilda sputtered between bouts of laughter.

Fear lodged in Nelwina's stomach. Where was she? Spenceworth was familiar, but strange at the same time. And the roads, traveling boxes and raucous birds?

She must have spoken her thoughts because Hilda stepped up and touched her arm.

" 'Tis a new time you're in. The other must want to return to this time in order for you to return to yours. I know not if or how this will happen. For now, *this* is your destiny. 'Tis best to settle in."

"What are you saying?" Nelwina frowned in confusion.

"You are in the future. Some things are much the same, but many things have changed. You must make your way in this world now."

"But how?"

"You must stay at Spenceworth. 'Tis both the most familiar to you and where your future lies." Hilda brushed the dust off the back of her skirt. "I'll be off now. I've much to do, you know. I can't be gadding about."

"But where are you going?" Panic inched up Nelwina's throat. "How do I find you?" She reached for the Gypsy's arm. "What if I need you?"

Hilda grinned. "If you need me, I'll find you." Then she cackled, quite pleased with herself.

Adam knocked on Jocelyn's door. When there was no answer, he cautiously pushed the door open only to find the bed neatly made and the woman gone.

"Jocelyn?" he called out, thinking she might be in the loo.

There was no answer.

Relief swept over him, followed closely by guilt. He was responsible for her injury. He couldn't allow anything else to happen to her.

So Adam searched the manor, calling her name and checking each of the rooms. Surely she was around here somewhere, he thought as he opened the door of the salon and searched amid the furniture still shrouded in dust covers. He'd made the new wing, the study and the foyer livable, but the rest of the manor still looked like a series of storage rooms with a good layer of dust. Eventually he'd get to them.

Exhausting his search of the manor, he grabbed his keys and went to his car. Maybe she had decided to return to Ramsgil. But the town was a good thirty-five miles away. Surely she wouldn't attempt such a walk.

He rounded a curve and there, leaning against a low stone wall, were Jocelyn and Hilda, the woman from the first-aid office. Who the bloody hell was that weird old woman, anyway? And what was she doing this far from Ramsgil?

This wasn't good, he thought. No, it didn't bode well at all.

Adam pulled his car to a stop, his gaze locked with Hilda's. What was she up to? It was evident that Jocelyn suffered from some serious aftereffects of her fall. What she didn't need was help from *that* woman.

And she thought her name was Nelwina. Why she would pick such an odd name was a mystery to him. Should he call her that? She'd gotten so agitated last evening when he called her Jocelyn. It was probably better if he went along with her wishes.

He'd get Joc . . . Nelwina to a real doctor, recalling the doctor's name he'd been given on the tour company's business card. As he stopped the car beside the two women, Nelwina straightened and jerked around, surprise widening her gaze. She stepped back until the stone wall stopped her.

He shut off the engine.

"There's no need for you to walk back to Ramsgil." Adam got out of the car. "I'll take you back."

He couldn't make out Hilda's whispered words, but Nelwina gave the woman an uncertain look and shook her head.

"Aye, you must," Adam heard Hilda say as he crossed the lane. She gave Nelwina a gentle nudge toward him.

What the hell was going on here?

Nelwina looked frantically between him and Hilda.

" 'Tis your destiny." Hilda gave her another nudge.

"Come on, Nelwina, let's get you back to Ramsgil.

45

You can get your own clothes and then I'll take you back to your hotel."

With one last glance at Hilda, Nelwina nodded and stepped over to Adam.

"Take me back to Spenceworth, my lord."

"Spenceworth?" Adam opened the car door. "No, I think after we gather your things in Ramsgil I should take you to London. We'll find Dr. Seabrook there or the company can recommend another physician." What had Hilda said to Nelwina? Why did she now want to go back to the manor?

"Nay!" Nelwina fairly shouted the word and gripped Adam's arm. "You can't take me to London. I must return to Spenceworth."

"But you need a doctor."

She shook her head. "Nay, I'm fine. I'll be fine at Spenceworth." She gripped her hands in front of her, twisting and turning them, agitation evident in every line of her body.

"But—"

"*Nay.* You must take me back to the manor." Tears glistened in her eyes and her shoulders shook.

"Okay." Adam spread his hands in front of him. "Calm down; I'll take you back. Just stay calm." She wasn't well and it was his fault. He should have left her alone and let her dodge the re-enactment. He never, ever should have tossed that coin. He was responsible for her predicament now. He'd get her back to the manor and find a doctor.

From the way Nelwina got into the car, one would think she'd never done it before. Adam closed her

46

door and she jerked in surprise. He read her fear as she turned her gaze to him.

Why was she so frightened?

He circled around the front of the car, got in and started the motor.

Nelwina gripped the wrinkled material of her skirt and squeezed her eyes closed, swallowing against the nausea rising in her throat and the fear shooting through her body. Hilda had given her a brief explanation of this contraption she was riding in, but it didn't make it any more comfortable. The speed with which they traveled astounded her; the closeness of everything made her sick.

If Adam said anything to her during the ride back to Spenceworth, she didn't hear it for the roaring in her ears. She wasn't sure if it was the noise from the thing they were in or from the anxiety pounding in her veins.

But she heaved a sigh of relief when the vehicle went still and silent. She opened her eyes, catching sight of Adam walking around to her. With a click and a squeak he opened the door and Nelwina wasted no time getting out.

"You travel in that often?" She pointed to the thing Hilda had called a car.

Adam gave her a disbelieving glance. "Of course. What else would I use? A horse?"

" 'Twould be a lot quieter and safer." She turned and headed for the front door of Spenceworth. Stopping at the foot of the stairs, she gazed up at the manor. 'Twas nearly the same as when she'd lived here. It was weathered a bit more, but the welcoming warmth was still evident.

She climbed the stairs, eager to reacquaint herself with Spenceworth. But first she needed to visit the loo again. There were some things she could appreciate in this time.

Adam climbed the stairs after Nelwina, puzzled by her behavior. Why had she insisted on returning to the manor? He rubbed his forehead. What he needed was a cup of strong hot coffee. He walked quickly to the new wing of the house.

A modern section had been added to Spenceworth some fifty years earlier. The new wing had been both cheaper and less invasive than remodeling the old structure and Adam was grateful for it. He'd seen other ancestral homes that had been updated with electricity and heat and found that they'd lost some of their charm. His uncle had run electricity to an outlet in the study and the chandelier in the foyer, and luckily, he'd stopped there.

As an architect, Adam appreciated the lines of the manor and the workmanship evident in the details that gave it character. As the new owner, he worried how he would manage the cost of upkeep. He'd started his own architecture firm in London, but it was still in its infancy and hardly turning a profit. Adam wasn't sure if it would ever make enough to cover the maintenance of the manor.

It was a shame he couldn't share the grandeur of Spenceworth with the public.

Adam walked down the hall past Nelwina's door

and his own to an open doorway. He entered an efficiency kitchen. From a cabinet he pulled down a large mug and a paper filter. He filled the coffeemaker with water, placed the filter in the top and measured coffee grounds into it. Flipping the switch, he reached into another cabinet and pulled out a package of Mallows. Munching on one, he leaned against the counter, impatient for the coffee to brew.

He'd just poured a cup when a loud rapping of the knocker on the front door startled him. Who the bloody hell could be calling this early?

"Adam?" the high, shrill voice called. "Adam, sweetness, are you here?" He froze, his cup raised to his lips.

"Damn." Carefully he put down his cup, grinding his teeth in frustration. Why now? Why did she have to show up now?

"Adam, dear?" The sound of clicking heels echoed in the entry hall.

God, he didn't need this right now. Maybe if he stayed quiet she'd go away. He glanced around the kitchen, searching for a hiding place just in case she came looking for him. But unless he could shrink himself down to the size of a whiskbroom, he'd find no haven here.

"Oh buck up, old man. Maybe she's just stopping by," Adam mumbled to himself as he left the kitchen and strode down the hall to the stairs. "And what's the likelihood of that?"

Adam stood at the top of the stairs. Just what he needed. He gazed down at yet another uninvited guest.

"Oh, there you are, love. I thought you could use a little company. You know it's not good for you to close yourself up in this musty old manor."

Adam's gaze traveled from his mother's smiling countenance to the mountain of luggage piled near the door and groaned.

It looked like she was laying siege to Spenceworth.

Chapter Four

Adam took a drink of his coffee and grimaced. Cold. Wasn't there a rule somewhere that said guests should not arrive before lunch? He was sure there was, and if not there ought to be. Dumping the cold brew into the sink, he poured a fresh cup from the coffeepot.

Settling himself in the nearest chair, he leaned back, his mug cradled in both hands. He brought it to his mouth and inhaled the scent of strong coffee, enjoying the quiet of the house.

Like an instant replay, the knocker banged at the front door. He'd never get to drink his beverage while it was hot at the rate the interruptions were going.

He went downstairs and opened the door to find Niles Jefferson standing on the step, two travel cases in his hands and one sitting beside him.

"Lord Spenceworth." Adam nodded. "The hotel asked that Miss Tanner's belongings be delivered."

Adam stared dumbfounded at the bags and then looked up at Niles.

"Miss Tanner was to have checked out this morning. The tour company included the things she left in their office."

Adam ran a hand through his hair.

"Where shall I put these, sir?"

Adam moved out of the way, and motioned Niles in. With a distracted wave of his hand, Adam said, "Anywhere will be fine."

Niles put down the two bags and then retrieved the third.

"How's Miss Tanner feeling?"

Pulling himself from his stupor, Adam met Niles's gaze. "Fine." No sense dragging anyone else into this, Adam thought.

"Wonderful." Niles turned to leave. "Nice to see you again, sir."

"Mr. Jefferson?

Niles stopped just outside the door.

"Yes?"

"Do you know anything about the attendant at the first-aid office?"

Niles shook his head. "I'd never seen her before yesterday. Why, is there a problem?"

"Well, only that I don't think she's qualified."

Niles frowned. "Shall I check into it for you, sir? Usually the doctor is available, but as I mentioned yesterday, he's in London until next week."

"That might be a good idea."

"I'll see to it then." Niles descended the stairs to his car parked in the gravel drive.

"Thank you, Mr. Jefferson."

Niles nodded and climbed into his vehicle.

Adam closed the door and stared at the luggage.

52

Things were going from bad to worse and it was just past nine. Bloody rotten day it was going to be.

He took a deep breath. Before he tackled any more problems this morning, he was having his coffee. He dared anyone to get between him and his caffeine fix.

Adam started to grab the handle of the largest bag, but stopped when he noticed the luggage tag. He flipped up the protective leather flap and read:

Jocelyn Tanner, 402 Magnolia Way Apartment A, Summerville, South Carolina

Adam frowned. Why did Jocelyn think her name was Nelwina? He really needed to get in touch with Dr. Seabrook. Unfortunately, he didn't know where the symposium was being held and since it was Sunday, the doctor's office would be closed. He'd have to wait until tomorrow. But come the morning, he and Jocelyn/Nelwina, whatever she called herself, were going back to London where she could get proper care.

Maybe some of his guilt would leave once he'd seen her in competent hands.

He picked up the two smaller bags, tucking one under his arm and clutching the other in his hand. Then, hefting the largest one with his free hand, he climbed the stairs. The smell of coffee floated down the hall to him. His mouth watered.

Stopping at her door, Adam put the large suitcase down and raised his hand to knock. At his touch, the door swung open and he stuck his head in the room.

"Joc . . . er, Nelwina?" The sound of splashing water reached him from behind the bathroom door and he quickly put the luggage in the room and left, closing the door behind him. He'd talk with her after he had his coffee.

In the kitchen he dumped the cold coffee and poured himself a fresh cup. The house was quiet, but he knew it was only a matter of time before hell was unleashed.

And he had no doubt that it would happen.

He grabbed the bag of Mallows and, coffee in hand, left the new wing. If he wanted to extend his peace and quiet, he'd have to escape to the old study. It was the only room in the manor that was uncovered and cleaned. The rest of the rooms were just as he'd found them; covers over the furniture and a layer of dust on the floors. He'd get to that later.

But right now, he was going into hiding. If he was lucky, it would take his mother a few hours to find him.

Nelwina walked out of the loo, still marveling at the wonders of it. What she'd mistaken as a poorly made window was actually a moving wall behind which she found a bathing tub. This one was somehow attached to the walls and when she turned one of the handles coming from the wall, water had poured out of the spigot.

What an extraordinary convenience, she thought as she glanced at the room one more time and closed the door.

Gazing around the bedchamber, wondering what other curiosities she might find, Nelwina saw three traveling bags beside the door. She didn't remember seeing them before, but then everything was so new it was hard to take it all in.

Going over to the bags, she placed her hand on the wall for balance and leaned over to pick up the smallest one. Her hand slid down, hitting a square box.

She squeaked in alarm as light burst into the room. Shocked, Nelwina looked up and squinted against the glare. She hadn't noticed the bowl on the ceiling before now. But how did the candle get lit?

She glanced at the box beneath her palm. She leaned on it again. Something shifted and the candle was extinguished. Keeping her eye on the dish, she leaned again on the box, trying to see how the fire got to the candle.

The room filled with light again, but there was no discernable spark. Was this another one of the marvels of the time?

She leaned against the wall and the candle went out. How clever, she thought, to have light simply by leaning on a wall.

Nelwina smiled, leaning on the wall once again, enjoying the power she felt at being able to illuminate a room so easily.

She turned her attention to the bags at her feet. Kneeling before the smallest of them, she turned it this way and that, trying to find the flap that would open the top of the bag. When she couldn't find one, she pulled on the leather handles, frustrated when they remained stubbornly closed.

Mayhap it wasn't a traveling bag, she thought, turning it upside down. The contents shifted, thumping around as she flipped it back over.

But then what was it?

A leather tag caught her attention. Canting her head, she read, *Jocelyn Tanner.*

Nelwina sat back on her heels, staring at the bag.

"Ah, Jocelyn, are you as confused as I?" She let go of the tag. "Do you understand what happened? Or why?" She shook her head. "For I know I don't. Are you now searching for a way to return? Forgive me, but I'm a bit relieved to be away from Haslett. I wonder, did you manage to do the same?"

The bag sat there, giving up none of the answers.

Hilda's words echoed in Nelwina's mind.

'Tis a new time you're in. The other must want to return to this time in order for you to return to yours. I know not if or how this will happen. For now, this is your destiny. 'Tis best to settle in.

How was she to settle in when she knew nothing of her surroundings? And she had no idea when this time was.

She glanced back at the bag. "Well, you're simply going to have to open because I know not where else to search for answers."

Nelwina traced the line dividing the top of the bag and discovered a silver medallion attached to a metal tab. With a gentle tug, the medallion moved to the other side, exposing the interior of the bag.

Nelwina's eyebrows shot toward her hairline. "Well, imagine that?" She ran her finger along the rough edge of the opening. "Ah, Jocelyn, please forgive me for invading your privacy."

Nelwina pulled out a pretty pink satin bag with a closing similar to the travel bag. Setting this aside, she withdrew a round blue bottle made of a strange flexible material. The darker blue top came off easily and she sniffed at the contents.

"Oh, it smells wonderful." Holding the bottle up, she read, "Freesia body wash." She twisted the lid back on and pulled out another container. This one was body cream and smelled like the wash.

"It would seem Jocelyn is a woman of privilege. How can Hilda expect me to step into her life?"

Next Nelwina found a fold of papers. Curious, she opened them up, glancing at the printed pages, but she could understand little of it. Scanning the print in the upper right hand corner, she gasped.

The paper fell to her lap. Nelwina clapped her hands over her mouth, stifling the screech threatening to rip from her throat.

Two hundred years had passed? Nay, how could that be?

She glanced back at the paper, shaking her head. Hilda had said another time, but Nelwina hadn't realized exactly what the Gypsy had meant.

Frantically, she scanned the room, unsure if she sought a way back to her own time or a means of confirming what she'd just read.

But the room, with its strange carpet touching the walls and the odd hat-wearing stick on the table, neither confirmed nor denied anything.

Stuffing the papers back into the bag, she grabbed the blue bottles and returned them to their places.

Her fingers curled around the pink satin bag and

she gazed at it a long moment. The contents shifted under her touch and curiosity got the better of her.

Nelwina opened the bag much as she had the travel bag. Inside she found long, shiny cylinders with different-colored creams. Sticking her finger down into one of the metal tubes, she came away with a glob of soft, pink cream. Turning the container over, Nelwina read the bottom. "Pink Carnation Lipstick." 'Twas lip rouge.

And then it dawned on her and she riffled through the rest of the items. Her eyes stretched wide in horror.

'Twas cosmetics, face paint.

What sort of woman had she traded bodies with? Was Jocelyn some man's mistress? For no proper woman Nelwina knew painted her face.

The sound of muffled footsteps startled Nelwina and she quickly stuffed the items in the satin bag and placed it back into the travel case.

She jumped to her feet, her heart thumping in her chest. She was confused and embarrassed. And strangely, she felt like a thief.

She gulped in a deep breath and stepped out of her room and into the hall. A wave of weakness shook her knees and she leaned against the door. Lord, but she was hungry.

"Oh, gracious."

Nelwina turned her head. The girlish voice was at odds with the white hair framing the speaker's face. Her warm brown eyes scanned Nelwina from head to hem, but Nelwina felt too badly to worry about the shabby state of her dress.

"My dear, are you ill?" The woman was beside Nelwina now, her hand on Nelwina's arm.

The weakness passed, leaving her feeling a little shaky. " 'Tis but hunger, I believe." She raised a trembling hand to her face.

"Well, come along, then. We'll just pop into the kitchen." The woman tugged at Nelwina's arm, guiding her down the narrow hall. "And have a bracing cup of tea and something to eat. I often get a little woozy when I haven't eaten in a long while. It's the blood sugar, you know. Gets low and you feel quite puny. If you're not careful you can faint from it."

The woman continued to chatter as she swept them both into the room. Adam's housekeeper was a talkative woman, Nelwina thought. And then she took in the woman's clothing and swallowed a gasp.

What kind of house was this? Though the woman was of mature years, she wore a skirt reaching only to the middle of her calf. And her hair was cut nearly as short as Adam's.

"Now you just sit here and I'll take care of everything."

The woman smiled at Nelwina who numbly sat in the chair the woman pulled out from the table. Leaning her elbows on the flat surface, Nelwina cradled her head in her hands and closed her eyes as an ache began behind them.

"Here then, dear." The woman placed a plate piled with cheese and biscuits on the table. "While I fix the tea, why don't you eat a bit of this and you'll feel better."

Nelwina nibbled on a piece of cheese and one of

the biscuits as the woman bustled around behind her.

Feeling somewhat better, though the headache was still there, Nelwina looked around.

Sunlight spilled in through a long window that looked out on the woodlands beyond Spenceworth. There was another small round window near the floor, but it was dark and she couldn't tell what the view would be. But one would have to be a small child to look through it, she thought, not understanding the purpose of a window so close to the floor.

As her gaze moved on, she saw a large white box sharing the wall with the door through which they'd entered. Might it be a pantry? Turning around, she looked for another door, but found none. Aye, it must be, though 'twas strange looking.

She frowned. Where was the hearth? How did one cook in this kitchen?

Something hummed behind her and the smell of eggs cooking filled the room. Then a rattling noise joined in and Nelwina turned around and watched Sophia pour steaming water from a pitcher into a teapot. How had she heated it? Nelwina wondered with a frown, for there was no fire.

The humming stopped and a strange high-pitched sound filled the room.

"Oh, the eggs are done." The housekeeper opened the small door of a cabinet on the counter and pulled out a bowl.

How could a box cook eggs?

Nelwina turned back to the table, rubbing her eyes. Everything was so strange to her. How would she ever find her way?

"Here, now." The woman came to the table, putting down cups and saucers. A teapot, a pitcher of cream and a bowl of sugar appeared next. Then she placed a plate of eggs in front of Nelwina. "And here's the salt and pepper. Oh, and some silverware." The woman placed a knife, fork, and spoon beside Nelwina's plate.

"Now." The woman settled in the chair beside Nelwina with another plate of eggs. "I'm afraid we haven't been properly introduced. I'm Sophia Warrick, Adam's mother."

Nelwina brought her shocked gaze up to meet the older woman's. Adam's mother? Her cheeks burned with embarrassment. She'd mistaken Adam's mother for a housekeeper of questionable virtue.

"I'm Nelwina Ha—Honeycutt, Adam's betrothed, my lady." 'Twas the one thing she was certain of amid all the strangeness around her. Since she was no longer married to Haslett, Nelwina preferred her maiden name to that of Haslett's last name, Ham.

"Betrothed?" Sophia's eyes widened in surprise. "He never mentioned." A watery sheen sparkled in her eyes and she leaned over and hugged Nelwina. "Oh, my dear, I'm so happy for you both. You must tell me everything. How did you meet? How long have you known each other? When did he ask you? How did he ask you? Was he very romantic?"

Nelwina's mind spun with Sophia's questions. "We've only just—"

"Oh, so he just asked you." Sophia straightened. "So tell me everything."

61

"Actually, my lady, I don't think you'll be too pleased."

"Oh, pish posh. Of course I will." Sophia waved her hand in the air.

Nelwina took a deep breath. "You see, my lady, he purchased me at a wife sale."

Sophia frowned and Nelwina braced herself for the woman's anger.

"Oh, splendid." Sophia clapped, startling Nelwina such that she dropped her fork. "At the re-enactment in Ramsgil—you were on the block and he offered the highest bid." Sophia beamed at Nelwina.

Nelwina looked at Sophia a long moment, wondering if the woman was addled. No mother of a noble family would want her son to marry a commoner, especially one he'd purchased.

While the law turned a blind eye to the commoners' practice of dissolving a marriage through a wife sale, she didn't think the law would view it quite the same when it involved a titled gentleman. 'Twould cause such a scandal

Mayhap they weren't of the nobility, Nelwina thought. But no, how then could Adam be the earl of Spenceworth?

"Have you set a date yet?" Sophia's question interrupted Nelwina's thoughts.

"No, my lady."

"Will you want a large wedding? Where are your people from? Will they attend?"

Nelwina bit the inside of her lip. What would Sophia think if she knew Nelwina was a bastard? Mayhap that was more information than the lady needed. "Nay, I've no family."

"Oh, Nel, I'm so sorry." Sophia's eyes filled with sympathy and Nelwina turned back to her eggs. Sophia reached out and patted Nelwina's hand. "Don't you worry, we'll do away with that silly notion of the friends and family of the bride and groom sitting on opposite sides of the church like they were enemies come to fight."

A few minutes later Sophia stood up, taking the empty plates to the sink. "Are you feeling better now, Nel?"

"Yes, my lady, thank you."

"Well, then, shall we explore the manor?"

Nelwina rose and Sophia hooked her arm through Nelwina's. "I always wanted a daughter, dear. Not that I'm not proud as punch of Adam, but it would have been wonderful to give him a sibling." She patted Nelwina's arm. "So you're the answer to my prayers, dear."

Nelwina swallowed the lump in her throat as she gazed at Adam's mother. How she missed her own dear parent.

They left the kitchen.

"Have you always lived at Spenceworth?"

"Gracious, no. The last time I was here was when Adam's father was alive, twenty-five years ago. I just closed up my flat in London. Since Adam inherited the manor, I thought I'd come for a nice long visit."

They'd reached the stairway when Sophia stopped and turned to Nelwina. "Shall we start with the dining room?"

Together, the women descended the stairs to the foyer. Following Sophia's gaze, Nelwina glanced up at the chandelier, still wondering about the strange candles.

"It needs a good cleaning, don't you think, dear?"

Nelwina nodded and opened her mouth to ask about the candles, but Sophia smiled and moved off to a door.

She opened the door and together they stepped over the threshold.

"Oh, gracious," Sophia mumbled.

The room was cast in shadows, the heavy drapes closed against the morning sun. The long dining table that took up the center of the room was covered with a large cloth. The chairs were grouped together, a cover haphazardly draped over them. The walls were bare of paintings and part of the sideboard was exposed, the dust cover having slid partway off.

Sophia left Nelwina's side. Marching smartly to the window, she flung wide the curtains and sunlight streamed in.

A cloud of dust billowed from the material and left Sophia coughing and waving her hand.

"This place is a mess." Sophia coughed again. "I thought Adam's uncle would see that the place was cleaned on occasion."

"Did he not live here, my lady?"

"No." Sophia backed away from the window and wandered around the table. "Charles became ill some ten years ago. He closed up the manor and moved to London to be nearer the doctors." She ran a hand over the dust cover of the table, coming away with dirt on her palm. "He never really cared for country life and spent very little time here." She dusted her hand off. "But I thought he would have someone come in to clean."

"But where are the servants, my lady?" The manor should never have been neglected like this.

"Servants?" Sophia laughed. "Nel, you're so quaint." She smiled, taking the sting from the word. "I think the queen is the only one with servants these days. Of course, it's politically incorrect to call them such. They're secretaries, or domestic engineers or some such nonsense."

"Did you not spend summers here?"

Sophia shook her head. "No. In fact, we visited very little. We only came here a few times, and we always spent our time in the new wing."

"But why? Spenceworth is a beautiful manor."

"Yes, it is, isn't it?" Sophia looked around. "Charles, Adam's uncle, was going to update it, but when he realized the high cost of the work, he stopped." Sophia wrinkled her nose. "After that he began spending more and more time in town."

"You mean Lord Spenceworth has a house in London as well?"

"Yes, he's got a small flat." She glanced at Nelwina. "Oh, you mean Charles? Yes, he did, but Adam had to sell it to settle Charles's debts." Sophia gave a negligent shrug. "But I daresay Adam didn't mind. The place was awful. I visited him once—just a duty call, mind you, but the place was a shambles even then. I asked him if he would like me to arrange a cleaning lady, but he declined—and none too graciously, I might add. Charles was a solitary man."

" 'Tis a shame."

"I'm sure if you want a place in town after you're married, Adam will do his best to find a larger one for the two of you."

"Oh, nay. I but meant 'twas a shame that Lord Charles was so alone. Did he not marry?"

Sophia laughed. "No, I doubt there's a woman on earth who could abide the man. Mean and crotchety." Sophia walked to the door. "Let's see the rest of the manor. I know there are rooms I've never been in. Charles discouraged anyone from wandering around."

Leaving the dining room, Nelwina asked, "Have you seen the salon?" They walked to the door opposite the entrance to the manor.

"Yes, I popped my head in once, but Charles got rather upset, so I didn't really get to go into it."

" 'Tis a beautiful room. 'Tis where Lady Spenceworth entertained her friends. Oftimes she and the old earl would have tea together there." Nelwina opened the door.

This room too was cast in shadows. She went to the windows and pulled back the drapes. "In the old days, the curtains were a bright yellow and the upholstery was green and white." She looked up from the dark red fabric and met Sophia's gaze.

"We should make a note to change the drapes, then. It would be wonderful to bring Spenceworth back to what it used to be."

Nelwina lifted a corner of a dust cover, exposing the seat of a straight-backed chair. "Why, this belongs in the dining room, my lady." She shook her head.

"We'll need to uncover all the furniture and group it by rooms. 'Tis a lot to do."

"Well, it will give us something to do while we get to know one another better." Sophia smiled and it felt as though someone had covered Nelwina with a soft, warm blanket.

Next they went upstairs.

"This is the lord's chambers, my lady." Nelwina opened the heavy, carved wooden door and inhaled. Mixed with the dust, she could just make out the smell of the old earl's tobacco.

"Do you smell it, my lady?"

Sophia sniffed. She frowned and sniffed again. "Dust, but there's something else." She turned to Nelwina. "What is it?"

Nelwina smiled. "The old earl would smoke here in this room. And sometimes in the study when Lady Spenceworth was visiting. 'Tis cherry."

"How do you know?"

"I asked the earl once what made the room smell like him." Nelwina walked around the dusty room, removing the cloths covering the wardrobe and armoire. She sneezed.

"Bless you."

Nelwina glanced up. "Thank you." She pushed the pile of cloth aside with her foot. "He told me that his tobacco was flavored with cherry root." She smiled at the memory. "The smell was always stronger in the study. 'Twas where he spent most of his time."

Nelwina took a deep breath and straightened her shoulders. "Now, through this door is the dressing room and beyond that is Lady Spenceworth's room."

They walked through the dressing room.

"What is this?" Sophia opened the door to a very small room. In the ceiling two rusted hooks held a small rusty chain.

" 'Tis the powder room, my lady."

Sophia looked around and up and down. "But . . ." She frowned in confusion. Nelwina understood. She'd felt the same way the first time she'd seen it.

"After Lady Spenceworth had her hair combed and styled, she would come in here and scented powder would be sifted down upon her from above. 'Twas the fashion."

"Oh." Sophia's eyes widened in understanding. "Nel, you're simply amazing. It's as if you lived here back then."

"Aye."

From there they went to the kitchen. 'Twas the place Nelwina was most familiar with.

"My goodness, do you think this is the original table?" Sophia ran her hand over the long, scarred, wooden table.

Nelwina bent over and looked at the place where the legs joined the top. And there she found the letters "NH" carved in a childish hand. She smiled, recalling when she'd done that. 'Twas when the earl and his lady entertained. Cook was bustling around the kitchen and bumped into Nelwina one too many times. He ordered her out, but it was cold, so Nelwina had hidden beneath the table. She'd taken a small knife from the table and etched her initials in the leg.

She straightened. "Aye, 'tis the original table."

"Really?" Sophia came over beside her and started to bend over. "How can you tell?"

Nelwina took her elbow and pointed to the top of the table. " 'Twould take many, many years to make a table look like this, wouldn't you think?"

"Yes, I suppose it would." Sophia brightened. "Can you imagine the cook kneading bread on this table?"

If Sophia only knew how easy it was for Nelwina to bring the picture to mind. If she closed her eyes, she was certain she could smell the yeast lingering in the kitchen.

Nelwina closed the door to her room and leaned against it. Wandering through Spenceworth, she had been flooded with wonderful memories and a kind of peace had settled over her as if she, once again, belonged within the walls of the manor.

'Twas like coming home, she thought with a sigh.

But the tour of Spenceworth and tea with Sophia had sapped all of her strength, drained her of all emotion and energy. Sitting on the bed, she took off her shoes and stretched out atop the coverlet. A short nap would make her feel much better.

What was wrong with him? Adam closed the door of the study and sat in the chair behind his desk.

He'd followed his mother and Nelwina as they wandered through the manor. Eavesdropping on their conversation, he was surprised at Nelwina's knowledge of Spenceworth. And every time he reminded himself that he had work to do, he found himself lingering beside an opened door, listening to Nelwina speak or watching the gentle sway of her skirts as she moved. She seemed so comfortable with the material swirling around her legs.

It was like a tour of an eighteenth-century townhouse he'd taken while in school. The guide had spoken much like Nelwina, but with Nelwina it seemed natural. Not once did she stumble over " 'tis" or " 'twas" and she always addressed his mother as "my lady."

He was drawn to her soft voice and her turn of phrase. It was a combination that had him thinking about a candlelit dinner, champagne . . . and seduction.

He shook the idea from his head, nudging thoughts of Nelwina aside, and opened a folder, forcing himself to concentrate on business.

His mother blew into the study a few minutes later. "Adam, dear, she's wonderful. The exact daughter I've dreamed of. Why, she's perfect for you."

Adam looked up from the papers on his desk.

"And she knows just everything about Spenceworth. But then you knew that, didn't you?" She gave him a mischievous grin. "Following us around like that, dear. Well, it was just too sweet."

She rushed on without pausing for him to respond. "But why didn't you tell me?" She pouted. "You could have called your mother with the news, you know. I'm so looking forward to dandling my grandchildren on my knee. Oh, Adam, you've made me the happiest of mothers." She beamed at him.

"News? Dandling grandchildren?" What the bloody hell was she nattering about? God, he hoped she'd wind down. It was as if she had a prodigious amount to say and needed to get the bulk of it out quickly, which required no participation from him.

"Don't you worry about a thing. Nel and I will whip Spenceworth into shape." Sophia frowned. "Though it will take a great deal of help." She brightened. "But we'll manage it. And here I worried about an extended stay."

She managed to have one-sided conversations as well, jumping from subject to subject. Rather like mental Olympics, he thought, bemused by it all.

And then her last statement hit him.

"An extended stay," Adam choked out.

"We'll be such fast friends, I can feel it." Sophia fluttered around the room like a butterfly on a sugar high, while Adam watched her in shocked silence.

"Such an unusual girl, with an unusual name. Though to be honest, I prefer Nel. Must be the 'wina' part of her name that puts one off." She shrugged. "She'll make the perfect daughter." Sophia finally settled in one of the leather chairs facing Adam's desk. "Do close your mouth, Adam, dear."

Bloody hell. Adam snapped his mouth shut. "Mother?" How does one tell one's mother that she isn't welcome to an extended stay? Adam resisted the urge to put his head down on his desk and moan.

And what was this nonsense about a daughter? Surely she wasn't taking Nelwina under her wing? Of course she was; that was the way she treated anyone near his age. He or she was instantly adopted, like it or not.

"Rather eccentric in her dress, don't you think,

dear?" His mother's brow puckered in a frown. "Though she does fit in with the manor, doesn't she?" She met Adam's gaze and smiled.

Adam closed his eyes, hoping to forestall them rolling back in his head. Sophia could be dizzying sometimes.

"Mother?" Adam raised his voice and opened his eyes. Sophia jerked her head around from perusing the books on the shelf beside the desk.

"Adam, don't raise your voice to me."

"Sorry, Mother, but how long did you say you were staying?" Adam sent a silent prayer heavenward. He didn't need another person to look after. He still had to get a doctor for Nelwina and see her back to London. And he had the manor to take care of, not to mention a dwindling bank account.

Sophia smiled back at him, her hands folded primly in her lap. And Adam groaned.

"Actually, I've closed up my flat. Birdie Higginbotham practically ran me out of town. The woman was stalking me, Adam. She was everywhere, bragging about her son buying a country home. Trying to pry information about your inheritance from me." Sophia shook her head. "Even after all these years, she still feels the need to compete with us." She straightened in her chair. "The manor is exactly what I need right now. Birdie will never find me here. Besides, I'm tired of all the hustle and bustle of London."

Adam ran his hand through his hair. Damn Birdie Higginbotham. He couldn't turn his mother away, but she couldn't simply stay here. He didn't have time to keep her entertained.

"I'm just so thrilled to have a country retreat." Sophia broke into Adam's thoughts. "Think of the time we can spend together."

"Mother, the manor needs a lot of work. It's not ready for guests." The light on his desk flickered. "See there, the bloody electricity goes out constantly."

"Oh, pooh, dear. I've got a torch in my car. I'll just bring it in and keep it handy." She flipped her hand in the air. "And I'm not a guest, I'm your mother. The new wing is in good order. It won't take Nel and me long to get the rest of the manor up to scratch." She gave him a challenging stare.

"But Mother—"

"If you didn't think the manor was ready for company, why did you bring Nel here?" Sophia cut in. "I wonder if I can find a gown like hers."

Adam took a deep breath, gathering his frayed patience. "It's a costume provided by the tour company. And I didn't bring—"

"Oh, yes, the tour company. Smashing idea, Adam." She smiled at him. "Very romantic."

The costumes. Damn, another thing he needed to see to. "I'll have to get the costumes returned." He rubbed his temple. "And I need to talk to her, as well," he mumbled.

"Well, then, I'd best get busy, don't you think, dear?" Sophia rose from her chair.

Adam nodded. He needed an aspirin, he decided, as his head began to throb.

Sophia reached the door and Adam raised his head. "Busy? Busy doing what?"

Glancing over her shoulder, she smiled. "Why, the wedding, of course." She shook her head. "You two should really decide on a date." She opened the door. "You can never have too much time to plan, you know."

And the door closed.

Adam blinked. Wedding? What wedding?

Chapter Five

The knocking woke Nelwina from her nap. Rubbing her eyes, she crawled off the bed and padded to the door.

Opening it, she found Adam on the other side and ran her fingers through her short hair. It felt so odd, these short locks of hers.

"Oh, I'm sorry, I didn't realize you were napping."

" 'Tis no matter, my lord. I should not be lying about in the broad of day." Her gaze ran over him, drinking in his masculine charm. Oh yes, she'd done much better than Haslett.

"I was wondering if you'd join me in the study." He glanced at her gown and Nelwina brushed self-consciously at the wrinkles in her skirt. "Once you've had a chance to change, that is."

"Of course, my lord," she replied, mortified that he should see her in such disarray. Blood rushed to her face, firing her cheeks. She must look a mess after having slept in her dress twice now and with no comb to bring order to her hair.

"Oh, and if you'd bring the gown down with you." He nodded to her. "I need to return our costumes to the tour office in town."

"Aye, my lord." She bobbed a quick curtsey and closed the door.

He was taking her clothes? What did he expect her to wear? "I certainly can't appear in the study clothed in only a smile."

Her gaze landed on the bags beside the chest. "The clothing of a woman who uses face paint?" Her cheeks burned. "But what else can I do?"

Taking a deep breath, she picked up the largest of the bags and placed it on the bed. Opening it, she found men's trousers with the same teethed closures as the travel bags. There were sweaters made of such soft yarn and so finely knitted they hardly seemed like sweaters. Bodices with buttons and little stitched holes they fitted into. 'Twas amazing, these things.

In another travel bag she found an assortment of very brief corsets and scanty garments like the ones she discovered she was wearing when she visited the loo.

Recalling her meeting with Adam, Nelwina searched through the pile of clothing on her bed and found what she hoped was appropriate daytime wear.

Returning to the smallest of the bags, she emptied its contents on the bed and discovered a comb as well as the sweet-smelling body wash and lotion.

She glanced from the bottles to the door to the loo and she bit her lip. Dare she make him wait? She slumped. It would make her feel so much better, but how would Adam react to having to wait?

She shook her head. "I doubt he's nervously pacing the study awaiting my arrival."

Grabbing up the bottles, she went to the loo and pushed open the window. On her knees, she reached in and set the plug and turned the handle nearest her. Water rushed from the spigot. As steam rose from the water, she turned one of the other handles and the water cooled.

Nelwina smiled. 'Twas wonderful to have hot water whenever you wanted, she thought. There was no need to carry buckets of water up from the kitchen in order to bathe. So she could bathe as often as she wished. The idea was quite intriguing.

"But what does this handle do?" She gave it a twist and screamed when water came down, drenching one side of her head.

Adam had just settled into the chair behind his desk when Nelwina's scream rattled the windows. Shooting to his feet, he was out the study door and up the stairs before he realized it. Running to Nelwina's door, he flung it open to find a half-drenched Nelwina, her terrified screams assaulting his ears.

"Calm down." He grabbed her shoulders giving her a little shake. "Calm down. Everything's fine."

Her screams subsided and Adam saw water streaming down her cheeks. He wasn't sure if it was tears, or water from the shower he heard running.

He glanced at Nelwina and choked back a chuckle. One side of her head was dripping wet, her hair was plastered to her head and half her bangs hung in her eyes. A little river of water wound its way down into the top of her dress, a damp stain marking its progress.

Her chest heaved with each breath and her shoulders shook.

"Don't you hate it when the shower is left on?" He smiled at her and gave her shoulders a gentle squeeze. Reaching up, he smoothed the damp hair from her cheek. When his fingers touched her warm skin, heat radiated up his arm, then raced through his body. He gazed into her green eyes and, of its own volition, his head moved toward hers. His mouth was a mere breath from hers when he caught himself, and straightened up, breaking eye contact.

Damn, what was wrong with him? Didn't he have enough to deal with? Didn't she?

Stepping around her, he turned the showerhead off and adjusted the temperature of the water.

He straightened to find Nelwina behind him.

"Shower?" She glanced from him to the tub.

Adam smiled, forcing his gaze from her mouth. Otherwise, he just might give in to the urge to kiss her. "Well, I'll leave you to it then." He stepped around her. "See you downstairs in a bit."

Nelwina's confused gaze stayed with Adam as he made his way back to the study. She'd acted as if she'd never seen a shower before. An uncomfortable feeling of dread settled low in his stomach. But he wasn't certain if its cause was her confusion or his attraction to her.

Nelwina stripped off her damp clothing and settled into the tub. " 'Tis a rather puny body you left me,

Mistress Jocelyn." She opened the bottle of body wash, pouring a little in her hand.

She hesitated a moment, feeling awkward bathing a total stranger's body. She'd helped her mother bathe without a thought, but that had been her mother. And these circumstances were much different.

" 'Tis foolish to be squeamish over this. 'Tis just a body, after all." Glancing down at her chest, she mumbled, "And not much of one at that." Rubbing the creamy soap into a lather, she inhaled, enjoying the wonderful soft scent of flowers filling the air. 'Twas a luxury she'd never known before.

As she washed her arms and legs she forgot about the smell of the soap and realized just how thin she was.

It didn't make any sense. How could a woman of privilege lack food? Did she spend all of her coin on cosmetics and scandalous garments?

"Well, that might be what Jocelyn did, but I'll see this body fed and more appropriately clothed. It could do with a few more curves."

She lingered in the tub a little longer. Upon getting out, she dried herself with the thick fluffy towel hanging on a bar. Mayhap later she could take a nice long bath.

But Adam waited below and she didn't want to test his patience any longer.

Later, she descended the stairs, the silky fabric of her skirt swirling around her legs. Holding the neatly folded gown in one hand, Nelwina smoothed her free hand over her skirt one last time before knocking. Her heart thudded painfully in her chest and she found it difficult to take a deep breath. 'Tis a momentous occasion, she thought and wondered if it boded well or ill.

"Come in." Adam's deep voice penetrated the thickness of the door and sent a shiver along her nerves.

Opening the door, she stepped inside the room.

He sat behind the old earl's desk, filling the space with his presence. An aura of mastery surrounded him and Nelwina caught herself fidgeting under his gray-eyed stare.

"Lord Spenceworth." Clutching the gown to her chest, she bobbed a curtsey and lowered her gaze from his eyes to his chest and the white material stretched so tight across it.

My stars, Nelwina thought. 'Tis most indecent. She could see every muscle move and flex as he stacked papers together and set them aside.

Adam glanced up from his desk. "Please, Miss Ta—er—Nelwina, call me Adam."

"Aye, my—Adam." She caught herself, not certain if she was comfortable with the informality. He *was* an earl, after all, and she a commoner. But then she was soon to become his wife, so the familiarity could be permitted.

"Please." He smiled, motioning to the chairs before his desk. "Sit down."

Nelwina walked quickly to the nearest chair and slid onto the seat. Her knees were near to knocking, her nerves frazzled. She inhaled and the smell of the old earl's pipe tobacco eased her. She let out her breath, calmer now.

"Just leave the dress there in the chair beside you."

* * *

Who was this woman? Adam wondered as Nelwina folded her hands primly in her lap. She was so stiff and proper. Where was the woman from the bus, the one who'd slumped in her seat? Physically, Nelwina and Jocelyn were the same, but that was as far as the resemblance went.

He studied her face. She wore no makeup, but with her dark eyebrows and creamy complexion, she didn't need any, he thought. Her green eyes, fringed with long dark lashes, stared back at him.

He lowered his gaze to her lips and swallowed. Lord, they were perfect, made for long, slow kisses. Adam shifted in his chair and glanced away from her face to her sweater and the sheer black scarf she wore. He traced its path until it disappeared into the neckline. Pulling his gaze from her chest, he marveled at the delicateness of her collarbone and the elegant line of her neck.

"You wished to speak with me?"

Adam glanced up, meeting her gaze. "Yes."

What was it he had wanted to discuss with her?

She canted her head, waiting for him to speak and suddenly his tongue felt glued to the roof of his mouth.

He swallowed, glancing down at the papers on his desk as he gathered his thoughts.

"How are you feeling?"

"Quite well, my—" He looked up, arching an eyebrow.

"Adam," she finished with a smile. "And yourself?"

"I'm fine, thank you." He took a deep breath, wondering why he didn't have a good feeling about this conversation. "No headaches? Dizziness? Nausea?"

"Nay, I'm well."

"If you're sure?"

She nodded.

"Then we need to contact your family. I'm sure they're worried about you."

"I've no family to worry."

"You don't have any family?"

She shook her head.

"Shouldn't you be contacting your employer, then? When was your holiday to end?"

"Employer?" She shook her head. "I'm not on holiday."

"But what about the tour?"

Her eyebrows drew together in confusion.

"The wife sale."

Her face brightened. "Aye, and I thank you. Though I don't understand why you participated in the sale, I am grateful."

He waved off her thanks.

"Don't you miss your home?"

"Home?" She sighed. "Oh, nay." She glanced around the room. " 'Tis much better than the cottage I lived in. 'Tis a wonderful place to make a home together."

"A home together?" A sickening feeling settled in the pit of his stomach.

She pinned him with a fierce glare. "Do you now think of the scandal of your actions?" He opened his mouth to reply, but she rushed on. "Are you not a man of honor? Does your word mean so little? You purchased me before witnesses. 'Twas a wife sale. Did you not want a wife, you should have kept your coin in your pocket and moved on."

"But it—"

"We are betrothed," she cut in. "Whether I like it or not, 'tis the way of things. You bought me before witnesses." A tear streaked down her cheek and her lower lip trembled.

He sat there stunned. She truly believed every word she said. The line between fact and fantasy had somehow blurred for her, no doubt due to her fall.

She needed a doctor and he'd better find one quickly before things completely unraveled in her mind. He'd call first thing tomorrow and see if he could get her an appointment. Until then, he figured the best thing to do was go along with her delusions.

He stood up and went to her side, placing his hand on her shoulder. She looked up, wiping a tear from her cheek. "I understand that you wish to break off our betrothal; you are titled while I'm . . . a commoner."

"Nelwina, titled or commoner, it doesn't matter anymore."

She grasped his hand and rushed on, " 'Tis folly to court such scandal, but I've no place else to go. There is much work to be done here. The rooms require cleaning, the rugs a good beating. The banister hasn't seen beeswax in some time, judging from the dull wood. And the gardens are a sin."

He patted her hand, anxious to calm her down.

"You look exhausted, Nelwina. Why don't you rest a while? We'll worry about this later."

He looked down into her eyes and she nodded, offering him a tremulous smile as she stood up. His hand grazed her scarf, the strange feel of it catching his attention.

Bloody hell. That's not a scarf. He stared at the sheer black material draped around her neck.

With quick steps, she reached the door. Adam's gaze locked on the small white tag hanging down from the center of the black material.

It was a pair of bloody panty hose.

The door closed on Nelwina's back and Adam ran a hand through his hair. First thing tomorrow he was calling Dr. Seabrook; something was really wrong with Nelwina.

Once outside the study, Nelwina allowed the tears to fall. Adam meant to turn her out. What would she do now? She had no idea of Jocelyn's life. Did she have family? Where did she live? Who was she?

"Oh, Nel. There you are."

Nelwina dashed the tears from her cheeks, straightened her shoulders and turned to Sophia.

"My dear, what's the matter?" Sophia gasped as she took Nelwina's arm, steering her away from the study door. She shifted her gaze from Nelwina to the door and frowned. "Did Adam upset you, dear?"

"I believe Lord Spenceworth wishes to cry off, my lady." Nelwina blinked back new tears threatening to tumble down her cheeks. "I can understand his reticence; a titled gentleman must never marry below his station." She swallowed hard and looked at Sophia.

"But what am I to do now? I must stay at Spenceworth, else I'll never find my way back."

"Well, I never. I thought I'd raised my son better than that. He's only been an earl a short while and he's already putting on airs." Sophia shook her head. "Well, I won't hear of it." She rubbed Nelwina's hand. "Don't you worry about anything. I'm going to have a word with my son. We'll get this straightened out, don't you fret."

Sophia started to turn away from Nelwina, but stopped and frowned. "Find your way back to where, Nel?"

"To where I belong," Nelwina muttered. "Wherever that might be."

"Well, I happen to believe you belong right here. With all your knowledge of the manor, where else would you live?" She squeezed Nelwina's hand. "Besides, who will keep me company while Adam's busy?"

Sophia marched toward the study. "Why don't you go upstairs and put a cool compress on your eyes while I take care of my son?" She smiled at Nelwina as she grasped the handle of the door. "Off you go, dear. And don't worry, everything will be fine." Sophia wiggled her fingers and disappeared into the study.

Nelwina fled upstairs, but instead of going to her room in the new wing, she turned and went to the old wing, climbing the stairs to the servants' rooms.

She found her way to the room she had shared with her mother a lifetime ago. Flinging the door open, her gaze swept the familiar walls of her childhood home.

Through a film of dirt, faint sunlight filtered in through the two windows. She stepped into the room, remembering hours spent here sewing with her mother. This room was at the back corner of the wing, given to her mother because of the light afforded from the windows.

Nelwina glanced around. Gone was the large bed they'd shared. In its place was a small cot, its thin mattress bare of a coverlet or blanket. A mix of furniture crowded the walls. A washstand with a thick layer of dust dulling its surface sat next to a battered wardrobe with its handles missing; an odd assortment of chairs sat betwixt and between the larger pieces. An old rug was rolled up and lay in front of the furniture.

How she wished she could stay in this room filled with memories of better times. A time when her mother heard her prayers at night and tucked her in; when they cuddled together for a little extra warmth, loath to leave their warm cocoon to put a bit more coal in the brazier.

She could put this room to rights. It would be her haven, the only familiar comforts she knew.

Tears burned in Nelwina's eyes. Somehow she had to convince Adam to let her stay.

"Adam, what is this nonsense I hear about you breaking your engagement with Nel? Since when do titles mean anything?"

Adam glanced up from his work to meet his mother's glare as she stormed into his study.

"Mother, there was never an engagement to break."

He put his pen down. "Nelwina isn't well. I think the fall did more damage than I first thought—"

"Well," Sophia interrupted, standing in front of him, "all I can say is I'm sorely disappointed in you. I thought I'd raised you better." She shook her finger. "For heaven's sake, you're engaged to her. You can't up and change your mind about something like that. It just isn't done."

"Mother, would you listen to me for once?" Frustration put an edge to his voice.

"Adam," his mother gasped. "Is that any way to speak to me? I'm not the one in the wrong here. You are."

"Me? I haven't done anything." He gathered up the papers for the second time today. He'd never get anything accomplished with his mother slamming in and out of the study.

"No? Then you and Nel are still engaged?" She pinned him with a glare.

"We were never engaged."

"Adam." Her eyes went wide with surprise and then, the light of understanding brightened them. "You're just suffering a bout of cold feet. Why, I remember your father going through exactly the same thing just after we became engaged. But you simply must deal with it yourself. You can't drag Nel through your ups and downs." She pointed toward the door. "The poor thing is crushed."

"Mother, it's not a case of cold feet. It was just a re-enactment. She thinks it was real. I'm taking her to the doctor tomorrow and then—"

"She's ill?" Sophia frowned. "She didn't seem ill.

Oh, you mean her dizzy spell. Well, that hardly requires a doctor, Adam. She just needed something to eat."

Does she do this on purpose? Adam wondered. Had she really not heard him or was she just ignoring what he said?

"Mother, she fell and hit her head."

"Oh, yes, I did notice that rather unsightly bruise on her forehead. Do you remember when you were knocked unconscious playing that game? Lord, I lost a good ten years off my life when they carried you from the field." Sophia took a deep breath. "And then the time you ran into the light post in front of the apartment. You had the ugliest knot on your forehead and just the day before your class pictures. I still have that photo in my purse."

Adam brought both hands up, rubbing the sides of his face and then running his fingers through his hair. Was she trying to talk him into a coma?

"But really, Adam, Nel is a lovely woman and I know you'll both be very happy together. And don't worry, those doubts will melt away."

"Mother—"

She held up her hand. "I know, I know. You don't need my advice. I'll just keep it to myself and not interfere."

She was going to stop interfering? Now? After a lifetime of it?

"Later on today, when you've a free moment, would you take me into Ramsgil and introduce me around? I know I have my own car here, but I get so turned around on these country roads. Thank heavens for that nice Mr. Jefferson, else I might not have found the manor at all. He gave excellent directions."

"Mother, as I told you before, I've got a lot of work to get done here. I can't be your tour guide to Ramsgil. Besides, I don't know anyone in town."

"Well, dear, then you need to get out as much as I do. And we'll take Nel along and introduce her around, too. Oh, this will be a wonderful family outing."

Adam groaned as she turned from the desk and started wandering around the study.

"Mother, I'm don't have time to entertain. I'm not going on an outing. And Nelwina will be gone in a few days."

"Now dear, my sensibilities aren't the least bit offended by Nel's presence here. I'm a modern woman, I know you young people like to test drive your relationships. And since you're so busy, I won't bother you with outings and such. Nel and I will just keep each other company until you come up for air."

"Mother, you'll just be bored here. Why don't I take you back to London tomorrow when I take Nelwina to the doctor?" Hope bloomed in his chest.

His mother sighed and slumped down in the chair, closing her eyes. "I don't think I can deal with Birdie Higginbotham, Adam. She's like a vulture circling overhead." Sophia opened her eyes a bit. "Besides, as I've told you, I've closed the flat."

Adam didn't need this right now. He had more than his share of things to do. "Mother—"

"You know, Adam, if you've so much to do, you could have a doctor come here if you think Nel needs medical attention. It would save you a trip to town."

She was wearing him down. When Sophia got an idea in her head, dynamite couldn't dislodge it. He simply had to work around it. One would think he'd have learned that lesson long ago.

"All right, Mother." And if he were really lucky, the physician would make it out quickly and Adam could try to get his life back in order.

"She's such a wonderful girl, Adam. And she knows just everything about Spenceworth. We'll get along famously and we won't be a bit of a bother."

Adam very much doubted that.

"Mr. James, what're you doing here on a Sunday?" The front desk security guard gave Philip a friendly smile.

"I just stopped by to pick up some things."

"Sorry to hear about the layoff. Had any luck finding anything yet?"

"No, but then I've just gotten my resume pulled together." Philip stepped around the security desk.

"Mind signing in, sir?" The guard held a pen and clipboard out to Philip. It only served to remind him that he wasn't a part of the firm any longer. And that's why he had come in today. He didn't want to encounter anyone else while he picked up the things he'd forgotten.

Philip let himself in with his key for the last time. He'd leave it on the secretary's desk when he left. He went to his office and took the umbrella and coat he kept on a hook on the back of his door. With a quick glance around the empty office, he closed the door and went up the hall.

The only thing left to get was the picture hanging in Jocelyn's office. He'd brought it from home to hang in his office, but there wasn't room, so Jocelyn had hung it in hers. He'd just never gotten around to taking it back.

He entered her office and went to the picture hanging on the wall beside her desk. As he passed he glanced in the metal basket on her desk which was filled with a pile of incoming mail. The envelope on top caught his attention and he picked it up.

He read the return address. "Dudley Titchlark, Esquire." Philip chuckled. "What a name." He wondered if anyone took the man seriously. "Better you than me, buddy." He dropped the letter back in the basket and took the painting off the wall, still wondering what Dudley Titchlark, Esquire, wanted with Jocelyn.

Why would Jocelyn be getting mail from England? He picked the letter up again and turned it over. What would an English attorney want with her?

The envelope wasn't sealed very well; a little steam and anyone could open it.

Including him.

Leaving Jocelyn's office, he went to the staff kitchenette. Finding an old kettle in the back of a cabinet, he filled it with water and placed it on the stove to heat. When the water started to boil, he held the back of the envelope over the plume of steam.

He was right, it didn't take much.

A finger of guilt tapped him on the shoulder as he peeled the flap open. But he shook it off. He'd seal it back up and no one would be the wiser. He was just curious, that's all. Even though he wasn't part of her life anymore, he was still concerned for her. This could be important.

He scanned the page and frowned.

"A legal matter?"

Chapter Six

Nelwina gave the room she'd shared with her mother one last look before closing the door. She didn't know if Adam would give her the opportunity to put the room to rights or if he would send her off to find her own way in the world.

As she returned to her room in the new wing, she fought back the panic and fear threatening to overwhelm her. What would she do if Adam made her leave? Where would she go? How would she manage in a place full of strangers where nothing was familiar? A tear slid from her eye and she bit back a sob.

"There you are, dear," Sophia called as Nelwina grasped the knob of her door. Quickly drying her eyes, Nelwina turned to the older woman.

"Aye, my lady?"

Sophia's smile faded and she rushed to Nelwina's side. "Oh, Nel, you're crying again." She opened Nelwina's door and nudged her into the room. Walking her to the bed, Sophia pushed aside the clothing scattered on it and drew Nelwina down next to her.

Nelwina gazed into Sophia's eyes and a powerful pang of longing streaked through her heart. How she missed her mother and the comfort of her love. Adam was lucky to have his mother so close.

Nelwina looked away from Sophia's caring gaze and swallowed back her tears.

"There now, don't you worry." She patted Nelwina's leg. "Adam's over his case of nuptial jitters. So no more tears."

Relief pulled the tension from Nelwina's spine and she slumped. She met Sophia's smiling gaze.

"Oh, my lady, I can't thank you enough." The betrothal was still intact. Spenceworth would be her home, at least for now. Mayhap she could restore her old room. She smiled and reached down to squeeze Sophia's hand.

"Oh, pish posh." Sophia's hands fluttered and then the woman frowned.

"What is it, my lady?" Panic straightened her spine.

"What is that you're wearing around your neck, dear?" She turned Nelwina's shoulders.

Nelwina twisted to follow Sophia's gaze. " 'Tis a scarf."

Sophia tsked. "No, my dear, those are hose." She plucked them from around Nelwina's neck. "They go on your legs."

"Oh." Nelwina took the garment from Sophia's hands and held it up before her. They looked nothing like hose to her, connected as they were, and so sheer she wondered how they could ward off the cold.

She glanced at Sophia and saw the frown puckering her forehead. Heat warmed Nelwina's cheeks. Everything was so strange to her. How was she to learn about all of this? What was her place? She wanted so badly to confide in Sophia, but what would the woman think if Nelwina told her she was from two hundred years in the past?

Sophia watched Nel hold up the panty hose, confusion knitting her brow. It was strange that Adam's fiancée seemed so much at home in the old part of the manor. And rather like a child on her first day of school, staring at her surroundings in wonder and confusion, when she was in the new wing.

At first Sophia thought it was the costume that made her feel that way. But the modern clothing Nel now wore seemed out of character for her. And whatever possessed her to use her hose as a scarf?

Sophia shook the confusing questions from her mind and thought about Adam. He was being difficult. She hadn't missed him following her and Nel around the manor earlier. That was the action of a man in love. Whether he would admit it or not, there was something between Nel and her son. It just needed a little tweaking.

Sophia glanced around at the garments lying on the bed. "Would you like me to help you put your clothes away, dear?"

"Oh, no, my lady." Nel slid off the bed. "I'll tend to it right away."

Sophia rose. "Nel, please call me Sophia. Since we'll be family, there's no need to stand on formality."

"I shall try, my lady . . . rather, Sophia."

"I'll leave you to tidy up, then." Pondering the situation and the best way to correct it, she left Nel.

Nelwina's voice pulled Adam to her half-opened door. She stood at the foot of her bed, an opened magazine in her hand.

Her eyes rounded. "I believe Victoria's secret is out." She quickly flipped the page.

"My stars, does no one feed these women?" She turned another page. "And where are their clothes?"

She snapped the magazine closed and put it aside and picked up a silky bit of lingerie. She canted her head as she held the garment up by a strap.

"And what good is this nightdress?" She folded the nightie up and set it aside.

Adam swallowed as images of Nelwina in the red, satiny gown, the hem brushing the tops of her thighs, popped into his mind. He closed his eyes and rested his forehead against the door jamb, enjoying the picture a moment longer.

Oh, he could tell her the benefits of that bit of stuff. Rather, he could show her.

"And these?"

He stifled a moan and opened his eyes.

"Why have so many short corsets?" She held up a lacy bra. "One is plenty."

Adam swallowed as he watched the bit of intimate apparel swing on her fingertip.

He pushed away from the door with a frown, remembering the panty hose draped around her neck. And just now she'd used archaic terms for a nightie and bra.

Tomorrow couldn't come soon enough for him. He'd locate a good doctor and schedule Nelwina for an exam.

And it was all because of a pink foil star and him that she was in this condition, he thought, regret clinging to his conscience.

He went to his room to retrieve his computer. There was more space in the study. He had to get something accomplished today, and maybe the work would take his mind off Nelwina.

Thank heavens his uncle had wired the study with electricity along with the foyer. And he was glad that he'd hidden the outlet behind a piece of baseboard molding. It didn't draw attention or compromise the authenticity of the room.

"Nel, dear, will you tell Adam that lunch is ready?" Sophia turned from the counter with a platter of sandwiches in her hands. "He's probably in the study." She placed the food in the center of the table. "Oh, and tell him to put on a decent shirt, will you?"

"Aye, my la—Sophia." Nelwina bobbed a quick curtsey before she could stop herself. She simply wasn't used to the informality of the time. Sophia had explained as they prepared lunch that one only curtsied to members of the royal family.

Reaching the study, Nelwina knocked and waited for Adam to bid her enter.

"What is it, Mother?"

She smiled and opened the door.

" 'Tis me, your lord—" Adam looked up and frowned at her. "I mean Adam. Your mother wished me to inform you that luncheon is served." She bobbed another curtsey and pursed her lips in irritation. Why couldn't she remember not to do that?

"Thank you, Nelwina." He smiled. "But you don't—"

"Aye." She cut him off. "Your mother has told me the protocol of this time. 'Tis a habit hard to break, I fear." She stepped back and then stopped. "And she requested that you wear a proper shirt to the table."

Adam's brow arched. "A proper shirt?"

Nelwina nodded and left the study.

Adam appeared as she and Sophia were sitting down at the table in the small kitchen. He wore a deep green shirt tucked into his faded breeches. Nelwina quickly forced her gaze to the sandwich on the plate in front of her, before she shamed herself by ogling Sophia's son.

What was wrong with her that she couldn't keep her eyes off Adam when he was about? And why did her heart double its beating whenever he looked at her?

The chair beside her scraped the floor as Adam pulled it out and sat. From the corner of her eye, she saw him shake his napkin out and drop it onto his lap.

"So, Adam, have you had a productive morning, dear?" Sophia chirped as she poured a sweet, bubbly beverage into her glass. Nelwina had enjoyed her first taste of Coca-Cola earlier, startled at first as the bubbles worked their way down her throat.

"Yes, things are coming along fine." He took a bite of his sandwich and Nelwina watched as the tendons in his neck flexed with the action. She picked up her drink and took a sip, forcing herself to focus on the food and not Adam.

"Nel and I are going to explore the attic this afternoon." Sophia smiled and patted Nelwina's hand. "We're looking for treasures."

"That's nice, Mother. Just be careful, will you? I haven't inspected the attic yet. God only knows what kind of shape it's in. There might be any number of spiders and rodents up there." He took a swallow of his soda. "Maybe I should go up first and check things out."

"Oh, no, Adam. I'm sure Nel and I can handle the spiders and rodents. They're more afraid of us than we are of them." Sophia turned to Nelwina. "Isn't that right, dear?"

"Aye, they are." She folded her hands in her lap and, gathering her courage, she turned to Adam. " 'Tis a very kind thing you've done for me, my lord, and I thank you. I will endeavor to be of help and place no burden on your time."

The words sounded stiff to her ears, but she didn't feel that Adam would appreciate an emotional declaration. Especially after their meeting earlier.

She must show him that as his wife, she would not give in to fits of weeping, that she was strong and dependable.

Adam shifted in his chair. "You're welcome, Nelwina."

"Well, if everyone is finished eating, let's get cracking." Sophia stood up and Nelwina scrambled from her chair, taking the plates from the table to the sink.

"We've treasure to hunt, Nel." Sophia headed for the door. "Leave the dishes for Adam. We cooked, he can clean."

The plates rattled in Nelwina's hands and she turned a cautious glance to Adam, expecting to see outrage stamped on his face.

He just grinned. "Don't look so surprised, Nelwina. Mother has always had that rule. I'm quite proficient with soap and water."

"But—"

"Come along, Nel. We need to change into jeans before we go to the attic. You did bring jeans with you, didn't you?"

Nelwina followed Sophia from the kitchen, glancing back to see Adam fill the sink with water. The picture of him standing before the sink stayed with her all the way to her room and while she sorted through the wardrobe for the mysterious jeans she was to wear.

Standing with Sophia in the attic, Nelwina wondered where to start. Furniture was stacked among boxes and a hodge-podge of other things.

At the far end of the room, Nelwina spotted the chairs that belonged in the hall. Against another wall with several boxes stacked on top of it was the table that should be beside the front door.

"Oh, Nel, look at all the treasures." Sophia clapped happily beside her.

"Aye, my lady, they're treasures, but we've got our

work ahead of us to get to them." Nelwina moved a box out of the way and began making a path down the middle of the room. They would be at this all day.

Sophia and Nelwina worked side-by-side through the day until they were able to get to the chairs for the hall. It took both of them to carry each chair down to the old kitchen, where Nelwina would clean and polish them later.

"We'll have to get the seats recovered," Sophia said, eyeing the chair critically.

Nelwina brushed at the faded petit pointe cover. "If you've the canvas and thread, I can make new covers."

Sophia looked at Nelwina, surprise rounding her eyes. "You can?"

"Aye. I'm fond of needlework."

Sophia smiled. "We can make a trip into Ramsgil to get what you need."

As they climbed the stairs, returning to the attic, Sophia turned to Nelwina. "Nel, I know you haven't been at Spenceworth long, so how do you know such intimate details of the manor?"

Nelwina's mouth went dry. How could she explain it to Sophia? Heavens, she still wasn't quite certain herself what had happened. All she knew was that she was here, among things both familiar and strange.

Nelwina longed to tell Sophia her story; she needed confirmation, to somehow learn how all this had happened.

She glanced at Sophia, whose kindly brown gaze looked expectantly back at her.

"You can tell me, Nel, dear." Sophia whispered to her as they reached the attic.

"Oh, my—Sophia, I would but 'tis impossible to believe." The words escaped Nelwina's lips before she could think.

Sophia cast her a calculating glance before stepping around her and into the attic. "You might be surprised at what I'll believe." She settled herself on a wooden crate and waited expectantly.

"Have you ever felt as though you don't belong?" Nelwina looked at the older woman. "Things feel both familiar and strange at the same time."

"You mean, déjà vu?" Nelwina gave her a blank look. "As if you've been here before or done something before?" Excitement filled Sophia's voice.

"Aye, that's it." A perfect way to describe how Nelwina felt. She smiled at Sophia. " 'Tis like I've lived here before." Nelwina held her breath, waiting for Sophia's reaction to her statement.

"That explains your knowledge of Spenceworth, Nel." She took Nelwina's hand. "Past life." Sophia squeezed her hand. "You've been here in another life."

Nelwina exhaled. Sophia didn't seem the least bit disturbed by Nelwina's words. Another life? Aye, 'twas another life, she thought as she considered Sophia's statement. It did fit, though not exactly. She was still in her present life. Wasn't she? Or had she died and then been reborn into this body? That would explain a lot of things, Nelwina thought, relief lifting her mood.

"Oh, Nel, you'll have to tell me everything. I've

read about past life regression and always wanted to experience it. I even went to a psychic, but she wasn't able to regress me. She says I first must trust her." Sophia frowned. "Now I ask you, would I go to her for sessions if I didn't trust her?"

Nelwina looked at Sophia, wondering what she was talking about, then shook her head to clear away the confusion blocking her thoughts.

Sophia rose from her crate and they started sorting through the attic again. Nelwina spotted a familiar iron bedstead. A little later, she'd pull it out and return it to the room she'd shared with her mother. She would make that room her haven, a place to go when all of this became too much for her.

"Yes." Adam shifted the cell phone to his other ear as he climbed from bed and padded to a nearby table for pencil and paper. "Next week will be fine. How long will you be in town, then?"

He nodded, jotting down a few notes. "Right. I'll have the plans drawn up with the changes by then." He wrote down the number. "Yes, I'll see you on Saturday then."

Punching the end button, he smiled. He hoped his first client would approve the plans for the seaside cottage, and he could get the construction underway.

He needed more than one client in order to make a go of his own firm. But it was a start, he thought.

Shuffling through the papers on the table, he finally found the card with the doctor's number. Since he was up, he might as well get this taken care of.

"Yes, sir, the doctor does make housecalls, but he's

at a symposium in London until next week. If this is
an emergency—"

"No, no—"

"Would you like to make an appointment, then?"

"There isn't a physician taking his calls?"

"No, sir."

"But Miss Tanner fell during the tour company's
re-enactment." Bloody crazy way to run a business,
he thought. "They gave me his number to contact."
Miss Tanner could sue the company, didn't they realize that?

"Oh, yes. Then you'll need to make an appointment
for her so the paperwork can be completed. Shall I
make it for you?"

Running a hand through his hair, Adam sighed.
"Yes, that would be fine."

"I've an opening a week from Thursday at half past
two. Would that do?"

"That's the soonest you have?"

"Yes, sir."

"But she's hurt now."

There was a long silence and then the receptionist
said, "Did she break anything?"

"No." His patience thinned. "She hit her head and
was unconscious for a spell."

"How is she now?"

"Physically, she's fine, but mentally, she's rather
confused."

"Oh, well, that's to be expected. Usually clears up
in a few days. But if you think she needs a doctor
before next week, I'd take her to emergency. Would
you like the appointment?"

"Fine. I'll take it then."

After giving the receptionist the information she needed, he hung up.

It didn't feel right, waiting so long for Nelwina to see a doctor. But maybe the receptionist was right and her confusion would clear up. He sure hoped it did. No telling what she'd be wearing when she came downstairs next.

He'd have to enlist his mother's help in watching Nelwina. In a way, her presence at Spenceworth was a godsend because he would be in London Friday through Monday.

Leaving early on Friday would give him enough time to get to his flat, print up the new plans, and make a few calls. Saturday would be spent with his clients, leaving Sunday for some time to himself after he tied up any loose ends.

His small flat just outside of town doubled as an office. While it was convenient, it was yet another expense to deal with.

Somehow he had to solve his financial woes and find a balance between Spenceworth and his career.

Nelwina relaxed her grip on her seat as Sophia brought the car to a stop and the noisy thing went silent. The trip to Ramsgil this afternoon had robbed her of her voice and set her nerves on edge. She much preferred the horse and cart to the modern car.

"Come along, Nel." Sophia closed her door with a noisy slam, bringing Nelwina from her thoughts.

Nelwina fumbled with the handle until she discovered how to open the door. Climbing out, she joined

Sophia in front of a little shop displaying a rainbow of threads and material in the window.

Inside, Nelwina gazed in wonder at the selection. Every color imaginable was available in several different types of thread and floss. She found a small, tightly woven canvas in maroon, perfect for the covers of the chairs for the foyer. Selecting a variety of floss and beautifully crafted shiny needles, Nelwina glanced at Sophia.

"My lady?"

"Did you find everything we'll need for the cushions?"

"Aye." Nelwina hesitated. "But I've no funds." Color heated her cheeks as she whispered her confession.

Sophia smiled. "I certainly don't expect you to pay for this. It's for the manor, after all." She patted Nelwina's hand. "Are you sure you have everything? Scissors?"

"Oh, aye, I'll need a small pair, if they're not too expensive."

"Now, you're not to worry about that. Besides, they can't cost much."

As Sophia and Nelwina left the shop with their purchases, an older gentleman approached and Sophia's face lit up with pleasure.

"Oh, Mr. Jefferson. How nice to see you again."

"Mrs. Warrick." The man nodded to Sophia, his gaze touching on Nelwina briefly before returning to the older woman. He smiled and Sophia blushed prettily.

"I wanted to thank you for your directions to Spenceworth. Without them, I'm sure I'd still be touring the countryside searching for my son." She glanced at Nelwina. "Oh, I'm sorry. Let me introduce Mr. Niles Jefferson." She turned to Niles. "And this is Adam's fiancée, Nelwina Honeycutt."

Niles frowned, scratching his chin. "Thought your name was Jocelyn Tanner."

"Oh, no. It's Nelwina Honeycutt." Sophia smiled and Niles simply shrugged, his gaze softening as he looked at her.

"Would you join us for tea, Mr. Jefferson?"

Niles's face blossomed a bright red and Nelwina bit the inside of her lip to keep from chuckling. He was much like a lad in the throes of first love.

She glanced at Sophia, noting the hope shining in that lady's eyes.

"Mrs. Warrick, I would be honored, but—"

"Wonderful. It's always nice to be in the company of a proper gentleman." Sophia linked her arm with Niles's and turned him around, propelling him to the door of a teashop. Nelwina followed behind, feeling much like a chaperone.

Chapter Seven

"Sophia."

Sophia hesitated just a moment. She recognized the high-pitched squawk, but pretended not to hear it, loath to put a topper on an already disturbing day.

As she'd done the last few days, she'd come to Ramsgil and spent a wonderful hour or so having tea with Niles. From the first time they had met, when he gave her directions to Spenceworth, she'd felt something special spark between them. With each meeting they became a little closer.

But today she sensed that he was resisting the attraction, drawing away. She tried to remember if she'd said something to cause it, but for the life of her she couldn't. It wasn't that Niles wasn't kind and attentive; she just sensed a tiny bit of a chill. She shrugged. He probably had something on his mind.

"Oh, Sophia dear." The thud of footsteps alerted Sophia to the inevitable.

Pasting a smile on her face, Sophia turned. "Why

Birdie Higginbotham, whatever brings you to Ramsgil?"

Birdie preened like a mangy parrot, her skinny little neck stretching in the process.

"We heard you closed your London flat and came to the country. Imagine running into you here of all places."

"Yes, just imagine." She didn't fool Sophia for a minute. The minute the old bat had found out about Adam's inheritance she'd pestered Sophia constantly. But Sophia had kept the details to herself. Apparently, Birdie had found out where the manor was and couldn't wait to investigate.

"You know our Ludlow just purchased a country estate."

"Did he now?" No doubt there was a coop on it just for Birdie.

"Yes. Ludlow's little Earlene is about to make us grandparents."

"My, how nice." Sophia gritted her teeth. Little Earlene outweighed Adam, for the love of heaven. There wasn't anything little about Earlene except her brain, Sophia thought.

"So tell me about this manor house Adam has taken on. I imagine it's just a small thing, hardly as nice as Ludlow's, I'm sure." Birdie fluffed all ten of the hairs on her head. "He paid a tidy sum for Runnymede. But it was worth every pound. Earlene is furnishing it with antiques of the period."

"Yes, well, that's nice." Sophia turned around, resisting the urge to sprint down the street to her car.

"We'd so love to visit you and Adam at his manor. What was the name of it again?"

"Spenceworth." Sophia glanced over her shoulder at the woman.

"Yes, Spenceworth." Birdie stood there, her head canted, waiting for an invitation. Sophia narrowed her gaze.

She and Nelwina were making good progress on the manor. With Niles's help, they'd hired a couple of the ladies in Ramsgil to aid with the cleaning. He'd also put her in contact with a handyman. The extra help would come in on Saturday while Adam was in London. They should be able to finish most of the downstairs before Adam returned.

Oh, how she'd love to see the look on Birdie's face when she saw Spenceworth, and Nel would put Earlene to shame by simply breathing. Just to get the woman to shut up for a while. Put her in her place, Sophia thought with glee.

"Shall we say a week from today, around seven, then?"

"Perfect, dear. Ludlow and Earlene will be thrilled." Birdie smiled at Sophia. "And, Maynard, of course will join us."

Sophia cringed at the thought of the Higginbothams sitting at the formal dining table at Spenceworth, but decided it would be worth the look on Birdie's face when she saw the manor and Nel.

Why, old Birdie would be green as a parrot.

"Damnation," Adam muttered as he drove up the drive to Spenceworth. "The bloody electricity must be out."

After spending three long days in London meeting with finicky clients and making an appointment with a new one, he was tired and longed for a quick snack and his bed.

The manor was pitch black. He pulled the car up to the front, grabbed his briefcase from the seat beside him and got out. The lights from the car would stay on for a few minutes and at least allow him to get inside, but from there he'd be completely in the dark. He'd have to remember to put a torch in the car, he thought as his feet crunched on the new gravel of the drive.

The car lights went off just as he opened the door and he was surrounded by total blackness. Tonight was a moonless night, making the darkness complete.

Adam set his briefcase down and closed the door, fumbling with the lock.

Stretching his arms out, he made his way to the stairs. But his toe snagged on something and he struggled to retain his balance. Pitching forward, he grabbed for purchase on anything. His hand brushed smooth wood. The next instant the wood crashed to the floor, followed by the sounds of breaking glass.

Adam landed on his knees. He put his hand down to push himself up and cursed at the sharp cutting pain to his left palm.

He looked up as a halo of light appeared from the back of the hall. He watched as Nelwina rushed to his side, candle in hand.

"My lord, are you hurt?" She supported his arm and tugged him up. The light from her candle illuminated his hand. She gasped. "You *are* hurt."

"It's just a cut."

"Come along, we need to tend to your hand." Gently grasping his left arm, she led him to the old kitchen.

What the hell was she doing in there? Adam wondered as he descended the few stairs to the door.

Nelwina pushed the door open and Adam stepped into the room. Several candles chased the darkness into the corners. A fire burned brightly in the huge hearth.

"Sit here, please." Nelwina guided him to a chair beside the worktable in the center of the room.

Adam turned his gaze from the fire to watch Nelwina. She looked so prim and proper with her high-necked, long-sleeved nightgown and fuzzy slippers peeking out when she moved. He didn't know many women who wore flannel gowns anymore. But rather than putting him off, Adam was even more attracted to Nelwina. Perhaps it was the mystery of what lay beneath all the material. Or was it that she'd been on his mind the three days he'd spent in London?

With a towel in hand, she took an old kettle from the hook over the fire. "I was warming water for tea. It shouldn't be too hot yet."

"What did I trip over?"

She glanced up from pouring water into a bowl she'd taken from a cabinet. "I imagine it was the small table and vase. The chair that sits beside it is still in the attic. We didn't expect you until tomorrow, else I would have put it out of harm's way."

She returned the kettle to the fire and sat down beside him. Dampening the towel, she took his injured hand in hers and dabbed at the blood pooling in his palm.

He sat mute under her ministrations, admiring the smoothness of her skin, the dark fan of lashes against her cheeks as she wiped his cut. His gaze clamped on the tip of her tongue as it made a circuitous route, moistening her lips. He closed his eyes, swallowing a groan as his body reacted to her.

"You're not going to faint, are you?"

Adam opened his eyes at the sound of Nelwina's concerned voice and found himself leaning toward her. His gaze met hers and he leaned closer, drawn by the warmth in her eyes. He brought his right hand up and palmed her cheek. Her skin was warm and she stilled under his touch.

"No, I'm not going to faint, Nelwina." He ran his thumb over her moist lips and his nerve endings hummed. "But I am going to kiss you."

With those softly spoken words, Adam brought his lips to hers, inhaling the soft floral scent that surrounded her.

The first touch of his hand stole Nelwina's breath; the gentle brush of his lips set her blood to pounding. He kissed the corners of her mouth, then the center. His groan vibrated against her lips and the pressure increased. His hand moved from her cheek to her shoulder and she leaned into him, the towel still pressed against his wounded palm.

He traced her lips with his tongue, and Nelwina was lost. She'd never been kissed like this before, so gentle and warm.

She'd missed Adam these three days. She found

herself wandering the halls, listening for his voice or the tread of his feet. She'd poked her head into his study simply to inhale the scent of old leather and sunshine. Smells that reminded her of Adam.

Without him here it was as if the sun had ceased to shine. She'd been listless, not looking forward to rising in the morning, knowing he wouldn't walk into the kitchen, his hair a bit rumpled, wearing what Sophia had called a tee shirt and jeans.

And here he was kissing her, making her heart pound and her blood sing through her veins.

She sighed beneath his lips and Adam took advantage and deepened the kiss. He was losing himself in her. Needing to feel her against him, he started to rise, pulling her with him. But the movement broke the moment and Nelwina stepped away from him, her fingers touching her lips, her eyes large with surprise.

He offered her a smile. "Yes, I know. Did the same thing to me." Damn, but he wanted more.

"How is your hand?" she asked in a shaky voice, turning to the fire.

Adam blew out a breath. He never thought he'd find flannel nightgowns so bloody sexy. She bent over the fire, poking at the glowing wood with a poker. The material stretched across her backside, accentuating the narrowness of her waist. Adam shifted his gaze to the fire now licking at the wood.

"Your hand?"

Nelwina's question pulled his attention from the flames in the hearth, so like the ones heating his blood.

"It's fine." He moved the towel, offering his palm

up for her inspection. "It's just a small cut."

She nodded. "Would you like some tea?" She motioned to the end of the table where he noticed dishes set out. But it wasn't tea he wanted from her.

As if reading his thoughts, she stepped back and out of his reach, folding her arms across her chest to let him know that the intimate moment was gone.

Fatigue washed over him then. It had been a long few days with little sleep. He'd spent his time between his clients, his flat and trying to track down the plans for Spenceworth's gardens.

"No thanks." If he stayed any longer, they wouldn't be sharing tea on that table, but something substantially more. He walked to the door, turned to her and held up his palm. "Thank you."

"You should take a candle, else we'll be tending another wound." She smiled, taking a candle from the mantle and offering it to him.

He retraced his steps and took it from her. "Yes, I don't need to trip over anything else, do I?" *My heart is enough,* he thought with surprise, and quickly left the kitchen.

Sophia stepped away from the kitchen door and headed to the stairs, her penlight zigzagging a path in front of her.

She'd had her doubts about this engagement. But after watching Nel mope about the last few days and catching a glimpse of the heated kiss shared between Nel and her son, her worries were banished. She smiled. Yes, things were coming along quite nicely.

"Mother?"

Sophia turned at the stairs. "Adam, what a surprise. I thought you were to return tomorrow." .

"I finished early."

"Well, we're glad you're home, dear." Sophia started climbing the stairs. "Oh, and we'll be having dinner guests next week."

"What?" She glanced over her shoulder, flashing her light on Adam.

"Dinner. You know, the meal you eat in the evening?"

"Mother, I know what dinner is. What I don't know is who, and why you invited anyone."

"The Higginbothams."

"Not Ludlow and his parents?" Adam groaned.

"And little Earlene too, dear."

"I've got too much to do right now, Mother. I don't have time for this. You're going to have to ring them and cancel."

"Well, I'd love to, but they're on holiday and I can't reach them. Besides, I'm looking forward to seeing the look on Birdie's face when she sees Spenceworth. Ludlow has purchased a country place and Birdie couldn't say enough about it. One would think Spenceworth was a caravan, for heaven's sake."

"But Mother—"

"For once I'd like to render the old bird speechless. It's time she found out that we're not chopped liver." She opened the door to the new wing. "Now, don't worry about a thing. Nel and I will take care of everything." And Sophia disappeared down the hall. Her light flashed across the floor, marking her progress.

* * *

Around dawn, Adam finally gave up on sleep. Every time he closed his eyes he saw Nelwina in her nightgown, the fire of passion charging her gaze.

Glancing over the banister as he went downstairs, he stopped when he caught sight of the foyer.

Early morning sun created a patchwork of light on the rugs covering the floors. Beside the front door was a half-circle table, a small silver tray shining brightly on top.

He came down the rest of the stairs and turned to look at the back of the hall. On either side of the door to the salon stood two massive chairs, intricately carved with high backs, the wood gleaming as a shaft of sunlight reached into the shadows.

Portraits hung on the wall, the pursed lips of the subjects adding to the old feel of the room. All the cushions on the chairs were faded, but care had been taken to remove any dust. The table he'd knocked over the night before was righted and the glass swept up. No doubt Nelwina had tidied things up last night.

So this was what Nelwina and his mother had been up to while he was in London. The transformation was remarkable. He felt like he'd just walked into someone else's home a couple of hundred years ago.

Philip signaled the bartender again. A minute later, another drink appeared before him and his pile of bills got a little smaller.

He'd been out on more interviews than he could count, and still hadn't found a job. Severance packages were fine, but that wouldn't last forever. But more than that was the damage to his self-esteem.

First he was fired and then he couldn't find another job. The job market wasn't supposed to be that bad.

He sipped his drink, ignoring the newcomers and their jovial laughter. It wasn't that many Fridays ago he'd come here, joking and having a good time, himself.

"Hey James," one of the newcomers called to him. "Found a job yet?"

Philip looked up. "No, but I haven't tried that hard either. Thought I'd take a vacation—sit around, watch soap operas and eat bonbons."

The guys laughed. They sat down on either side of him, leaving one man to stand behind Philip.

"Have you heard?"

"What?" Philip took another sip of his drink.

"Jocelyn hasn't come back from vacation. It's been over a week since she was due back."

The bartender brought beers for the men around Philip. They were regulars. Every Friday you could count on seeing these men come in for a few beers before they went off to either their wives and home or out to dinner.

"They haven't heard a word from her." The guy took a long pull from his beer bottle. "Weird, huh? I mean, Jocelyn was always so conscientious. Hell, I don't think she's ever been late to work once."

"Maybe she liked England so much she decided to stay," Philip offered, wiping the moisture from the outside of his glass.

"Yeah, but you'd think she'd call the boss and let him know."

"I heard they were pulling all her accounts and

were going to audit them. Bet they think she's embezzled money and then left the country."

"Wasn't there an internal audit being done on one of her accounts already?"

The other man shrugged.

Philip choked on his drink. "Jocelyn would never do that." He put his drink down. "When are they doing the audit?"

The guy shrugged. "Don't know. Probably take them a couple weeks to gather everything up. You know how these things go. They've locked up her office and the auditors will go in and work there. But first they have to get the auditors scheduled."

"Hell, that could take more than a couple weeks."

"I think the company feels safe enough. They've transferred all the funds she had access to into new accounts."

"Do they really think Jocelyn would steal from the clients?" Philip's hand shook as he brought his drink to his lips.

"No. It's standard procedure, James, you know that." The guy shoved his empty toward the bartender. "But you have to admit, it does seem rather suspicious—she goes out of the country on vacation and never comes back."

He took a drink from a new bottle. "Of course, she could come home tomorrow and with a good explanation, the whole thing would probably come to a halt. Those audits cost the firm big bucks."

Philip fought to control his panic. He finished his drink as casually as he could and then excused himself.

He had to find Jocelyn, and quickly.

Chapter Eight

Nelwina hadn't slept well in days. Not since sharing that kiss with Adam. Each time she heard his voice, her heart beat a little faster; each time his gaze met hers, her stomach fluttered nervously.

Padding to the kitchen, she leaned against the wall to illuminate the room and went about making herself a cup of tea. It still amazed her how quickly and easily things could be done in this time. Reaching into a cabinet, she pulled out the package of Mallow cookies. Only one remained. With a shrug, she took a knife from the drawer and cut the cookie in half. Closing up the package, she took her sweet and, clutching the mug of tea, left the kitchen and climbed the stairs to the servants' quarters. She would spend her day cleaning and arranging the furnishings in her old room.

The more she learned about this time, the stronger her need to stay at the manor became. It was home to her, a reminder of happier times. And it was familiar. When the modern contraptions became too much for her, she could find comfort in the old section of the manor.

In Sophia, Nelwina had found a mother figure offering guidance, understanding, and safety. But Adam was a different kettle altogether, especially after that devastating kiss. He'd turned her world topsy-turvy.

"Mother, you didn't find any old drawings of the gardens in the attic, did you?" Adam poured a cup of coffee and reached into the cabinet for his cookies.

"What happened to the Mallows?" He held up the package for his mother to see the mutilated remains of one cookie. "She's been pilfering them again. Look what she did to the last one." He tried to look severe, but he couldn't quite control the smile pulling at the corners of his mouth.

"Are you sure it was Nel, dear?"

Adam looked pointedly at his mother. "Was it you?"

Sophia laughed. "No. I guess Nel shares your love of them. But at least she didn't take the last one." She shook her head. "I don't see how either of you can eat them first thing in the morning. Frankly, they'd give me a stomachache."

"Not much of a breakfast," Adam grumbled, biting into the remains of the cookie.

His mother nodded, smiling into her teacup. "Even if it were a whole cookie, it still wouldn't constitute breakfast in my book." She swallowed a sip of tea and said, "But to answer your question, dear. No, we didn't see any drawings of the garden." She silently offered Adam a piece of toast. "Why?"

Absently, Adam took the slice and bit into it. "I'm restoring the gardens and I'd like to do it as near to the original plans as I can."

"Have you asked Nel?"

"Why would I ask her?"

"Because she lived here in the late seventeen hundreds, dear. No doubt she knows how they were laid out."

"Mother, please don't start that again. It's preposterous."

"You can think that if you wish, dear. But all one has to do is talk to her to realize that she knows everything about this manor, and in such detail." His mother rose from her chair and took her dishes to the sink. Looking over her shoulder at Adam, she said, "It couldn't hurt to ask her, could it?" Heading to the door, she called over her shoulder, "I'm off to Ramsgil this morning. I'll see you around lunchtime."

"Would you get another package of Mallows while you're out, Mother?"

"Of course, dear," she called from the hallway.

Adam pondered his mother's words while he drank his coffee and finished his toast. Ever since she'd gone to that psychic, she'd come up with some mad ideas, but this was the craziest. He shook his head.

Finished with his breakfast, Adam knocked on Nel's door. Maybe she could help him locate the plans. When she didn't answer, he headed downstairs in search of her.

He pushed open the door to the old kitchen and stepped inside the tidy room. Memories of the night they'd kissed rushed back to him. He hadn't been in here since then.

There'd been an old-world quality about that night—the candles and fire illuminating the room, Nel in a long flannel gown, heating water over the fire. He stared at the table, recalling the feel of her lips against his. His body jerked to attention.

He shook the memories from his mind. "Nel?"

There was no answer.

He poked his head into the darkened downstairs rooms, absently noting the absence of the dust covers, and then he headed to the attic. If he didn't find her there, he'd go ahead and search for the elusive garden plans. It was strange that they weren't with the rest of the manor's papers. He'd found a couple old journals and some papers, but nothing on the garden.

If he didn't find anything in the attic, he'd thumb through the journals again. There had to be information on the designer of the gardens. Maybe he'd missed it the first go-round.

The attic door opened easily beneath his hand. "Nel?" He glanced around the room and whistled low.

His mother and Nel had done a nice job bringing order to the room. He recognized furniture that had been downstairs before Nel had arrived, along with boxes stacked and labeled. A path had been cleared down the center of the attic, the furniture on one side and boxes stacked on the other.

Scanning the labeled boxes, he didn't find anything pertaining to the manor itself, just dishes and linens and other miscellaneous items. In a far corner, he found a box labeled "books" and pulled that out. He'd

123

take it down to the study and examine the contents.

He left the attic carrying the box. As he descended the stairs, he heard a door open and saw Nel step out of a room at the end of the hall.

"There you are." Her head snapped around and her hand went to her chest. "I wondered where you'd gotten off to."

"I was just . . . uhm . . . cleaning."

"Up here?"

She nodded.

Adam put the box down next to the stairs and walked to Nel. She wore a pair of jeans that hugged the curve of her hips, hips that were taking on a decidedly sexy fullness, he thought with a smile. He'd found her attractive on the bus, but now she was downright sexy. He allowed his gaze to travel over Nel's body again.

"Need some help?"

She bit her lower lip and shook her head. Adam smiled again, and a flush crept from her neck to her cheeks.

God, she's delectable.

"Is there something you needed?"

Images swept through Adam's mind, images that would surprise Nel, no doubt.

Shaking the thoughts from his mind, he focused on a safer topic. "I've been searching for the garden designs."

Nel's eyes brightened and she smiled. "So you'll be putting the gardens to rights, then?"

"Yes, but there isn't much left to guide me. The hedges are monstrously overgrown, the paths are weed-infested, and it's difficult to recognize what the original design was."

"But my . . . Adam, I can help you with that." Excitement filled her words.

Adam grinned. "You know where the plans are?"

Nel shook her head. "But I believe I remember the way of the garden. Come." She stepped around Adam.

Adam turned and followed her.

"Mind, I might not recall all of the flowers." She glanced over her shoulder, concentration knitting her brow. "But I'm certain I remember the paths and such."

Adam rubbed his face. Not this again. His mother kept harping on Nel's past life. He didn't need Nel taking up the banner.

He hurried after Nel, grabbing the box of books and taking it downstairs. Leaving it beside the door of his study, he followed Nel to the gardens.

They wandered the paths with Nel stopping here and there explaining the plantings in this bed, describing the flowers in another. From her, Adam began to get the feel of the gardens.

"Where did you find the plans?" Adam interrupted Nel's narrative as they reached the center of the gardens.

"Oh, there aren't any plans. The old earl had a row with the designer and he destroyed all the information."

Adam snorted.

"I don't rightly know what the argument was about.

I was young then and only caught the whisperings among the staff."

"Nelwina, please, not that past life stuff again."

She glanced at him and frowned. Narrowing her gaze, she finished, "I only know that the old earl sent the gardener on his way, destroyed the plans and set to making the garden his own."

Adam stared at Nel. In his search for the layout of the grounds, he'd heard similar stories, but he'd discounted them. But since he couldn't find any plans, could the stories be true?

He shook the absurd thoughts from his mind. He was beginning to think like his mother. And that was a frightening thought.

Nel moved along the paths, stopping here and there to pull a weed growing in one bed or another.

He cleared his throat. "I wanted to thank you."

"For what?"

"The foyer. I assume you had a hand in it?"

"Aye. But you've no need to thank me. 'Twas my pleasure and a promise I made to you. We've completed the dining room and the salon, as well. Mayhap when your mother returns we'll tour the rooms."

"You did all that in three days?"

Nel laughed, a light sound that caressed his ears.

"Nay, we've been working on them for over a week now. You've been so busy you haven't noticed." There was no accusation in her tone, but understanding and a note of approval.

And Adam found it meant something to him, that she approved of his work ethics.

Nel turned to him, a freshly plucked weed grasped

126

in her hand, her head tipped to one side. "Would you like me to draw up what I remember of the garden, my lord?"

Damn, but she was charming, Adam thought, smiling, even when she forgot and called him "my lord." He could picture her in a long gown, her hair tucked up under one of those frilly caps he'd seen in old portraits.

He blinked. Now where had that come from?

"I could do it, my lord. If you're wanting to restore the gardens, I can help."

Her earnest plea drew his attention. He had no doubt that Nel could draw up a nice set of plans. She'd done wonders in the foyer. Other than a very brief glimpse he had yet to see the other rooms. But instinct told him they would be even grander than the foyer.

Why not let Nel try her hand at drawing the gardens? He could use some help with them. The design had to compliment the architecture of the building. If he were to draw visitors from Ramsgil, the gardens had to be spectacular, especially if that was the only thing offered on tour. And Nelwina did seem to have a feel for the place.

He glanced back to her, the weed clasped in her fingers twirling around in a nervous circle. She looked so damned attractive standing there in the late-morning light, the sun glinting off her burnished hair.

His gaze snagged on her lips and, for the hundredth time, he recalled the kiss they'd shared. And for the hundredth time he craved another.

"I'd like that, Nel." He glanced around the garden.

Was his reply in answer to her question or his body's desires? He wasn't sure.

He forced himself to turn from her and walk back to the house before he took her in his arms and kissed her till they were both dizzy.

He stepped through the garden doors into the drawing room and inhaled deeply. He had to get control of himself. Nel was a complication he didn't need right now. No sense in getting more involved. Eventually, she'd have to return to her own life in the States.

The odd part was, she didn't seem inclined to do so. Every attempt he'd made to learn more about her—her career, hobbies, friends—she simply shrugged and changed the subject.

But surely there was someone worried about her; her employer, a friend, someone. He recalled seeing her handbag in her room and he considered searching through it for information. It would be prying and normally he wouldn't do it, but this was no ordinary situation. He had to consider it. He already shouldered enough guilt where Nel was concerned. If she caught him going through her things . . . well, it didn't bear thinking about.

But why didn't she know at least something of her life?

Pulling his thoughts from Nel and the confusion surrounding her, he looked around the drawing room. It was a jumble of mismatched furniture with an air of neglect about it, dust covers strewn half on and half off some of the pieces. Would Nel be able to work her magic here as well? Would it have the same charm as the foyer? As Nel?

He rubbed his brow. He had to curb these thoughts. But the image of her blushing when she was in his presence and the way she smiled at him made it damnably hard to do. Did she share his interest or was Spenceworth the only thing she was passionate about?

No. He shook his head. There was their kiss. It nearly scorched his skin, he thought as his lips warmed at the memory.

"Bloody hell."

He left the drawing room to return to his study, determined to go through the box of books he'd found in the attic and put aside the crazy thoughts racing around in his mind.

In the foyer he stopped and cast an appreciative gaze around the room.

Damn, he'd love to open the place up for tours. No doubt it would draw a lot of notice. But his uncle's will was quite specific.

"Bloody waste."

He entered the study and opened the box, unloading its contents on the table between the two chairs in front of his desk. But try as he might, he couldn't banish Nel from his mind.

Leaving the books piled on the table, he went to his desk. In the bottom drawer he found a sketchpad and watercolors. Just the things Nel would need to draw out the garden.

Not stopping to think his actions through, he went back to the garden, hoping she hadn't left yet.

Gazing through the drawing room windows, he watched Nel pull weeds from a weathered planter.

Nelwina tossed the weed aside and was reaching for another when the sound of a closing door brought her around.

She bit her lower lip and watched as Adam came toward her. She'd just been congratulating herself on controlling the tremors that racked her body whenever he was near. She'd managed to step away from him before, but she didn't know if she had the strength to do it again.

"I've brought you a sketchpad and watercolors."

Nelwina inhaled deeply, forcing her riotous pulse to slow. Dusting her hands off, she cautiously came to her feet, unsure whether her legs would hold her up. She stepped toward him before she even realized it.

Nelwina took the pad he offered, clutching it to her chest. Adam stepped closer, holding out the watercolors.

"You'll need these, too."

She nodded, taking the thin box from him, careful not to touch his hand.

Adam captured her wrist and tugged her gently to him.

"Nel." Her name whispered from his lips, the sound so deep and masculine, set her pulse to racing and the tremors started anew.

He canted his head to the side and she watched, mesmerized, as he slowly brought his lips to hers. His eyes closed, offering her a glimpse of the fan of his dark lashes.

She breathed in his scent, a clean manly smell that went straight to her head. He nibbled at the corner of her mouth as his fingers stroked her wrist.

With a groan, he wrapped his arms around her waist, pulling her close, the sketchpad still clutched against her chest.

His lips moved over hers, firm but gentle, coaxing yet demanding. Her knees wobbled and she grasped his shoulders, the sketchpad forgotten as it slid to the ground.

Adam traced Nel's lips with his tongue, begging entrance. His body jerked to full attention when she tentatively opened her mouth. He tasted her sweet warmth, his tongue leading hers in a dance of passion and seduction.

Her intensity matched his, fanning the flames of desire. He held her closer, bringing his hand up to cradle her head as he deepened the kiss. He dropped his other hand from her waist to her hip, pulling her against him to share the heat of his desire. A groan rumbled up his throat at the intimate contact.

Lost in a sea of yearning, the watercolors fell from her grasp. In a frantic dance of passion, she explored the breadth of Adam's shoulders; her hands clutched the muscles of his arms and finally found their way to his neck, where her fingers slid through the silky strands of his hair.

His groan vibrated against her mouth, and Nelwina sighed in response.

Adam pulled away, kissing the corners of Nel's

131

lips, then her eyelids, before resting his forehead against hers, the raspy sound of his breath warring with the pounding of his heart.

Nelwina opened her eyes when Adam moved away, mumbling something about a cold shower. She watched him retreat, disappearing through the drawing room door.

Her entire body shook as she knelt down to gather the sketchpad and watercolors. Holding them against her chest, she glanced once more to the door through which Adam had gone.

She missed him already.

It had taken every ounce of Adam's control to end that kiss and walk away. He could still feel Nel's lips, her body pressed against his. Desire throbbed through his body. Damned if he didn't need that cold shower.

A surge of pride flowed through him. He knew that Nelwina wasn't ready to take the relationship to the next level and although his emotions wanted him to press on, sensibility told him that the timing was wrong. Work at Spenceworth was progressing nicely, his trip to London was productive, no need to rush romance. Yes, sensibility ruled.

I am in control and life is good.

He had started to climb the stairs when a movement in the window caught his eye. He turned around and peered outside.

"Damn. The doctor." Adam had completely forgotten about the appointment. He opened the door to the doctor's knock.

"Lord Spenceworth?" The doctor was a short, balding man. His thick glasses magnified his brown eyes, making him look like a wide-eyed innocent. His jacket was at least twenty years old and the bottom of his trousers slouched over his shoes.

A country doctor personified, Adam thought, wondering how much help the man would be for Nel.

Adam held out his hand. "Dr. Seabrook. Thank you for coming."

"My pleasure, sir." He stepped over the threshold and gazed around the foyer. "Been a long time since I've been here."

"Oh?"

"I tended your uncle until he moved to the city."

"Oh, I hadn't realized you knew him."

"Yes. It was a good thing he moved to London to be closer to the specialists. I told him he'd find the doctors he needed and that he should get someone to care for him daily as well. It was dangerous for him to be in a place this size by himself."

"Yes, well—"

"So where's the patient?"

"If you'll step this way." Adam opened his study door. "I'll bring her in here, if that will do?"

The doctor glanced around the room. "Fine, fine. This will be fine." He pushed his glasses up and looked at Adam. "What kind of problem is she having? Not the feminine kind, I trust."

Adam shook his head. "No. She fell and hit her head."

"Hmm." The doctor frowned. "Oh, yes, the tour company."

"Yes, that's right. She fell off the block and lost consciousness."

The man put his bag down on a chair and pulled out a manila file. "Let me see, now, I have to complete these reports."

He asked Adam questions concerning the accident, jotting down his responses.

"And you brought her here."

"That's right. There was an elderly woman attendant in the first-aid office, but she didn't seem qualified."

"Hmm. Well, I can't think who it might have been. But then the tour company probably brought someone in. How's she been since?"

"Physically she's fine, but she seems rather confused."

"That's to be expected." He placed his medical bag on the floor beside a chair. "Well, let me take a look at her, eh?"

"Oh, Dr. Seabrook?"

"Yes?"

"It might be easier if she didn't realize you were a doctor at first."

"Fine, fine. Some people are squeamish around medical professionals."

Adam nodded. At the door he turned back to Dr. Seabrook. "Oh, and she prefers to be called Nelwina." He turned from the surprised look on the doctor's face and left the study to search for Nel. He found her in the hall, coming from the drawing room.

"Nel, I've someone I'd like you to meet."

"Oh?"

He led her to his study and opened the door, allowing her to precede him.

"Nel, this is Mr. Seabrook."

Nelwina looked at the elderly bald man standing before her, peering at her through impossibly thick spectacles, a tentative smile on his lips.

"Mr. Seabrook, this is Nelwina Honeycutt."

"Miss Honeycutt, pleased to make your acquaintance."

Nelwina bobbed a quick curtsey before she could stop herself. "The pleasure is mine, sir." The man gave her a startled glance before turning his gaze to Adam.

"Mr. Seabrook would like to talk to you about your fall in Ramsgil."

She looked from Adam to the gentleman standing beside him. What interest could Mr. Seabrook have in it? She frowned.

"Ah, yes, that's right, Miss Honeycutt." He moved away from Adam. "Shall we have a seat here, then?"

Nelwina looked to Adam. He gave her a reassuring nod. "It's okay, Nelwina. He's here to help."

"But Adam, I do not need his help." She allowed Adam to guide her to a chair.

"He just wants to ask you some questions." He patted her shoulder and, before she could form an objection, Adam left.

"Now then, Miss Honeycutt, have you had any headaches?"

Nelwina shook her head.

"Any dizziness?"

"Nay."

"Are you on medications?"

She frowned. "Nay, sir."

"Very good, then."

He held up his index finger in front of her. "I want you to follow my finger."

"And just where is your finger going, sir?" Nelwina stared at him. His questions were most odd, she thought.

"No, Miss Honeycutt. I shall move it from one side to the other. I would like you to follow that movement."

"Oh."

He moved his finger and she followed it as he instructed her.

"No. No. Keep your head still and follow it with your eyes."

"My stars." Frustrated, Nelwina glared at the man. "What is so intriguing about your finger that I should spend my time watching it?"

The man sighed. "Please, Miss Honeycutt, if you'll just follow my finger with your eyes, we can get on with this exam."

"Exam?" Now Nelwina was completely confused. "What exam?"

"Well, a neurological one, of course. When one has had a concussion it is customary to get a neurological exam."

Nelwina had no idea what the man was talking about. Mayhap he was a bit daft, she thought, but 'twould be faster just to do as he said and get it over with. She couldn't see the harm in humoring him.

She watched his finger. Then he held up the index

fingers of both his hands. "Now, watch my fingers and tell me when you can no longer see them."

She sighed. "How am I to watch the both of them? Where one eye looks, so looks the other."

Mr. Seabrook blinked several times and cleared his throat. "Yes. Well then, I'll just examine your pupils."

Nelwina shook her head. "But sir, I'm not the governess at Spenceworth. I have no students." And then it dawned on her. "Oh, you mean my eyes."

He squinted at her, leveling a measuring gaze on her. "Miss Honeycutt, I would appreciate your cooperation. I've a few others to see today." His kindly voice firmed. He reached on the other side of his chair and retrieved a black bag.

Nelwina frowned. "Are you staying at Spenceworth?"

He simply glared at her without answering.

From his bag he pulled out a small silver instrument that was flared at one end.

"Now, I want you to look over my shoulder."

Mr. Seabrook was certainly strange, Nelwina thought as she focused on the bookshelves behind him.

A light flashed in her eyes and she blinked, bringing her hand up to shield it.

"No, no, Miss Honeycutt. Keep your hands in your lap." The strident tone of his voice rubbed against her dwindling patience.

"But sir, the light could blind me."

He raised his eyebrows and pursed his lips. He was fast losing his patience with her, she could tell, but she did not have an unending source of it at the moment, either.

"I am going to do my job and examine you, Miss Honeycutt and the sooner you cooperate the sooner it will be finished." He brought his tiny wand-like instrument up. "Now, focus your eyes over my shoulder and do not blink."

So firmly were his instructions issued that Nelwina froze in her seat, trying hard not to blink when the magic of the instrument flashed brightly in her eyes.

The man turned back to his bag. Upon seeing it, Nelwina realized just what this man was, a doctor.

She pushed to her feet. "You'll not be using your lancet on me today, sir." All the memories of her mother and the doctor who came to treat her came rushing back. She stared at the bowl with a strange lid atop it that the doctor placed on the table. "And you'll not need your blood bowl, either."

He glanced up at her and his forehead wrinkled and the top of his head turned pink.

"Miss Honeycutt, I assure you, I haven't a lancet in my case. And this bowl is part of my lunch." He pulled out a jar and Nelwina stepped back behind her chair.

"And you can put the leeches back as well. You'll not see me to my end as those of your ilk did my mother."

"But Miss Honeycutt, these are not leeches, they're olives—for my lunch."

Swirling around, Nelwina ignored the man and beat a hasty retreat. She would have a word with Adam, make no mistake about it.

*   *   *

"My lord, I could find no neurological evidence of injury. But I am concerned about her confusion. She spoke of lancets and leeches. It was as if she'd never had a medical exam before."

Adam ran a hand through his hair. "What do you recommend, Dr. Seabrook?"

"I can't be certain, mind you, without a complete neurological workup, but I don't see any damage."

"But what about her confusion?"

"Well, as I said, I didn't see any injury upon first exam. Sometimes it simply takes time for a bruise to the brain to heal. She's suffered no physical effects. She's just confused." He closed his bag and walked to the door of the study and Adam followed behind.

Glancing over his shoulder the doctor said, "Just keep an eye on her. I think with patience and time, the confusion will clear up."

Chapter Nine

"Lunch was wonderful, Niles." Sophia smiled at the gentleman across the table from her.

"It was my pleasure, my lady."

"Oh, Niles, you simply must quit using that form of address. I'm certainly not entitled to it."

"But your son is the earl of Spenceworth now. As his mother you must be afforded proper respect."

"Oh, pish posh." Sophia frowned, waving a hand at him. "I'm exactly the same as I was before Adam inherited. Nothing has changed in my life." She canted her head, allowing an intimate smile to tip the corners of her mouth. "Except for meeting you."

"And I'm honored to be your friend."

"Why do I hear a 'but' hovering in the air?" Sophia sighed, wary of where this was going.

Niles glanced away from her a moment before bringing his gaze back to hers. "But we are from two different worlds and anything more than friendship would be impossible."

"Niles!" Sophia gasped. "Don't tell me you subscribe to that archaic belief of class separation?" Taking the napkin from her lap, Sophia busied herself with folding the linen, keeping her head down and blinking back tears.

"There's a perfectly good reason for it."

Sophia looked up at him. "Oh?" she challenged.

He shifted and turned his attention to placing his silverware atop his plate. "I am a commoner. I have no title, no pedigree. You deserve someone of your own station."

She tossed the napkin on the table and pushed back her chair. "So Niles, you believe I deserve a stodgy old stick in the mud?" She grabbed her handbag and stepped away from the table. "Well, all I can say is you certainly know how to insult a lady."

With that, she marched to the door of the restaurant, her heart pounding furiously in her chest.

Men! Imbeciles, the whole lot of them.

"Splendid." Adam beamed at Nelwina and his mother. "You've both done a bang-up job here." He gazed around the dining room. "But shouldn't the chairs be placed around the table?"

"Nel says that's the way it was done, dear." She patted his arm. "And Nel would know." She smiled up at him.

He frowned at his mother. She still clung to the notion that Nelwina was experiencing a past life. And he knew it was pointless to argue with her, especially since Nelwina seemed to share his mother's belief.

Or was his mother simply humoring Nelwina? That

thought gave him pause, and he looked at Sophia. She smiled at him again.

"I despaired of getting the place clean, what with no electricity to run the vacuum, but Nel showed us how to beat the rugs and clean the drapes like they did in her time."

The guileless look in his mother's eyes convinced Adam that she did indeed share Nelwina's belief.

Adam sighed. How could he convince Nelwina of the impossibility of her claim when his mother was supporting it?

A wave of guilt washed over him. He certainly hadn't done anything to disavow her of the notion. He wished he knew more about her personal life in the States—where she worked, who her friends were, anything. But each time he asked, she gave him a blank stare and shook her head.

The doctor had said it would take time and that he had to be patient. Surely, her people back home knew of her vacation in Britain and would be inquiring after her.

He had no answers, so the only option was to follow the doctor's recommendation. Be patient.

He turned around. This room, like all the other downstairs rooms, had been painstakingly cleaned, the furniture, knickknacks and paintings carefully arranged.

Together, they left the dining room behind and entered the salon. The room was cozy and bright with several windows looking out at the garden. Chairs and settees were grouped around the room with an old piano in one corner. A fireplace, its mantle carved with flowering vines, carried the outdoor theme inside to complement a similar print in the fabric of the drapes and upholstery.

A basket sat beside a chair in front of one of the windows, needlework spilling from it. Adam walked over to it and plucked the fabric from the basket. "What is this?"

"Petit pointe." Nelwina supplied from the doorway.

"The stitches are so small."

She giggled. " 'Tis why it's called petit pointe."

He held it close, noting the precise stitches forming a bouquet of flowers in the center of the material. "Did you do this, Nelwina?"

"Aye." She glanced down at the floor and then back to him. "The chairs needed new coverings."

"I didn't realize you were so talented." He looked into her eyes a moment before his gaze slid to her lips, remembering the kiss in the garden. He'd never been so obsessed with a woman.

He'd caught only glimpses of her as she and his mother went about the manor. They'd forbidden him entrance to any of the rooms they were working on, insisting that the results be a surprise for him.

"Thank you." A rosy hue climbed Nelwina's cheeks. "I've only two more to do to see the foyer finished."

He smiled at Nelwina. "Do you have any other talents I don't know about?" Her eyes widened and the pink staining her cheeks darkened.

Did she think of him as often as he did her? Adam wondered. God, he hoped so. It would be hell if this attraction were one-sided.

Placing the needlework back in the basket, he rejoined her by the door. Looking directly into her eyes, in a low voice he said, "Spenceworth looks wonderful, Nel."

Flustered, she turned and led the way from the salon.

As they stood in the foyer a shaft of sunlight hit the chandelier, sending prisms of color dancing round the room.

He'd loved Spenceworth's architecture before, but under Nelwina's careful hand it glowed with a warm, inviting atmosphere.

The proportions of the rooms were grand. With the intricate crown molding, the delicate plasterwork on the high ceilings and the ornately carved woodwork, Spenceworth was a shining example of seventeenth-century architecture.

He'd toured a few old mansions in his school days and they'd always felt devoid of life, like a museum, with a musty smell that spoke of years of disuse.

Somehow, Nelwina had banished the cold, musty feeling.

Now Spenceworth felt lived in.

The Higginbothams arrived for dinner that evening. Nel and Sophia had worked through the afternoon preparing the meal. And as Sophia led everyone into the dining room, Adam caught Nel nervously brushing at her dark dress.

The room shined brightly, from the freshly polished silver to the china dishes placed before the seven chairs arranged along the table.

"I thought this evening we would dine informally," Sophia was saying. "We are in the country, after all."

Adam clenched his teeth, wondering if the Higginbothams sensed the tension between him and his mother. From years of experience, he knew Birdie could be pushy and difficult, but why his mother insisted on trying to get the upper hand with the woman was beyond him. He frowned. And it rankled him to have no control over either his mother or whom he entertained.

He glanced at Nel. She wore a simple, soft black dress that flirted about her shapely long legs when she walked—legs he couldn't help but look at. She wore no makeup, but then she didn't need any. Her complexion was smooth and clear, her cheeks had a natural rosiness and her eyelashes and brows were a dark brown, drawing his attention to her clear green eyes.

Damn, but she was beautiful.

"Not at all, Sophia. Why, I imagine Ludlow will be doing just that when he entertains at his country retreat." Birdie patted Ludlow's shoulder as she took her seat.

"And when will Runnymuck be opened?" Sophia smiled tightly, and Adam bit back a chuckle as he turned his gaze to Birdie. This just might be an entertaining meal after all.

"Oh, Sophia." Birdie tittered. "It's Runnymede, not Runnymuck."

"Why, yes, of course."

Adam listened to the conversation, at first trying to participate. But Sophia was determined to direct the discussion, interrupting him to give the answers she thought best. He settled back in his chair, letting her have her way.

"Tell me Adam, have you and Nelwina set a date?" Birdie looked pointedly at the unadorned ring finger of Nel's left hand. "Or is there no need to rush?"

Adam ground his teeth. The woman was insufferable. Always had been, always would be.

Sophia jumped in before Adam could tell the meddling woman off.

"Oh, they've only just gotten engaged. There's plenty of time for planning."

Adam shot Sophia a glare and his mother went silent.

"So, Ludlow, where is Runnymede?" Adam met Ludlow's watery blue gaze.

"In the West Country. Beautiful country up there."

"I prefer Spenceworth." Sophia slid her comment in with a smile.

"Nelwina, what of your people?" Birdie leveled her gaze at Nel.

Nel opened her mouth to answer, but Sophia chimed in. "They're from America." Sophia turned to Nel. "Isn't that right, dear?"

"But your accent is hardly American. Wherever did you get it from?"

"Well, you see—"

"Nel went to school here." Sophia supplied the answer. Nel's eyes rounded and she started to say something, but Sophia rattled on. "Would you like a tour of the manor after dinner? Nel has whipped it right into shape. It's simply amazing what she's done. Isn't it, Adam?"

Adam smiled at Nel's stricken look. "Yes, amazing."

By the end of dinner, Sophia was looking frazzled. It couldn't be easy fielding all the questions in the conversation. Adam could not have cared less what the Higginbothams thought of him or the manor, but it mattered to his mother, so he'd tolerated it.

Adam couldn't help but share the pride evident on his mother's face as Nel took everyone on a quick tour of Spenceworth. The women had done a grand job in each room they entered and again Adam regretted that he couldn't share the manor with the public. Not only was the architecture wonderful, but the interior furnishings were arranged so artfully.

Adam stood with Sophia and Nel as the Higginbothams went to their car. "It was nice to see you again," he called out. "You should co—"

His mother dropped her heel on his toe. "Ouch." He met Sophia's warning glare.

"You should drive carefully. Ta ta." She waved her hand as the car drove off. "Are you daft, Adam? Wasn't one dinner with the Higginbothams enough?"

Adam grinned as Sophia turned and walked up the stairs, calling over her shoulder, "I'm completely done in. I can't recall a more exhausting dinner party."

Nelwina tapped lightly on the door to the study. She heard a noise through the thick wood. Turning the knob, she entered. "Adam?"

"Oh, Nel, it's you." Sophia leaned back in Adam's chair, her hand flat against her chest. "You scared the life out of me."

"I'm sorry, Sophia." She held out a paper. "I was delivering the drawing of the garden."

"Never mind that." Sophia waved one hand to Nelwina, a piece of paper grasped in her other. "Come and see this."

"Sophia!" Nelwina gasped. "You shouldn't be reading Adam's papers."

"Oh pish posh. I'm his mother." She dismissed Nelwina's objection. "He means to turn Spenceworth into a bed and breakfast."

"A what?"

"Bed and breakfast." Sophia looked up from the papers. "An inn."

Nelwina didn't understand. Why would Adam want to do something like that?

"I can't believe it. How can he do this, Nel? It will ruin the manor."

Nelwina shook her head. "Mayhap if you told him how you feel—"

"Oh, no. Adam wouldn't appreciate my input. He'd call it meddling."

Nelwina sighed, placing her sketch on Adam's desk. " 'Tis his property. I imagine he can do with it as he pleases."

"But really. There are plenty of rooms available in Ramsgil. Why would he want to compete with them?"

"I don't know."

"What's this?" Sophia picked up Nelwina's drawing.

"I promised to sketch the old garden for Adam."

"Oh, it's lovely, dear. I so envy you to have such knowledge of the past—to have lived at Spenceworth when it was in its prime." Sophia gazed off. "The country balls and the wonderful gowns." She sighed.

With a shake of her head, Sophia looked back to the papers in front of her, a worried frown knitting her brow. "I need to speak with Niles," she mumbled to herself as she stood up.

"My lady, are you certain this is a good idea?"

"Niles, will you kindly stop calling me 'my lady'?" Irritation lent a sharp edge to Sophia's words and she took a deep, calming breath before she continued. "I thought about it on the drive in and I don't see any other way. Surely you don't want to see the manor competing with Ramsgil for customers, do you?"

"But my—" Sophia shot him a glare.

He cleared his throat and continued. "This is quite an undertaking."

"It's less of an undertaking than turning Spenceworth into a bed and breakfast." Sophia put her hand over his, the warm contact immediately settling her nerves.

"I don't think Lord Spenceworth will be too pleased with your plan." Sophia curled her fingers around his hand when he gently tried to withdraw it. She noted the blush staining his cheeks and swallowed a chuckle.

There was a chemistry between them and she'd be darned if she'd let him put it aside simply because her son had inherited a title.

"Maybe at first, but when he sees how well it works out, he'll come around." Sophia looked into Niles's eyes. "And I'm sure Nel will agree to do the tours."

"I don't know, Sophia." She nearly crowed with delight when Niles inadvertently used her name. But her joy was short-lived when she read the doubt in his gaze.

She pulled her hand from his. "Well. I would love your help, Niles, but if you feel it compromises you, I understand." She pushed back her chair and stood up, blinking back tears. "But this is something I'm going to do, with or without your help." She'd so hoped he would help her. She wasn't certain she knew everything to do and Niles was so organized and informed.

Niles sighed. "Very well, Sophia. I'll help you out, I just hope this doesn't come back to haunt us both."

Sophia smiled at him and sat down, and for the next hour they worked out the details.

"Oh, Sophia, you shouldn't have." Nelwina stared at the pile of fabric, lace and buttons. " 'Tis too much."

"Oh pish posh, dear. I remembered you mentioning how you liked to sew and after what you've done with Spenceworth, you're entitled to this." Sophia held up the taupe material with its small white dots. "Besides, I've a plan."

Nelwina picked up the white fabric, her mind consumed with thoughts of a new gown.

"That's what the woman called white-on-white." Sophia smoothed out the material. "See the pretty little flowers in white there?"

"Aye." Nelwina had never seen such wonderful material. And to think it was hers. All she need do was stitch it up.

"There's shears, pins, chalk, needles, thread, buttons and a measuring tape there, too." Sophia pulled out each item as she named them off. "But there isn't a sewing machine here at Spenceworth. I should have thought of that and asked at the fabric shop. Maybe we can rent one."

"A sewing machine?" Nelwina turned from the fabric and notions strewn across her bed. "There is a machine that stitches?"

"Yes, dear." Sophia smiled, delight brightening her eyes. "And quickly, too."

Ah, the wonders of the modern age, as Sophia liked to call this time. "But I have no stitching machine." She shrugged. "And so I'll make the gown as my mother taught me."

"But won't that take you forever?"

"If I apply myself, I should be able to make the gown in a week." Nelwina went to the mirror and looked at her body. "Of course, I was accustomed to sewing for my other body. This one is much taller." Nelwina met Sophia's gaze in the mirror. "The proportions are a bit different." She shrugged. "But no matter, I can fit the gown."

Nelwina crossed back over to the bed and searched through the material. "And what was this again?" She held up a narrow, flexible item covered in white cotton.

"Boning. The saleswoman said it would help the bodice fit smoothly."

151

Nelwina nodded. "Aye, boning." She fingered the material covering. "And all I need do is stitch the cotton edges to the seams." She grinned at Sophia. " 'Tis wonderful. But what is it made of?" She flexed the boning. "Not bone, or steel or wood."

"Plastic. Remember the cups I showed you? The plastic ones?"

"Truly?" Nelwina stared at the boning, moving the fabric down to reveal the milky flat plastic. "This plastic is used in everything, it would seem."

Sophia chuckled. "Yes, we do seem to find a million uses for it, don't we?" She settled on the bed. "Now for my plan. And the reason for the gown."

Nelwina dropped the boning and turned to meet Sophia's gaze.

"I spoke with Niles while I was in Ramsgil. He was most upset about the thought of the manor being turned into a bed and breakfast. I was right, Spenceworth would be in competition with the ones in Ramsgil and the people of the town won't be too happy about it."

"But what can be done about that? Spenceworth is Adam's to do with as he wishes."

"Well, what if we were to show Adam that there's a way to make as much money without as much work and expense?"

"How?"

"By giving tours, of course."

"Oh." Nelwina thought a minute. "The butler often did that when the old earl was away." She smiled as she remembered. "He supplemented his salary quite handsomely, I believe."

"There you see." Sophia clapped her hands. "Niles is working on our brochures. And he'll handle the distribution of them to the tour companies."

"And Adam has agreed to this?"

"Nel, I don't want to tell him about this until I know it will work. We'll have a test run and see how much interest there is. I'd hate to get Adam's hopes up only to dash them if the tours were a flop." Sophia scooted from the bed. "And he has so much to do now, I don't want to burden him with any more."

"But why did you buy the material?"

"Well, dear, Niles and I were hoping you would conduct the tours. You know everything about the manor and the past residents. With you in period costume it would be as if the tourists had stepped back in time."

"I'm most flattered, Sophia, but is this such a good idea?"

"Oh Nel, I just want to make things easier for Adam. Do you know how much work it will take to bring the manor up to specs? And it will thoroughly ruin the atmosphere." Sophia gathered the cards of buttons. "Upkeep of Spenceworth isn't cheap and the taxes on this place must be enormous. But if the manor is opened for tours, part of the tax burden is lifted. Niles knows just what has to be done to meet the government's requirements. So you see, there are no downsides to this plan." She placed the buttons beside the material. "Please say you'll help, Nel."

In the face of Sophia's plea, Nelwina was lost. What else could she do? Sophia had treated her as a daughter, helping Nelwina adjust to the oddities of the time. Without Sophia, Nelwina didn't know what would have happened to her.

"Are you certain you can't tell Adam?"

"Oh, no. I want to be sure it will work first."

Nelwina fingered the material. She met Sophia's gaze. "Aye, I'll help."

"Oh smashing, dear." Sophia reached over and hugged Nelwina. "This is going to be so exciting. But remember, we want to surprise Adam."

Aye, it was going to be exciting, Nelwina thought. Good or bad was yet to be decided.

A week later, Nelwina stood before the mirror in her room. She adjusted her skirts and felt more like herself than she had since arriving at Spenceworth. She twirled around, her skirt belling out around her. She'd used an old sheet to make a petticoat and the ruffles helped to add fullness to her skirt.

Never had she worn such a beautiful gown. The taupe bodice and overskirt complemented her coloring and the snowy white-on-white of her underskirt was pristine and crisp. The boning that kept the bodice's fit smooth was much more comfortable than the wood or steel boning of her own time.

Her gaze traveled to the lace cap hiding her short, brown locks. 'Twas a shame her hair wasn't long. But it was much easier to care for. She simply washed and toweled it. There was no braiding or pinning needed.

She turned from the mirror, catching sight of the modern, white canvas shoes adorning her feet. Those she would never change for the boots of the past.

These were ever so much more comfortable.

"Oh, Nel, your gown is beautiful." Sophia walked into the room, her gaze traveling over Nelwina's dress. "You did a beautiful job. I so loved the fashions back then. The long skirts and such."

Nelwina soaked up Sophia's praise. She felt so out of place most times, 'twas wonderful to find acceptance in Adam's mother.

Recalling the look of surprise and pleasure on Adam's face when they'd toured the downstairs sent a ripple of pride up her spine. She'd seen a flicker of admiration in Adam. But later in the salon, there was desire mixed with that admiration and Nelwina remembered the kiss they'd shared beyond the doors in the garden.

And butterflies took flight low in her stomach.

Pulling her mind from such thoughts, Nelwina focused on Sophia, meeting the older woman's envying gaze.

"I could easily make you a gown, Sophia."

Adam's mother's eyes lit with delight. "I'd so love to have one." She frowned. "But it's so much work, my dear. I'm sure you have other things you'd rather do."

"Oh, no, my lady," Nelwina rushed to assure her. "I love to sew, and making a gown for you would be my pleasure."

"Are you certain?"

Smiling, Nelwina nodded.

"I could go out now and fetch the material." Sophia grasped Nelwina's hands. "And I'll ask the saleswoman if she knows where I might find a sewing machine to rent. It would take less time if you used a machine, you know."

"But my lady, I don't know how to use one."

Sophia clapped her hands together. "Well, between the two of us, we should be able to figure it out, don't you think?" Dropping Nelwina's hands, Sophia bustled out of the room, calling as she left, "I'll return as quickly as I can."

Nelwina nodded, smiling as she followed Sophia. Standing at the top of the stairs, she listened as Adam's mother descended the stairs, still chattering away.

"I should think a deep blue with a striped underskirt would look best."

Nelwina chuckled, her heart filling with love for the woman who had accepted her so completely. 'Twas a small thing to do to make Sophia so happy.

The bell over the door jingled as Sophia entered the shop.

"Mrs. Warrick, lovely day, isn't it?"

Sophia searched among the bolts of material to find the saleswoman. Spotting her between tables piled high with fabric, Sophia smiled. "Yes, it is."

"What might I do for you today?"

Sophia gazed around the shop, overwhelmed by the volume of choices available to her. On the drive from Spenceworth, she'd explored every conceivable design and color for her dress. She couldn't remember being this excited over something in a long time.

And looking over the array of fabrics, panic seized

her. How would she ever find what she wanted? There was just too much to see.

"How did the fabric work out?" the saleswoman inquired, holding two bolts of cloth in her arms.

"Oh, the dress looks wonderful. Nel is such a wonder with a needle." Sophia touched a bright red silk, but discarded the idea. Blue was what she wanted. "And she made it in just a week." She walked around a table of fabric, picking up a piece of black velvet and then putting it down. "Which is amazing, considering she did it all by hand."

"No!" The saleswoman gasped. "You mean she doesn't have a sewing machine?"

"No."

The woman placed the bolts on a table and came over to Sophia. "I didn't know anyone did that sort of thing anymore."

"I didn't either." Sophia spotted a royal blue bolt on the far wall. "And she's going to make me a gown, as well."

She went to the bolt and pulled it out. "Do you have a striped fabric to go with this?"

"Yes, ma'am." The saleswoman pulled a matching stripe from another shelf. "I've a nice flower print, if you prefer."

"No, that's perfect. Just what I pictured. I'll need lace trim, buttons, boning and muslin to make a petticoat." Sophia placed the bolt on the cutting table. "Do you know where I might find a machine to rent? I hate the thought of Nel sewing another gown by hand. She worked on hers day and night the entire week and I so missed her company."

"I've an old one in the back you're welcome to use if you like."

"Oh, that would be wonderful." Sophia stopped herself before she added how amazed Nel would be at the machine and how quickly it stitched seams.

"Mrs. Warrick?"

Sophia looked up from the lace she'd picked out. "Yes?"

"I do a lot of sewing for Ramsgil, making costumes and such for the re-enactments and other events here. Sometimes there's more work than I can handle. I was wondering if your friend would be interested in helping me out?"

Sophia thought a moment. With the cleaning and arranging of the manor completed, Nel might find herself bored. The sewing would keep her busy.

"I would, of course, pay her," the saleswoman added.

And give her a bit of money, Sophia finished her thought.

"I'll certainly ask her."

"Excellent. She could do the work at the manor if she preferred. Though I would like to meet with her before we finalized anything."

"Of course. Perhaps Nel and I can come to town for tea one afternoon. We'll drop by then."

An hour later, Sophia left the shop, the old sewing machine in the trunk, everything needed for her dress in two large bags in the backseat.

On the drive back to the manor, Sophia put aside her thoughts of the dress and Nel's possible employment, and recalled the looks that passed between her son and Nel whenever they were near.

Yes, Nel was perfect for her son. He'd made a wise choice. Sophia had stopped in to check on the progress of the brochures and while she was at the printer's, she'd picked out invitations for the wedding.

There was going to be a wedding at Spenceworth, make no mistake about it.

As the chimneys of Spenceworth came into view, Sophia thought about the brochure proof in her bag. The tours would be a raging success, she thought. Nel had brought the manor back and she'd make the perfect guide. Maybe Nelwina could write out a script of some sort and Sophia could don her costume and help with the tours.

Adam stared at the drawing on his desk. Nel had done a bang-up job, he thought. She'd drawn out the paths and beds, sketching in the existing large trees and low brick wall enclosing the garden. Each group of flowers, shrubs and trees was labeled and the beds outlined and placed uniformly around the gravel paths. It was lovely.

Down in the corner, she had listed the types of plants and quantities needed as well as a notation that the beds needed topsoil and a few of the low walls needed repair.

He'd glanced through some of the account books, but still hadn't found any information on the design of the gardens. But after examining Nel's drawing and comparing it to what remained, he thought she must have come fairly close to the original layout.

He'd turn Nel's drawing over to the landscape company he had hired for the seaside cottage project. Maybe they could tell him how closely her sketch resembled a seventeenth-century garden. And if her plans worked out, he just might be able to save a bit on the garden and get it finished more quickly.

Movement on his computer screen caught his attention.

"Damn," he muttered as his stock prices flashed on the screen. "I don't need another bad day on the market."

"What's wrong, dear?" His mother breezed into the room, a smile on her face.

"Nothing, Mother."

She stood beside him, leaning over to receive her customary peck on the cheek from Adam.

"Is it a bad day for the market?" She canted her head to the side, studying his computer screen.

"No worse than usual, I suppose." He hit a button on his computer and the screen went black. "What have you been up to today?"

"I went shopping."

Adam groaned. What was it about shopping that sent women into throes of ecstasy? His mother's face was rosy with pleasure, her eyes dancing in delight.

"Adam, you should see the dress Nel made. It's fabulous."

"I'm sure it is." Adam wasn't in the mood to discuss dresses and shopping. Those stock prices needed some consideration. While he couldn't sell off the ones connected with the manor, he could look into his own stocks. Maybe he should sell before they became worthless. Or maybe it was just something happening in the government that had sent them down. Damn, he really needed to look into this.

"And she's making one for me. I may have even found her employment." His mother blithely went on about her shopping trip and Nel's sewing abilities.

"That's wonderful, Mother, but if you'll excuse me, I've some work I really need to tend to." He didn't want to be rude, but he really needed to find out what was happening in the market.

"Oh, I'm sorry, Adam dear." She bustled to the door. "You tend to your business. Nel and I have a lot to do ourselves. Just put us from your mind, we'll be close as kittens, sewing away."

Adam stared at her retreating form. At the door she turned. "What kind of flowers should Nel carry?" She frowned. "Lilies? No, those always remind me of funerals." She brightened. "Wildflowers. Yes, that's it. Don't you think, dear?" She wiggled her fingers at him. "I'll take care of ordering them. I know how busy you are."

And the door closed and he shook his head. What the bloody hell was all that about?

There were some things he was better off not delving into—the workings of his mother's mind was one of them.

He flipped the power on for his computer screen and scanned the headlines. Maybe he should have brought a telly to Spenceworth. It would make it a sight easier to keep track of world events. If he didn't tend to things, find a way to pay the bloody taxes and make the repairs to the garden, there'd be no Spenceworth.

Chapter Ten

Philip flattened the sheet of paper and leaned his elbows on the table. Knowing Jocelyn, she would follow this schedule, even a year after the honeymoon had been cancelled.

He dialed the hotel number listed on the page.

"Jocelyn Tanner, please."

"One moment, sir." He heard a few clicking sounds and the woman came back. "I'm sorry, sir, Miss Tanner isn't a guest here."

"What do you mean? She's supposed to be registered there."

"I'm sorry, sir."

"Well, when did she check out?"

"I'm sorry, sir, we can't give out that kind of information."

"Listen, I have to find her. There's an emergency here and she has to return to the States."

"I am sorry, sir, but there's nothing I can do to help you."

Philip slammed down the phone. What in the hell

was he to do now? He had to find Jocelyn. His gaze landed on the letter from the attorney and hope bloomed in his chest.

Maybe she'd gotten in touch with him. Quickly, Philip dialed the number.

"Solicitor's office."

"Yes, is this Dudley Titchlark's office?"

"Yes, sir. How may I help you?"

"I'm trying to locate Jocelyn Tanner."

"Sir?"

"Jocelyn Tanner. Mr. Titchlark has been in correspondence with her. She's in England now. Perhaps she's contacted him?"

"Tanner." There was a long pause on the other end of the line. "Oh, yes, Miss Tanner. I recall now. Mr. Titchlark is handling her inheritance."

"Can you tell me how to get in touch with her?" Finally, Philip thought, someone who knows her.

"Oh, I'm sorry, sir, but we've not heard from her."

A dead end. Now, what did he do?

He thanked the woman for her help and hung up the phone.

Damn it all, he needed Jocelyn here, but how would he get her home when no one knew where she was?

He cradled his head in his hands, massaging his scalp with tense fingers.

What were his options?

He could wait around for Jocelyn to come home, but by then he could be in jail. Or he could go to England and search for her. At least then he'd be out of reach when results of the account investigations came in.

Reading over the itinerary again, he was thankful for Jocelyn's compulsion for planning things out. He folded the paper and slipped it inside the ticket jacket. Surely he could retrace her steps and find her.

He had to.

"Nel?" Adam caught a glimpse of her skirt's hem as he left the study.

"Yes, my lord?" She appeared at the head of the stairs, her hands behind her back, and Adam caught his breath.

She looked as if she'd just stepped out of an eighteenth-century movie set, from the lacy cap covering her hair to the hem of her dress brushing the floor.

She started down the stairs, her white sneakers the only clue of modern times. She fit, he thought. From her graceful descent to the curtsey she bobbed at the bottom of the stairs.

And he smiled.

The old-fashioned dress emphasized the curve of her waist and the sway of her hips and fitted her perfectly.

"Adam?" The softly spoken word brought him from his thoughts.

"Oh . . . yes, Nel." Adam stepped back, fighting the urge to pull her into his arms and kiss her. He looked into her gaze and narrowed his. "What do you have behind your back?"

Her cheeks pinkened and she glanced away. "What?"

He folded his arms over his chest. "Behind your back." He moved to the side, but she scooted around.

He fixed her with a severe glare. "Is that the last Mallow?"

He watched her eyes widen, then darken with guilt. He grinned and she held out the mangled half of the cookie with a sigh. "Aye, 'tis the last one, but I left half for you."

He was tempted to take it from her, just to see her reaction, but when he looked up from the serviette on her open palm and met her twinkling gaze, he couldn't. But neither could he let her get away scot-free.

"So now I won't have any breakfast, eh?"

He watched her gaze dart back and forth as she thought a moment. Then she smiled and his knees went weak. "You may eat this half now and the other for breakfast." She bobbed her head once, seeming quite pleased with her solution as she extended the cookie to him.

He chuckled. "No, you go ahead, but I'm going to be hiding them from you in the future."

" 'Tis a good plan, but I warn you, I've a passion for them and will, no doubt, be able to sniff them out wherever you might stash them."

Adam tipped his head back and laughed. But the laughter died when he looked at Nelwina as she took a bite of the cookie. For a long moment he was mesmerized as the tip of her tongue swept over her lower lip, capturing a stray crumb. She seemed not to notice.

Nodding to him, she asked, "What have you there?"

"The plans." He glanced at the rolled-up drawing in his hand.

"The plans?" She popped the last of the cookie in her mouth, wiping her fingers on the serviette.

"For the garden." He cleared his throat. "You've done a marvelous job on them. Thank you."

"You're most welcome." She smiled. "I hope it will be of help to you."

"Yes, it will." Turn away, idiot, he told himself. "Do you have a few minutes?" *What the bloody hell am I doing?*

"Of course, my lord."

She followed him out to the garden. He walked a little way down one of the overgrown paths and turned around.

Nel stood with the manor as a backdrop, the sun shining down on her. The picture she created standing there as if she'd just stepped out of a very old painting was unnerving.

And for a moment he envisioned her amid a proper English garden, flowers blooming and the paths freshly graveled. The image fit her perfectly.

She stood still under his gaze, her head canted.

Adorable. She was utterly adorable. And he wanted her.

He stepped toward her and she shifted, an alertness widening her gaze. Had he frightened her with their last kiss? Or was he being presumptuous in thinking she shared his interest?

He frowned, recalling the moment when their lips met and his arms wrapped around her. She had felt so right, so utterly perfect there as she shared his passion.

No, he thought, the interest was shared. Perhaps things were going a little too fast for her.

He cleared his throat and his mind.

"I've a question about your drawing." He unrolled the paper in his hand.

Nel moved to his side. "Yes?" Her sleeve brushed against his arm and she stepped back.

Adam offered her what he hoped was a reassuring smile and pointed to the center of the picture. "You indicate a fountain here."

"Yes." She turned to the center of the garden. " 'Twas not large, but the gentle fall of the water was quite soothing." She smiled. "And the birds loved to bathe in it." She glanced up at him. " 'Twas most peaceful."

"Nel, let's not start that again, please."

She raised one of her brows.

Not wanting to get into an argument, Adam moved to the center of the garden, climbing over a few scraggly shrubs and kicking around the dirt. "But I don't see any hint of a fountain here." Ah ha, he thought, caught you.

Nel shook her head. "Who knows what became of it over the years?" She turned in a slow circle. "The garden was my favorite place. I didn't often get to come here, but when I did it was special."

"I'm sure." He refused to encourage her in this. He'd gone along with it at first because the hospital had told him to keep her calm, but the doctor had pronounced her fit. His patience was near an end. It was time she quit this nonsense.

She smiled. "I had chores to do, my lord. Things were not as easy then as they are now." She walked down a path to a large tree off to the side. "This tree was not here then." She turned to him. "So much has changed. Just there was a rose bush." She pointed to the corner of one of the beds. "I tore my petticoat one day and the old earl ordered cloth from London for a new one. 'Twas the finest one I ever owned." Sadness filled her eyes.

Adam stepped back onto the path. "Come on Nelwina, this is a good story and all, but—"

"My mother was seamstress to the manor," she went on, ignoring his comment. "She made Lady Spenceworth's gowns as well as many of the servants' clothes." Nel plucked a leaf from the tree and walked toward Adam. "Oftentimes, Lady Spenceworth would take tea here in the garden." She turned to the right and pointed. "There in the corner near the wall." She went to it, a distracted frown wrinkling her forehead. "I forgot to put that in the drawing. 'Twas a small area paved in brick with a table and two chairs in the center. Sometimes the old earl would join her."

Nelwina looked over her shoulder at Adam. " 'Twas those times and when they entertained I was forbidden to enter the garden."

Adam glanced from Nel to the corner. He would like to see her taking tea there and, somewhere inside, he knew it would please her.

Please her? The thought caught him unawares.

He should be focusing on getting the garden in

shape for tours, not on pleasing Nel. He should be trying to get her to recall her real life, not nattering on about a past life.

Besides, who knew how long she'd be staying? She could leave tomorrow and where would that leave him?

He veered away from answering that question, pushing from his mind the depressing thought of Spenceworth without Nel.

"What type of fountain was it?" Okay, he'd play along. Maybe she was a landscape designer in the States? It would explain the plans she'd drawn for him. If he got her talking about her job, it might help clear up her confusion.

" 'Twas small. A beautiful young woman, rising out of a seashell. The water cascaded over her head and into the shell at her feet."

Adam eyed the area where Nel said the fountain had been. It would be the perfect touch.

Sophia settled in the chair behind Adam's desk. He and Nel had just gone out to the garden and Sophia needed to learn Adam's schedule. If she happened to discover a clue as to why he was so worried, well, so much the better.

She knew she couldn't just ask him what weighed so heavily on his mind. For some reason he felt the need to shield her from problems.

It had started shortly after his father died, this need to protect her from worry.

Adam had been just a child, but whatever problems he'd had, he'd chosen to handle them without her help. Not that she'd been much help, devastated by the loss of her husband and the financial difficulties that followed.

She'd turned to her husband's older brother, the earl of Spenceworth, but the man had refused to help out.

She'd known her brother-in-law didn't approve of her, claiming his brother could have done better in choosing a wife, had he any sense at all.

Sophia didn't care that he cast aspersions on her, but his insult to her dear husband was beyond bearing. It had cost her much to turn to the earl in her hour of need.

Sophia sniffed back tears. No wonder the man never married, as foul-tempered as he'd been. What woman would want him?

In the end, she hadn't needed his help. She and Adam had managed. And once out on his own, Adam hadn't forgotten her; he'd sent her a monthly allowance. Not that she really needed it, but she knew it made him feel better, so she accepted it.

She shrugged off the memories. It had been a long time ago and her brother-in-law was dead and her son now held the title. There *was* justice in the world after all, she thought.

Shuffling through the papers on Adam's desk, Sophia wondered just what was in the will. Adam had gone to the solicitor's office alone. But he'd brushed aside her questions later, saying only that he'd inherited the manor and title.

Sophia found an investment statement. Scanning the report, she frowned. From the looks of it, Adam's stock was taking a beating. No wonder he was worried.

But then why was he so set on the bed and breakfast idea? Surely it would take a lot more capital to update the manor.

Well, things would turn around once they started the tours.

Putting the statement aside, she searched around for his day planner.

Niles, bless his heart, had helped her proof the brochure and ordered the print run. All she had to do was find out when Adam was scheduled to be away for a weekend.

What if Adam wasn't to leave the manor? What then?

Sophia shook her head. If there was a problem, Niles would find the answer. The dear man was simply brilliant.

She'd finally gotten him to call her Sophia, a step in the right direction by her estimation. It became apparent that she would have to pursue the man. He was so set on this class thing. It was beyond frustrating.

She smiled. They had yet to kiss, but she was planning her move, rather like chess, she thought. One planned one's moves, adjusting for the play of the opponent. She was good at chess—she would be good at Niles!

She finally found Adam's day planner. Flipping through the pages, she smiled when she came across a notation.

Perfect!

She snapped it closed and put the planner back where she found it.

The timing was perfect, she thought as she left the study.

It was fate.

"Nel?"

Nelwina glanced up from the sewing machine in her room to find Sophia standing in the doorway.

"My lady?" She stood up, the skirt of Sophia's gown in her hands. "What is amiss?" The older woman's brow was furrowed.

"I'm afraid things are worse than we first thought. It seems Adam is having a bit of financial trouble."

"Oh, my. But my lady, how do you know this?"

"I was searching for his schedule and came across his investment statement."

"My lady," Nelwina gasped. "You went through his papers . . . again?"

"Well, how was I to know when we could plan our tours?" Sophia shook her head. "That isn't the point, my dear." She sat in the chair by the window. "I'm afraid Adam's stock isn't doing well. I've been wondering what has him so worried." She glanced out the window. "I wondered why he hadn't started any of the renovations on the manor." She looked at Nelwina. "He hasn't the money, Nel. And that's what's been bothering him. I know it."

Nelwina went to Sophia. "I do wish I had funds to give him."

"And if you did, he wouldn't accept it."

Nelwina understood this. Adam, like most titled

men, was proud and independent. He would keep his finances private. At least he would try, she thought, thinking of Sophia's determination to help her son.

She'd seen a worried frown on his face on several occasions, but felt powerless to do anything. She couldn't very well ask him what the problem was. 'Twas not her place, as such matters were handled by men.

Was Adam in danger of losing Spenceworth? The thought crashed to a halt in her mind.

"Nel, can you be ready for the tours by next weekend? Adam has scheduled a trip to London and he'll be gone the weekend."

"Aye." Nelwina pleated the material of her modern skirt. "But are you certain we should be doing this? Mayhap we should ask him?"

"No, and we can't. He wouldn't let us help. He'd be embarrassed if he knew we were privy to his financial problems."

"If he's having problems, why hasn't he thought of the tours? Why not ask him now?"

Sophia shook her head. "Then he'd know that we know about his finances. And trust me, he'd close us out and be mad in the mix." Sophia stood up and paced in front of the bed. "No, we must do this and surprise him. Once it's done, we'll have to weather the storm, but he'll come around."

"Are you certain this is the best way to do it?"

"Trust me, my dear." Sophia stepped over to the sewing machine. "How is the dress coming?"

"Oh, my lady, the machine is a wonder. Why, I could sew two dresses a week and still have free time." Nelwina smiled, standing and holding up the skirt. "Thank you for helping me learn to run the machine. I should have your gown and petticoat finished by tomorrow."

"Oh, smashing." Sophia gave Nelwina a quick hug. "Now, I've got to run into town."

"And will you be seeing Mr. Jefferson?" Nelwina smiled. Sophia had spent a lot of time between the manor and Ramsgil. And she'd had quite a lot to say about Mr. Jefferson after each of her trips.

Sophia blushed and Nelwina swallowed back a chuckle.

"Well now, dear, love isn't just for the young, you know."

"Oh, my lady." Nelwina hugged the older woman. "Of course it isn't. I'm so happy for you."

"Yes, well . . ." Sophia gave Nelwina one more quick squeeze. "I'd better run then. Niles and I will get everything arranged." Going to the door, she stopped and met Nelwina's gaze. "And you're not to worry over anything. Adam will be so proud when we show him how well the tours go."

"I'm sorry, sir, but we've so many guests. I just don't recall Miss Tanner."

"But it's an emergency."

The man behind the desk at the London hotel just shrugged.

"Didn't we send her bags to Ramsgil?" a woman mentioned as she walked behind the man, earning a glare from him.

Philip smiled. At last he had some information.

"Thank you. Thank you very much." He turned and left the hotel.

On his way back to his hotel, he stopped by a tourist office and purchased a map of England. First thing tomorrow he'd rent a car and go to Ramsgil and find Jocelyn.

Things were looking up, he thought.

Chapter Eleven

"Where are you two bound for today?"

Nel and Sophia stopped at the front door and turned to face Adam. They glanced at one another before his mother spoke.

"Shopping." She chirped the single word and smiled, wiggling her fingers in farewell.

It was the same answer he'd gotten the last few days. Either his mother or both women left every day.

They sure were acting odd these days. For his mother that was nothing new, but for Nel . . . well, come to think of it, she'd always seemed a bit different, too. So how was he to tell when she was acting stranger than normal?

He didn't know how they could shop day after day, but Nel was wearing new clothes that fit her better than her old. It was all those Mallows she kept pilfering. He grinned. He rather liked the results, though. The image of Nel's nicely rounded hips encased in close-fitting pants sprang to mind.

He shook his head. Better not go there, he thought.

He glanced out the window and watched as his mother's car disappeared. It had been almost a week since the doctor's visit and there'd been no change in Nel. The physician had said to be patient, but Adam wondered what would happen if Nel's confusion didn't clear up.

Somehow, he needed to learn a little more about her. Surely someone should be notified. He'd tried to get the information from Nel, but she always denied having family, friends or a job.

Leaving the foyer, he climbed the stairs and went to the new wing. He hesitated a moment, his hand on the knob of Nel's door. Feeling like a thief, he turned it and walked in.

He glanced around the tidy room, seeking any clue as to who Nel really was. He walked around the bed and on the floor he found a magazine and newspaper. He picked the items up, his gaze scanning the old edition of the *New York Times*. He placed it on the bed and turned his attention to the magazine. Thumbing through, he found an envelope stuffed between its pages.

He flipped it over. The return address was that of an American travel agency. Pushing back the guilt his prying brought on, he took out the contents.

Unfolding the paper, he read over the itinerary listed. He exhaled a breath. Nel had been due back more than two weeks ago.

Surely someone was worrying over her. Wouldn't he or she be making inquires?

He looked back down at the paper in his hand, Jocelyn's name catching his attention. The travel agency had sent the paperwork to Jocelyn in care of Dempsey, Daniel and Finch. Was that a law firm? he wondered.

Well, it was a start, he thought, folding the paper and slipping it inside the envelope. Putting the magazine and paper back on the floor where he'd found them, he went down to the study. He'd find the number and give them a call. Surely someone in personnel could tell him who her emergency contact was.

After a quick search on the Internet, Adam found the firm's number. Jotting it down, he put the note in his pocket. It was too early to call now; he'd have to wait until later.

With that bit of business done, he went back to work, pushing the anxiety of the future call to the back of his mind. He wasn't certain he wanted to learn anything about Nel. What if she were married? That thought stopped him. Surely she'd remember that, wouldn't she? He shook his head; he hadn't any answers. Not yet anyway.

He wondered how long his mother and Nel would be gone. How long can it take to do a little shopping? Adam shrugged.

No. Don't even go there, old boy.

"Do you think he's suspicious?" Nelwina asked Sophia as they climbed into Adam's mother's car. The machine still frightened her, but with each trip to Ramsgil the fear lessened a bit.

"Nel, dear, all a woman has to do is tell a man she's going shopping and suspicion is the furthest thing from his mind. They seem to shut down and get that delightful glassy look in their eyes." Sophia laughed. "Believe me, men want nothing to do with the sport."

Nelwina shifted in her seat. She'd left off her gown and worn a pair of trousers she'd purchased on their first trip to town this week. Sophia had pointed out that the effect would be better were they both to wear their gowns only for the tours.

"But we've given him the same excuse for the last three days."

Sophia shrugged. "It's the joy of being a woman. We can tell them we're going shopping and they won't ask any more questions."

They shot around a curve and Nelwina gripped the edges of her seat. Even after three days of Sophia's driving, Nelwina still felt faint at this one particular spot.

The road straightened out and Nelwina forced herself to fold her hands in her lap. She'd come to admire Sophia's ability to handle the car. It was something Nelwina would never be brave enough to do.

She watched the passing countryside.

Some things never changed, she thought, like Spenceworth and the low stone walls dividing the fields. Black-faced sheep dotted the green pastures just like they had two hundred years ago. She couldn't imagine living anyplace else.

Pulling her gaze from the scene out her window, she watched the road ahead and thought about their trip to town today.

"Will the brochures be completed in time?"

Sophia nodded. "The printer promised they'd be

ready today. And Niles said he'd see they were sent on to the tour companies this afternoon."

Nelwina gripped her hands together in her lap as Sophia negotiated another turn, barely missing an oncoming car.

"I'm so excited, Nel. Our dresses will be the finishing touch. And you'll be the perfect guide, what with all your knowledge of Spenceworth. I've such a grand feeling about this. It's bound to bring in a good deal of money, especially once we get to advertising the tours."

"And you're certain Adam will be pleased?" After many admonishments to refer to the earl as Adam, Nelwina had finally relented, though she still had trouble with it occasionally.

"Well, we had to do something to help him, didn't we?"

"Aye. But I'll be making a fine wage sewing for the fabric shop. Wouldn't that be a better way to help Adam?"

"Oh, Nel." Sophia glanced from the road to her. "That money is for you, dear. Every woman needs her mad money, you know." Sophia turned back to the road. "And the sums needed for Spenceworth far exceed your salary."

Nelwina slumped in her seat. "I suppose you're right."

"Of course I am. We've found the perfect way to solve at least a bit of his financial problems. Adam will be thrilled and relieved."

They approached a roundabout and Nelwina gripped the edge of her seat. As the car shot into the circle of traffic, Nelwina closed her eyes and muttered a quick prayer. These, above all, put the fear of God in her. How people avoided crashing into one another was beyond her comprehension.

With the roundabout behind them, Nelwina took a deep breath and replied, "I pray you are right, my lady."

"So do I."

Nelwina didn't think Sophia meant for her to hear that last comment. And Nelwina wished she hadn't, for her stomach knotted with anxiety.

Adam inspected the last of the repairs to the roof. He'd had to make a financial choice between the garden and the building structure and the building won out.

The integrity of the structure must always come first. There was no point in having wonderful gardens if Spenceworth was crumbling around his head. So he'd invested in the repairs.

With the roof finished, he had a few loose ends to tie up at Spenceworth and then he'd be free to head to London.

He'd told his mother of the trip and she'd seemed quite pleased, but not at all surprised. He'd met with a new client on his last trip and Saturday he'd present the plans he'd been working on for him.

He'd also received a call from an older couple asking for a Sunday appointment. So his weekend trip would be a busy one. But he wouldn't recognize any real income until the construction started.

And while he was in London he was going to pay

another visit to his late uncle's solicitor. He needed to sell some of the stock to pay the taxes and get the funds for the garden restoration, but he had to have the solicitor's approval first.

"Bloody stupid way to run things," he muttered as he closed himself in the study. But then, the entire will had been idiotic in the extreme.

"I hear you're quite the seamstress, Nel." Mr. Jefferson turned his smile on Nelwina and a blush heated her cheeks.

"Oh now, Niles, you've not told a soul about our little surprise, have you?" Sophia looked up from the brochure extolling Spenceworth's charms. "We want it to be a surprise."

"Mum's the word." He patted Sophia's arm and they headed to a little shop for tea.

Nelwina smiled, happy for the couple. The two are besotted, Nelwina thought, watching them as they gazed into each other's eyes. Sophia was such a vibrant, energetic person. She deserved someone who shared her zest for life.

They were perfect for one another.

Nelwina tamped down the envy pushing up from her heart. Would Adam ever look at her like that? Were her feelings written as plainly on her face as Sophia's? To be loved like that was a dream for her.

"Who you looking for?"

Philip turned to the oddly dressed old woman who'd spoken to him.

"Jocelyn Tanner." He glanced around Ramsgil's

neat little streets. "The hotel told me they sent her bags here."

"And just who might you be, then?"

"Her husband." He'd found out that he got more help if he claimed to be Jocelyn's husband than either a friend or a fiancé.

"That so?" The woman stood in front of him. The bracelets around her wrinkled wrists jangled as she propped her hands on her hips and squinted up at him.

Who the hell was this old hag anyway?

Her eyes widened and then narrowed. "Careful who you call a hag."

"Excuse me?" Philip frowned. Had he actually spoken his thought? No, he hadn't. He knew he hadn't.

But then how did she know? He snorted. Anyone looking like her had probably been called a hag a time or two.

Just a coincidence.

"Now that's the second time you've called me a hag. If you're wanting information, you'll catch more flies with honey than name-calling."

Philip blinked. He knew he hadn't said anything. This woman was giving him the willies.

"Sorry," he mumbled and stepped around her. She probably doesn't know anything about Jocelyn anyway.

"She didn't say anything about a husband."

Philip stopped and turned around. "You've spoken with her?" He moved back to the woman. "Where is she?"

"Well, now you want information, don't you? And

why should I answer your questions when you've been so rude to me?"

"I said I was sorry." He wanted to shake the old—

"Careful."

Philip didn't finish the thought. Could she read minds? No, he didn't go for that kind of trash. But if she did know where Jocelyn was, he wanted to know.

"Listen, she's in some trouble at home and I need to find her."

"Well, she isn't here."

Okay, now he *was* going to shake her.

"She was, but then she left."

"Where did she go?"

"Had an accident, she did."

"What?" Philip fisted his hands. "She's in the hospital?" Damn, that complicates things, he thought.

"Nay."

Relief washed over him.

"I tended to her myself." She preened. "Nasty lump on her head, it was. I treated her and she left. Simple as that."

"She hit her head?"

"Aye." Nodding to the small park across the street, the crone continued, "Right there on the green. Got knocked right off that block of wood. Hit her head and just went limp."

"You mean she lost consciousness?"

"Aye. But I brought her around quick enough. She was fine in no time."

"Where is she now?"

"Where she belongs." She cocked her head. "And you should be where you belong." She turned around and ambled off, disappearing around the corner. Philip rushed after her, but when he rounded the corner, the mysterious woman was gone. There was no sign of her anywhere.

Damn, that was strange, he thought. But if Jocelyn had been hurt, then the old woman couldn't be the only one who'd seen it.

Chapter Twelve

"My stars." Nelwina breathed the two words as she stared out at the two vehicles pulling up before the manor.

"Our first visitors." Sophia clapped her hands in glee. "Now remember, Nel, just be yourself and tell them a bit about Spenceworth."

Nelwina nervously brushed at her skirts and met Sophia's gaze. "Oh, my lady. Are you certain I can do this?"

Sophia adjusted the bodice of her royal blue gown. "Of course, my dear. And when Adam sees what a success you've made the tours, he'll be thrilled to have all his problems solved."

Since the inception of Sophia's idea, dread had settled over Nelwina. The older woman had more faith in Nelwina's ability than she herself did.

She shared Sophia's desire to erase the lines of worry etched in Adam's face, and she would do her best to succeed.

'Twas not as if it hadn't been done before, she

consoled herself. When the old earl was absent, the butler and even the steward had conducted tours for a fee. Surely she could do it for Adam.

"I only wish the gardens were renovated." Sophia sighed, leading Nelwina out of the room and down the stairs to the waiting tourists. "Think what we could do there."

Nelwina shivered. They'd dared much with this venture. What would Sophia do with the gardens? Nelwina didn't even want to think on that.

Niles Jefferson had agreed to sell the tickets in Ramsgil. Sophia would handle the grouping of the visitors so that Nelwina would take around twenty or so at a time. Each tour would take almost an hour, which meant that she would be repeating herself eight times.

Nelwina stood in the entry hall at the foot of the stairs and gave the hall one last cursory glance. At Sophia's insistence, Nelwina had set out the tea service, whipped up a batch of biscuits and set bread to rising. All in the attempt to make visitors feel as if they'd just stepped back into the eighteenth century.

The only room that would not be included in the tour was the study. She'd adamantly refused to touch anything in that room. 'Twas, after all, Adam's study with his business correspondence and such lying about. And while Sophia didn't seem to have any compunction about trespassing, Nelwina certainly did.

The first group entered with a noisy clamor and Nelwina took a deep breath, smiled at the visitors and bobbed a curtsey.

"Welcome to Spenceworth, my lords and ladies." Spying a couple of children holding tightly to their mothers' hands, she added, "And young masters and mistresses, as well." Meeting the enchanting gaze of a little girl with strawberry-blond curls she smiled and winked. The little one shyly smiled back, edging behind her mother's skirts.

And so the tours began. By the noontime break, Nelwina's mouth was dry and a dull ache lodged behind her eyes.

"We're doing splendidly," Sophia crowed as they sat down to take tea and sandwiches in the upstairs kitchen.

Pouring out the tea, Sophia glanced at Nelwina. "Are you ill, dear?"

Nelwina met Sophia's concerned gaze and shook her head. "Nay, my head is paining me some, is all."

"I'll fetch you some aspirins after we eat."

Nelwina propped her elbow on the table and rested her chin in her palm. "Mayhap I simply need something to eat and drink."

"If you don't feel better after lunch, I'll get those pills for you, dear. We can't have you getting sick. After all, you're the only one to give the tours."

Nelwina simply nodded and sipped her tea.

Th day was only half gone and already she was drained. Pray the tea and food would restore her.

Philip stepped over the threshold of Spenceworth and stopped, his gaze landing on the woman standing at the foot of the stairs.

Jocelyn.

The relief of seeing her made his knees wobbly.

After his encounter with the old woman, he'd questioned a few people and found out Jocelyn had been taken to Spenceworth.

"Good afternoon and welcome, my lords and ladies. My name is Nelwina Honeycutt and I'll be taking you on a tour of Spenceworth. The furnishings of the manor are as they were in the eighteenth century." She smiled. "Mind that you keep with the group and do not handle any of the bric-a-brac or sit on the furniture."

Philip pulled his attention back to her, focusing on Jocelyn. Had she put on weight? Her face was fuller. Scanning her dress, it was hard to tell just how fat she'd gotten. Distaste curled around his tongue.

It was a good thing they weren't really married. He couldn't stand fat women.

But why was she acting as a tour guide? And what was with the accent and the name?

He watched her scan the group and held his breath, anticipating her surprise as her gaze slid right over him and to the person on his right.

What the hell? Not even a flicker of recognition. Philip frowned. What was wrong with her?

Even after he begged off of their engagement, she hadn't treated him like this. She politely, if a bit coolly, greeted him whenever they chanced to pass in the hall at work.

She started climbing the stairs and the group followed behind her.

Philip was still trying to understand Jocelyn's lack of reaction to him as they trekked through the rooms.

She described them in detail, adding tidbits of trivia here and there.

How did she know all this? Maybe it was just a script she'd memorized.

The weird thing was it sounded so natural for her. And the way she moved in her costume—she didn't stumble or trip. In fact, she was quite at ease in it.

Something wasn't right here, Philip thought as the group headed back down the stairs.

He pondered the problem as Jocelyn led them through the rest of the rooms. It wasn't until they emerged from the dining room into the hall that he thought he had the answer.

It was the accident. She'd hit her head in the fall and was suffering from amnesia.

He shook his head. That only happened in movies, he told himself. But he was at a loss to explain the way Jocelyn was acting.

She was much too conscientious to simply walk away from her job. Hell, she loved that job—spent most of her waking hours at work, putting in over-time, seldom took vacation and was never out sick.

She wouldn't just quit.

The tourists were ambling away, out the door. Philip made his way over to Jocelyn.

"Nice tour." She turned around with a smile on her face.

"Thank you." She bobbed a curtsey. Canting her head to the side, she asked, "Did you have a question?"

"Ah, yeah." Philip searched for one, but the only thing that came to mind was why she was acting as if they'd never met. But something stopped him from asking. "I'd heard in town that you were hurt in a fall. I hope you're recovered." He studied her face, focusing finally on her eyes.

Her gaze widened in surprise. "Why, yes. Yes, I'm quite well, thank you for asking." Her brow wrinkled in confusion. "Excuse me, but have we met?"

"Do I look familiar to you?" Philip held his breath. Had Jocelyn just been playing him along? A little bit of revenge? Though she never seemed like a vengeful person, which had allowed him to beg off their wedding without fear of reprisals, people changed.

"Nay, I cannot say that. 'Tis just that you seem to know me."

"Jocelyn, it's me, Philip. Philip James." He smiled, hoping to end this farce and get down to business.

She shook her head. "Sir, I'm afraid I do not know you."

Amnesia. Sounded preposterous to him, but it could happen. And it just might make things easier, he thought.

"It's the fall. They say that sometimes a person will lose their memory. Must be what happened."

She gave him a blank look and he bit back the frustration, forcing his voice to be conciliatory. "We were very close back home."

"Close?"

He nodded. "Yes, we had a very close relationship. We were—"

"The coach is returning to Ramsgil, sir." The driver stood at the opened door of the manor, addressing Philip.

"I'll come back later and we'll talk."

Jocelyn gave him a vague smile.

With one last look, he left.

He'd better get back to his hotel and call Titchlark and make an appointment for Jocelyn. It couldn't hurt to get her inheritance before they left England. If he worked it right, he just might get his hands on that inheritance.

And then he'd call Mr. Dempsey and let him know what had happened to Jocelyn. Once he knew of her accident, he'd probably halt the audit of her accounts.

"Nel, who was that?" Sophia frowned after the departing man.

Nelwina turned from watching him leave. "A Mr. Philip James."

"Do you know him, dear?"

"Nay, I think not." She smiled at Sophia. "He'd heard about my accident and asked after my recovery."

"How odd." Sophia glanced at the closed front door. "But then Americans can be a bit . . . unusual."

Pushing the stranger to the back of her mind, Nelwina focused on Sophia. "Shall we have tea? I know I could use a cup."

"Just let me change, dear. I wouldn't want to risk spilling anything on my gown."

As Nelwina put the teapot on the table, Sophia entered the kitchen, wearing a pair of charcoal trousers and a dark pink sweater.

"Oh, Nel." Sophia smiled. "The tours were a hit, dear. You were marvelous."

193

Nelwina settled herself in the chair opposite Sophia. She was tired. She'd spoken so much today she didn't care if she ever talked again. And there were still tomorrow's tours to do.

"Are you all right, my dear?" Nelwina focused on Sophia's kind gaze.

"Yes." Nelwina poured herself a cup of tea, added a spoonful of sugar and took a sip. "Just a bit tired."

"I should say. The number of times you climbed those stairs, well, it's enough to tire anyone."

Nelwina shook her head. "It's not a physical fatigue. My brain is tired. I don't believe I've ever been so talkative."

Sophia nodded and silence fell over the kitchen as they enjoyed their tea.

A few minutes later, Sophia pushed a piece of paper toward Nelwina.

"Niles brought this around."

Nelwina pulled the paper closer to her.

"We did quite well, Nel."

Nelwina read over the figures and blinked in surprise. "I knew there were many visitors today, but I never believed it would equal this."

Sophia nodded. "And we really didn't advertise either. Just think of the possibilities when we do. During the summer we could do tours every day."

Nelwina's shoulders slumped with the sudden weight of the responsibility of handling so many tours.

"Of course, we'll have to find someone to help you with the tours." Nelwina glanced from the paper to Sophia and Sophia's eyes brightened. "Do you think

194

I could do it?" She scooted her chair closer to the table. "You've told me so much about the manor and how it was in the eighteenth century, surely I could help you?"

"Aye, my lady, that you could." Sophia's excitement was contagious. Gone was the weight from Nelwina's shoulders. If Sophia were to help, then mayhap it was possible. She glanced back to the paper. And if they did half as well during the week as they had today, surely Spenceworth could support itself.

"Just you wait until Adam sees this." Sophia picked up the paper and waved it around. "He'll be so surprised. He thinks I'm just an empty-headed old woman."

Sophia put her palm up to stop Nelwina's objection. "I know what he thinks. And I've used it to my advantage over the years. It wasn't easy raising a young boy without a father. I had to have some leverage." Sophia picked up her cup and put it in the sink, and turned to Nelwina. Her gaze hopeful, she asked, "I would so love to give Adam the good news. Would you mind terribly?"

"Oh, no, my lady. Please, 'twas your idea after all."

Sophia patted Nelwina's cheek. "I'm so very glad Adam brought you home, my dear. You're a gem. I'm ready for a nice long soak and a few hours with a good book. I'll see you in the morning."

"Good night, my lady."

The next morning it rained and Nelwina worried that the tourists would stay away. But the first coach arrived filled with visitors and the worry lines on her forehead vanished.

And so the day went and Nelwina found it was easier than the day before. She varied the tours, sometimes starting in the hall, other times the kitchen. Each tour was like a walk through her childhood.

The last tour had just arrived and Sophia caught up with Nelwina. "How are you faring, dear?"

"Wonderfully, my lady. 'Tis much better today, not quite as tiring. With each tour I recall yet another little memory." Nelwina smiled and turned as the last group entered the hall.

Sophia was using her heater again, Nelwina thought as the lights in her room blinked out.

She lit the candle she kept by her bed. It had taken some adjustment, having a room illuminate at the flick of a switch. But it was no hardship on her when the lights went out. She was more accustomed to candles.

The closing of a door somewhere outside pulled her from the book she read. Excitement curled low in her belly.

Adam. He was home.

Recalling the last time he'd entered the house without light, she scampered out of bed, threw on her robe and grabbed her candle.

She'd just reached the top of the stairs when he came through the door.

"Lights out again?" Adam looked up to see Nel standing at the top of the stairs, the candle in her hand casting a warm glow around her.

"Aye." The soft smile tilting the corners of her lips made his mouth water. The three days he'd been away from Spenceworth, all he could think about was Nel.

Was she making another gown, or a cover for the footstool she'd found in the attic last week?

And what had she and his mother been up to? Their whispers stopped abruptly every time he entered the room. And they'd spent a lot of time in town.

"Shall I warm water for tea, my lord?"

"What?" He focused on Nel, dragging his mind from his thoughts. "Tea? No, no, I'm fine, thank you."

He climbed the stairs and with each tread, his heart beat a bit faster.

Nelwina stepped back as Adam gained the landing at the top of the stairs. Fighting the urge to throw herself in his arms, she tightened her grip on the candleholder. The flames shimmered as her hand shook with suppressed desire.

My stars, she thought. In the candlelight the raindrops captured in his hair winked like diamonds. The corners of his mouth tipped up in a smile that set a hive of bees loose in her stomach.

She reached out to brush aside the damp locks falling on his forehead, but Adam captured her hand in his warm grasp. And Nelwina's knees went weak.

"Nel?" He felt the tremor run through her slim hand as it rested in his. Her skin was warm and soft and she looked up at him with startled eyes.

God, how he wanted to kiss her lips again. Her gaze flickered down to his mouth and then back to his eyes.

This had been building since they'd first met on the

tour bus. He'd tried to turn away from it, but he'd failed. He couldn't block her from his thoughts. She didn't have to be near to occupy his mind.

He could recall their kisses with clarity; the feel of her in his arms, the subtle flowery scent that surrounded her, the softness of her lips . . . and her passion.

And he wanted more. He wanted to watch her wander the garden paths, take tea where other Warrick ladies had and watch the birds gather at the fountain.

He wanted to see her descend the stairs in the long gowns that so suited her and share Mallows at the worktable in the old kitchen.

She'd carved a place in his heart. And right now, Adam had no intention of denying his feelings.

Nervously, she dampened her lips and his breath stopped in his chest.

He bit back a groan, but refused to relinquish her gaze or her hand.

Dropping his briefcase, he took the candle from her fingers and placed it on the nearby table.

And then he pulled her into his arms and their lips met.

Chapter Thirteen

'Twas a kiss to melt her soul. Adam's lips were both soft and firm, his breath minty.

His arms came around her and Nelwina knew safety. She felt cherished as his lips traced a path from her mouth to her neck and back again.

His hands roamed, leaving behind a white-hot ribbon of desire. His tongue outlined her lips and she gasped into his mouth. Her pulse thundered in her ears as his tongue dipped into her mouth.

Adam's knees shook as he tasted the sweetness of Nel's lips. He deepened the kiss, his arms wrapped around her, no longer to tantalize her, but to keep himself from crashing to the floor.

Their tongues met, hers tentative; as if she'd never kissed like this before. A molten wave of desire crashed over him with the sheer innocence of her response.

Reaching over, he snuffed the candle between his fingers and scooped Nel up to carry her to his room.

Their lips separated only when he laid her gently on his bed and shrugged out of his coat.

And then he joined her. Their bodies melded together as their lips met in a soul-joining kiss.

Fumbling with the belt of her robe, Adam rolled on his back, taking Nel with him. He shoved the sleeves down her arms and the soft pillows of her breasts pressed against his chest as she arched up to free the garment.

He groaned deep in his throat and rolled Nel to her back. Through her nightgown, he cupped her breast, and a shot of desire arced to his groin. He palmed her breast and his penis throbbed as her taut nipple grazed the sensitive center of his hand.

Nelwina struggled with the buttons of Adam's shirt, not wanting him to stop his caresses, but needing to feel his skin against hers. Passion roared in her ears and shot through her veins as Adam found his way beneath her nightgown. And a moment later, he pulled the garment over her head and tossed it to the floor.

Frantic now to touch the warmth of his skin, Nelwina tugged at the buttons of his shirt. His fingers joined her quest and then her palms lay flat against the contours of his bare chest.

His lips came down to hers again and she opened her mouth to welcome his exploration. The button of his pants dug into her hip and she moved her hands to remove the last barrier.

Again his hands were there to help. His lips left hers, moving down her neck to her collarbone. Her fingers tangled in his hair as he captured her nipple in his mouth, his tongue swirling around it until she moaned in surrender.

He moved up next to her again and the heat of his arousal pressed against her thigh.

And she opened for him.

Adam touched the bud of her femininity. Massaging it with small circles, he heard her breath catch and felt her body stiffen. A tremor vibrated through her and she cried out.

Through a haze of passion, Nelwina heard the sound of tearing paper. "Adam?" Her voice sounded low and husky to her ear.

"Shh." Adam positioned himself above her, dipping his head and kissing the base of her neck. He whispered, "Protection."

Before she thought to wonder what he meant, he started to enter her, slowly. Running her hands up his chest and down his arms, she held her breath as he went still. Her body cried out for him. She felt the shudder ripple down his arms and an answering one rolled through her.

She needed him within her, fully. Grasping his hips, she pulled him to her and hissed as pain greeted his entry. But the pain was fleeting and soon Adam carried her to another level of pleasure.

In his passion-clouded mind, Adam didn't recognize the barrier he'd breached. It wasn't until his mind cleared that it came to him, but he was too spent to do more than groan.

Bloody hell. She's a virgin. Or was a virgin.

He buried his nose in the sweet scent of her hair,

waiting for the tears he figured would come next. But he could barely hear her breath.

Nelwina had experienced that pain before, but without the pleasure. She never knew that coupling could be so wonderful. She'd come to dread those times with Haslett. But Adam never gave her a chance to think on what they were doing. He kindled her passion to a raging fire and once the fuel was consumed, the embers glowed on.

'Twas wonderful.

"Yes, it was." Adam's deep voice filled the silence of the room and Nelwina realized she'd whispered her thought.

Adam kissed her lips and then her eyes. Tugging back the covers, he rolled to one side, pulling her close as he covered them both. "Why didn't you tell me you were a virgin, Nel?" he mumbled into her ear.

Sated and warm, a long moment later, she murmured, "I didn't know myself."

And she heard Adam's even breathing and knew he slept.

Nelwina woke as the first rays of sun lightened the sky. She turned her head to see Adam's profile in the early morning light and smiled, remembering the passion of last night.

And the pain.

"Sweet mother of God, what have I done?" she whispered, the smile erased from her lips.

Untangling herself from the linens, she quickly found her nightgown and robe. Donning her clothing, she quietly crept from the room, grateful that Sophia wasn't an early riser to catch her stealing like a thief from Adam's room.

Once inside her own room, she took a shower, blocking any thoughts from her mind. She didn't want to think about what had happened last night or what it would mean today.

But the tenderness between her legs brought it all back. And with it came the uncertainty as well as the wonder.

She had lost her virginity not once as was customary, but twice. Her hands fell to her sides, a confused jumble of thoughts filled her mind.

What had she done to Jocelyn? 'Twas not her right to give another's virtue. Tears welled in her eyes. There was no way to undo what she had done. What would Jocelyn think when she returned? Would she hate Nelwina?

Why hadn't Hilda warned her of this? And where was the old Gypsy? Fresh tears streaked down her cheeks, the water from the shower washing them away. Nelwina should have tried to get back to her time. Guilt that wouldn't be cleansed away by the warm water settled over her.

If she'd put more effort into returning, none of this would have happened. She was ashamed that she'd done so little to find her way back. In her heart, she knew she didn't want to return, especially now, when her feelings for Adam had blossomed.

But she had no right to those feelings, she reminded herself. She was living another's life.

She braced her hands on the cool tiles of the

shower, letting the water beat down on her head. What was she to do?

At least, Nelwina consoled herself, she had suffered the brief pain and not Jocelyn. But she'd also denied the other woman the joy Nelwina found in Adam's arms.

A flash of jealousy left Nelwina stunned.

That joy was hers and hers alone. The thought of sharing Adam with another left her breathless.

But did she have any right to him? What if she were swept back to her own time tomorrow? What then? Would Adam find Jocelyn more to his liking? Would she find him as attractive as Nelwina did?

The questions spun around in her head, making her dizzy. She couldn't sort it all out.

There was one thing Nelwina held on to and that was the joy that Adam was the first and only one to know this body intimately. He had not taken Haslett's leavings. She nudged those thoughts aside, loath to tarnish last night with thoughts of another man.

Her blood heated and her heart beat faster.

She reached down and turned the hot water down, expecting steam to rise from her skin as the cool water fell on her overheated body.

Stop that this minute, Nelwina Honeycutt. You've experienced the attentions of a man before.

Aye, but nothing this passionate or pleasurable.

And the problems plaguing her swirled around in her mind again with the thought of Adam. Pain lodged in the area of her heart at the idea that she might have to leave him.

How could love be so painful?

There were things that were beyond her control. The realization brought a strange kind of quiet to her thoughts.

She had no idea if she would ever return to her time and what kind of fix her life might be in there. She would simply do the best she could and trust that Jocelyn would do the same.

Pray God that things worked out.

Resolutely forcing her mind to other things, she finished bathing. She dressed in a long cotton skirt and bodice . . . no, Sophia told her it was called a blouse now. The skirt she'd made and the *blouse*, she emphasized the word in her mind, was one from Jocelyn's bags. She glanced in the mirror, adjusting the collar.

The full skirt fell to just above her ankles, allowing her easy movement. It was a compromise between the skirts she was used to wearing and the fashion of the time she found herself in. She liked the look, she thought as she slipped on short hose Sophia had told her were called socks and her Keds. She grinned as she read the blue label at the heel of her shoes. Who would have thought to label shoes like that? And to what purpose?

She shrugged the question aside and glanced into the mirror once more. Satisfied with her appearance, Nelwina went to the old kitchen downstairs. She needed the comfort of the old surroundings and she was hungry.

In the kitchen she stoked the fire, put water on to boil and set about making fresh biscuits. The comforting warmth of the hearth and the familiar activity of baking calmed her nerves.

Adam rolled over, his hand reaching for Nel, but the bed was empty. He opened his eyes and squinted as sunlight poured in through the open curtains. He glanced at the clock, and remembered the power was out.

And that one thought brought on the memories of last night. He couldn't remember ever experiencing anything like it. Making love with Nel last night had reached far beyond the physical. It had reached his heart and connected with his soul.

He got up, eager to shower and find her. He'd met with the landscape contractor in London and wanted to show her what he'd ordered for the garden. He'd found the perfect statue for the fountain and even ordered a small white table and two chairs, to be delivered today, for the corner where she could take tea in the afternoon.

In the kitchen he flipped the breaker and reset the clock on the microwave. Crossing the hall to Nel's room, he knocked on her door, but there was no answer.

Thinking to find her in the garden, he left the new wing. At the top of the stairs the smell of cinnamon filled the foyer.

His stomach growled and with a smile on his face he headed to the old kitchen.

He pushed the door open and watched as Nel pulled a pan from the old-fashioned stone oven built into the wall of the fireplace.

Again it struck him how much better she seemed to function in the old rooms of Spenceworth. He'd never seen her do more than make tea and coffee in the modern kitchen, nor had she touched the oven there.

And here she was baking in an antiquated one. Where had she learned to do it?

Past life. He shook his head, knowing that if he asked, that would be her response. And he wouldn't ruin a glorious morning by asking. Maybe once her memory returned he'd find out who had taught her the fine art of hearth cooking.

He walked up behind Nel and wrapped his arms around her waist, inhaling the flowery scent of her hair.

"It smells wonderful. Is there enough for me?" He nuzzled her neck.

The pan clattered to the top of the worktable.

"My stars, you startled me."

"Deep in thought, were you?" He kissed the nape of her neck. "And were you thinking of me?"

He turned her around and saw a blush climb her cheeks. Damn, but she was cute, he thought. "I've been thinking of you," he murmured, bringing his lips to hers for a good-morning kiss.

His stomach grumbled and Nel smiled.

"I'm afraid I've only tea."

Adam glanced at the pan of biscuits. "Tea and fresh biscuits sounds perfect."

A moment later Nel had poured tea for them both and placed two plates with biscuits beside the tea.

He could get used to this, Adam thought as he savored the cinnamon flavor of the warm biscuit and Nel's quiet companionship.

Sophia descended the stairs, smiling as she passed through the foyer and heard the murmur of Nel and Adam's voices. Her mouth watered as the smell of baking cinnamon filled the air. The two lovebirds were sharing a breakfast Nel had made in the old kitchen. Today promised to be a marvelous day.

She headed into Ramsgil. Niles would have the receipts totaled for the weekend. The silly man had refused to tell her the total, so she'd gotten up earlier than normal in her excitement. And for that, Niles would have to treat her to breakfast. Just the smell of Nel's biscuits made her tummy rumble.

She found Niles at the back of the dining room of the tavern. He stood up as she approached.

"Well, Niles, how did we do?" She put her handbag on an empty chair.

He smiled and handed her a slip of paper.

"Oh my!" She threw her arms around Niles's neck and kissed him on the cheek.

"Er . . . Sophia?"

"Oh, Niles, we couldn't have done it without you." She felt the warmth of his hands at her waist and a tingle of pleasure shimmied up her spine. If only he'd really hug her, she thought wistfully.

She pulled away from him, just enough to see his face, and nearly laughed. The poor man looked both bewildered and embarrassed, but she noticed his hands were still holding her waist.

Their gazes met for a moment before Niles's

cheeks reddened and he cleared his throat, moving his hands to his sides. "Yes, well, I just hope we did the right thing, my dear."

Sophia smiled. So Niles felt the chemistry between them too. Oh, the day was getting better and better, she thought.

"Oh, Niles." She patted his hand. "I just know Adam will be pleased. We've solved his financial woes."

After breakfast, Niles walked her to the bank and they exchanged the money for a bank draft in Adam's name. She'd considered giving him the money, a pound at a time, but thought it would make a better impression if she gave him one bank draft. Much more businesslike.

Niles opened her car door, but before she could slide onto the seat, he took her hand and pulled her close, giving her a gentle kiss on the lips.

"Oh, Niles." She smiled, her heart beating like a young girl who's tasted her first kiss.

It had been such long time since she'd received the attentions of a man. Her stomach was all aflutter. She touched her lips and smiled. Yes, she'd bring him up to scratch. Her cap was quite set for Niles and Sophia would settle for nothing less than a life with him.

"I'll ring you later," he told her as he handed her into her car and closed the door.

With a wave and a smile, she pulled from the curb and headed back to the manor, quite pleased with the day's events and looking forward to the ones yet to come.

Thinking about the bank draft in her handbag, she

grinned. Oh, how she loved surprises. Adam would be dumbfounded. He'd be relieved. He'd be delighted.

And she couldn't be happier.

Chapter Fourteen

As she banked the fire in the kitchen hearth, Nelwina heard the crunch of gravel and the rumble of Sophia's car.

She grinned. Adam would be so pleased when Sophia gave him the draft for the money the tours had brought in over the weekend.

The women had agreed that they would tell Adam together after Sophia returned. Nelwina chuckled with excitement.

Adam had gone out to the formal gardens after giving her a long kiss that left her feeling warm and content.

Still feeling that glow, she poured herself one last cup of tea and then gathered the rest of the dishes from the worktable and put them on a tray. Though she preferred to cook in the old kitchen, washing the dishes needed to be done in the new one. Sophia had explained about the plumbing rules of this age.

Actually, Nelwina didn't mind, especially when the hot water came right out of the spigot. And the modern soap didn't burn or chafe her hands.

With a damp cloth, Nelwina wiped down the work-table and then swept the floor. She gave the kitchen one last glance and, with her teacup in hand, she went to the windows looking out on the kitchen garden. The sun shined brightly now, creating sparkling diamonds of the drops of rain still clinging to the leaves of the remaining weeds.

Stepping out into the morning air, she stood there picturing the garden as she remembered it and planning what she would plant and where.

Sophia bought the produce they ate in Ramsgil, so a large kitchen garden wasn't necessary and would be time-consuming to tend.

But an herb garden would be wonderful, and useful as well.

She wandered along the path between the beds, planning where she would plant dill, thyme, and rosemary. There also would be plenty of room for flowers. She could make sachets for the wardrobes.

Her smile died.

She'd vowed earlier to do the best she could, to live the life that wasn't hers in a way she thought Jocelyn would want. But how could she do that when Jocelyn was a total stranger?

Should she be making plans like this? Or should she teach Sophia how to do the tours? Find Hilda and make things right? She'd done what she could to help Adam; she should find Hilda and make her way back to her own time.

But after last night, the thought of leaving Spenceworth nearly tore her heart from her chest. Her feelings for Adam had grown since she arrived at the manor. But did he share her feelings?

Sighing, she nudged a stick from her path with her toe. And what if she was meant to be here? Would Adam come to love her? She knew she could live in a loveless marriage, but could she survive in a relationship where her affections weren't returned?

Would they even marry?

She shook her head. She didn't know. Sophia had told her that Adam paid no attention to the classes, but how could he not? 'Twas a thing of birth; one was either born to rank and privilege or not. And to make it worse, she had been born on the wrong side of the blanket. Illegitimate.

Could he ever put aside her birth and the class distinctions and return her love? For indeed what she felt for him was love, of that she was sure.

She felt so dishonest, taking Jocelyn's place, even though she'd had no control over it. She had tried to explain to Adam, but each time, he interrupted her and she sensed his anger. She knew 'twas difficult to believe this situation she was in, but 'twas even more difficult to live it.

Nelwina sipped her tea. A cloud passed over the sun, momentarily casting a gloom over her and the garden.

She had no answers to the questions. 'Twas easy to say that she would rattle along, doing her best, but with her future beyond her control, 'twas harder to do.

The uncertainty of it would drive her mad, she

thought as she walked back to the kitchen, her fine mood gone with the sunshine.

Adam wiped his feet before entering the old kitchen. Lifting the napkin that covered the leftover biscuits, he snatched one and glanced around the room.

Nel had cleaned up from their breakfast. Looking into the hearth, he saw that she'd also banked the fire. Was she planning on baking later?

He hoped so.

He took a bite of the biscuit and rolled his eyes appreciatively as it melted in his mouth.

Adam smiled and shook his head. "How does she manage to bake anything in that?" He opened the metal door and peered into the oven. "She's amazing."

He finished off his biscuit and went upstairs. He'd left Nel's drawing of the garden in his room. His client had approved the final plans for the house and had given Adam the next installment for his services. He'd used the funds to purchase plants for the garden. The delivery should arrive later today and he wanted to make sure he knew where the plants should be unloaded.

Following the sound of running water, Adam went to the kitchen and found Nel doing the dishes. He caught a glimpse of her face when she turned to pick up a cup.

Something was wrong.

"Nel?" She turned and offered him a watery smile, her eyes glistening with unshed tears.

No, he thought, don't ruin last night with recriminations or guilt.

But her slumped shoulders and the lost air about her tugged at his heart.

She rinsed the cup and put it aside to dry. Adam stepped up beside her and turned her to meet his gaze.

"What is it, love?" He wiped a lone tear from her cheek and took her into his arms and rubbed her back.

" 'Tis nothing." She wiped at her eyes.

"Nel, tell me what's bothering you."

Nel remained silent, her face pressed against his neck. He held her and turned his head to kiss her neck.

With a gentle squeeze of her shoulders, he moved back to look into her eyes.

"Oh, Adam, there's something I haven't told you."

Dread sank in his stomach. "What's that?" He held his breath.

Nel glanced away. "My father never married my mother." She looked into Adam's eyes. "I'm illegitimate *and* a commoner."

He exhaled and grinned. "And you think this matters to me?" He gave her his best mock frown. "This title I've inherited hasn't changed me, Nel. I've never paid attention to the class system." He squeezed her shoulders. "And as for the other, well, you had no control over it. Besides, it simply doesn't matter to me." He kissed the tip of her nose and smiled.

But something else still bothered Nel. He could tell by the sad shadows in her eyes.

"That's not all, is it?"

She shook her head. "I don't want to leave."

"And I don't want you to, either." Just the thought of Spenceworth without Nel brought a hollow feeling to the pit of his stomach. "Could you extend your holiday? I ordered plants for the garden. I thought you might like to supervise their placement." The idea had just appeared, but it sounded excellent to him.

He'd spoken with the personnel administrator at Dempsey, Daniel and Finch on Friday. The woman had been quite concerned, but assured him she would notify Nel's boss of the accident. Adam left his number in case there was a problem. But Nel had enough sick leave on the books that she could stay an extra three weeks. Of course, he couldn't tell her that, but he hoped talking about her job would jog her memory.

"You don't understand." She sniffled again and Adam changed from stroking to patting her back.

"Then explain it to me."

" 'Tis near impossible. I don't even understand it."

Adam clamped down on his impatience. "Let's go at this one step at a time." He tipped her chin up with his finger. "Shall we?"

Misery darkened her gaze, but she nodded.

"What is it you'd like to do?" Adam pulled out a chair for Nel. He took the one beside her and watched as she pleated the material of her skirt.

She took a deep breath and exhaled it with a sigh. "I'd so love to stay here." She met his gaze.

"And you can." A spark of happiness lit her round eyes, but a second later it was gone.

She shook her head. "How I wish it were so."

"Nel." Adam grasped her upper arms. "It is so. I

216

really do need your help with the gardens. And if you choose to stay in England, we'll get you a work visa." They'd deal with the logistics of a move later.

He was assuming she'd wish to stay after the confusion cleared from her mind; when in fact, she would probably wish to return to her life in South Carolina.

Confusion wrinkled her brow and then tears filled her eyes. " 'Tis no use, I'll never fit in here." She swiped at her cheeks. "I know not how long I'll be here."

"Nel, listen to me. No one knows how long they'll live. And you can stay here as long as you like."

"You don't understand," she wailed, scooting out of her chair and rushing from the kitchen.

Adam caught up with her in the hallway. Grabbing her around the waist, he turned her around.

"Then explain it to me, damn it." His patience was at an end. He was sick of her evasiveness.

"You won't believe me." She raised her chin to charge him with his crime. "You've never believed me." She shrugged off his hands.

"Is this about that past life thing?"

She nodded.

He closed his eyes. Why did the women in his life cling to the occult? Past lives, déjà vu, psychics, tarot cards, Runes. Rubbish, all of it.

But then images flashed in his mind.

Nel in her gown climbing the stairs. Nel trying to figure out how to operate the vacuum and screaming when he flipped the switch and the bloody thing had started up.

And Nel and the old oven in the kitchen. She knew

exactly when the temperature was right for baking. She could kindle a fire in the hearth and bank it. And the next morning, she'd add a few pieces of wood and stir it back to life.

And then there was Nel's drawing of the garden.

The contractor had been very impressed with it, commenting on how the design held a bit of Capability Brown's style. Brown had been a popular landscape designer in the eighteenth century, tending to design gardens with an eye to naturalism. But mixed with Brown's influence was the more common formal layout.

Maybe that was the rub between his ancestor and the designer.

He shook his head and opened his eyes. What was he thinking? So she had a few unusual skills. Skills could be learned, right?

But it wasn't just her skills, he told himself. There was a feeling, an air about Nel that he couldn't explain.

But what would happen when Nel recovered? How would it affect their relationship? Would she be the same?

He ran a hand through his hair and met her sad gaze. Or would she rush back to her life in South Carolina, her holiday just a memory?

"Nel, tell me how I can make this right for you."

Nelwina looked at Adam. How she wished it were that simple. If only he could assure her that Jocelyn was content living Nelwina's life, that she wanted to remain where she was.

If only he could guarantee that she wouldn't pop back into the eighteenth century without warning.

She brought her hand up and cupped his cheek. " 'Tis my fondest wish that you could make it right." She let her hand fall to her side. " 'Tis impossible, my lord."

She turned and left, making her way to the old servants' quarters. She would find comfort and solace in the room she'd shared with her mother.

If only she could find answers.

"Nel?"

Nelwina brought her head up. Sophia had returned and was searching for her. Nelwina wiped away the last vestige of tears, straightened her skirt and stepped out in the hall. Sophia stood at the first door, her hand on the knob.

"Oh, there you are, dear. I've the draft." Excitement filled Sophia's voice and a smile stretched her lips. "Come, let's give Adam the good news."

Sophia met Nelwina halfway and linked her arm with Nelwina's. Taking a slip of paper from her pocket, she showed it to Nelwina. "Beautiful, isn't it? We did this with little or no advertising and in only two days."

Nelwina steadied Sophia's hand so she could read the writing.

"We earned that much?" Nelwina gasped. Never had she even seen that much money. Certainly Adam's troubles were over now. At least she had earned her keep and helped Adam and Spenceworth.

Together she and Sophia found Adam in the garden, sweeping off the flagstones in the corner.

"Adam, dear, Nel and I have a surprise for you." Sophia wiggled like an excited child.

"I'm almost finished here."

"Oh, do come along, Adam. We've the most extraordinary news."

Giving the paving one last swipe, he propped the broom against the side of the manor.

"Okay, Mother, what is it?" He dusted off his hands, avoiding Nelwina's gaze, and took the paper Sophia proudly handed to him.

"What's this?"

Nelwina watched as his eyes scanned the print.

He frowned. "Where did you get this?"

Sophia flashed Nelwina a triumphant look. "The old fashioned way . . . we earned it." She chuckled.

"You earned eight hundred pounds? How?"

"Oh, Adam, Nel and I conducted tours of Spenceworth over the weekend. We both dressed in costume and," Sophia bounced on the balls of her feet, "Nel was wonderful. She held the visitors spellbound, I tell you. And look," she pointed to the draft, "that's what we earned. Isn't it wonderful?"

Adam's face filled with fury. Sophia stopped bouncing and her smile dissolved.

"Who the bloody hell do you think you are? Do you know what you've done?"

"My lord," Nel gasped. " 'Tis your mother you address."

He turned his head and glared at Nelwina. "Excuse me? Do either of you know what you've just done?" He stepped toward them, "Do you?"

"But Adam . . ." Sophia whimpered, backing up.

"Damn it, Mother." He combed his fingers through his hair. "What have you done?"

Sophia's face reddened and she raised her chin. "We tried to help you, you ungrateful wretch. If you turned the manor into a bed and breakfast you would have taken the business from those in Ramsgil. And changed Spenceworth completely. Our way was not invasive at all." Sophia squinted up at her son. "I happen to know that your stocks aren't performing so well. How did you plan on paying for the renovations?"

Adam opened his mouth to speak, but Sophia cut him a scathing look. "We only wanted to ease your worries. Granted, it was none of my business, but you are my son and your happiness is my business. Now you can either take what we've offered or we'll go shopping with it."

Sophia folded her arms across her chest, her toe tapping on the flagstone walk as she waited for his answer.

Some of his anger leaked away when he glanced at Nel and saw tears spilling from her eyes.

But then neither woman knew the cost of what they had done. His anger returned. It was time they did.

He'd always kept any financial problems from his mother. She'd struggled to raise him after his father had died and when he'd left university, he'd taken over the burden for her. He never wanted her to worry over money; that was his job, as he saw it. And look what it had cost.

221

"Mother, first of all, I was not going to turn the manor into a bed and breakfast."

Sophia started to argue, but this time Adam cut her off. "These plans you saw, I assume you were nosing around my desk?" He didn't wait for her reply, but continued, "I wrote them up before I spoke with uncle's solicitor and got a complete copy of the will. You had no business pawing through my desk. Now what you and Nel have done has cost me the little support the will afforded for Spenceworth. The will prohibited me from opening Spenceworth up to tours. Should I do so, the stock that supports the manor would be turned over to charity."

"Let the charity have it, Adam." She pointed to the check in his hand. "We did this in one weekend without any publicity. We don't need the dividends from the stock."

"Mother, listen to me." Adam's voice rose. "Without the dividends, your little contribution here will barely pay the taxes. It's little more than a drop in the bucket of what is needed to keep this place in repair."

Adam stepped around the stunned women. "Why couldn't you just have left things to me—had a little faith?" He entered the manor, closing the door behind him with more force than necessary.

He headed to his study. He'd call his attorney and see what could be done about the tours. There had to be a way around the will. He'd spoken with his uncle's solicitor and the man had assured him there was nothing that could be done. But Adam wasn't going to accept that. There had to be a solution.

"Adam?"

He glanced up from his desk and found his mother standing just inside the room.

"You were very harsh out there." She nodded toward the garden. "Nel is quite upset."

"Mother, I'm quite upset. Neither of you seems to realize what you've done. Because of your hare-brained idea, I may well lose Spenceworth. The bloody place will fall to rack and ruin, be taken over by the historic society, and in the end, it will be a tourist trap. And all thanks to a meddling mother and her eccentric partner in crime." He ran his hand through his hair again. "I should have left Nel to the ministrations of that crazy old woman. It's been one problem after another since I met her."

"Adam!" His mother gasped, her eyes narrowed and her lips pursed. "I thought I'd raised you better."

She spun around and left, slamming the door behind her. A few minutes later the front door slammed and he heard her car drive off. He glanced down at his desk and saw the draft.

Mother, you forgot your ill-gotten gains.

Nelwina fled through the kitchen door, the pain of Adam's words squeezing her heart. She had seen Adam frustrated, but never angry like this.

She was still grappling with the dictates of Adam's uncle's will. She had no idea what stock he spoke of. There were no animals at Spenceworth.

She left the kitchen gardens behind and headed to the woods off to the left. Unless . . . Her steps slowed. Unless he kept them someplace else. But what about the dividends? She shook her head. No, she didn't understand any of this.

But what she did know was that Adam viewed her as another problem. A problem he didn't need.

She bent and picked a yellow wildflower. Lord knows she tried to fit in—wearing the strange clothing, eating their packaged food. What more was she to do?

She spun the flower between her fingers. She had problems, too. Even now, most things were alien to her. She was much like a babe just learning to walk.

But Adam was consumed with his own troubles. And as long as she was at Spenceworth, he counted her among them.

She wandered through the forest, feeling sorry for herself, tears rolling down her cheeks. After a few minutes, she stopped beneath a huge oak tree, scrubbed the tears from her face and placed her hands on her hips.

"Well, this is a fine thing you do, Nelwina Honeycutt. As if feeling sorry for yourself is going to fix a thing." She tilted her head back, staring up at the canopy of leaves. "I have been through enough." She shook her fist at the tree. "Do you hear me? Enough."

She'd traveled through time, ended up in another woman's body and fallen in love. And Adam thought he had problems. She snorted. Hah! She could show him what problems were.

She was sorry she and Sophia had caused him trouble, but he was an intelligent man; surely he could work things out. And his mother was right. However these stocks he talked about brought money to him, the tours could do as well. 'Twas a bloody lot of money they'd handed over to him this morning.

She would simply march back to the manor and they would work this all out. She turned around and started back through the woods.

Her steps slowed as she recalled the look he'd given her in the garden. There was not a shred of love to be found in his gaze. And then the conversation with his mother she'd overheard. Her bravado leaked away and her shoulders slumped.

What was she to do?

"Jocelyn."

Nel looked up and saw a man striding toward her, waving his hand.

"Jocelyn," he called again and Nel looked behind her, expecting to see another woman. It took her a moment to realize he was calling to her.

And panic caught in her throat. It was the man from the tour. The one who'd asked after her health. She'd been exhausted that first day and hadn't the energy to wonder why he would be so concerned. A sick feeling settled in the bottom of her stomach.

Chapter Fifteen

"Jocelyn." The man huffed as he reached Nelwina, his dark blond hair blowing in the breeze. Dark glasses hid his eyes. "I'm so glad I found you." He stretched out his arms, and Nelwina stepped away.

"Mr. James?"

"It's Philip, Jocelyn." He let his arms fall to his sides. "You don't call your husband 'mister.' "

"Husband?" She stumbled back a step. "You're my husband?"

He nodded, taking off his glasses and smiling.

"But why didn't you say this after the tour?"

He looked down, fidgeting with the spectacles. "I thought you were still mad at me." A lock of hair blew across his brow and he looked up. "You were rather cool toward me, after all."

Nelwina frowned. "I don't believe I'm any warmer today."

"Well, that's because of the amnesia. At first, I didn't really believe it could happen. But then I caught a program on television the other night where a woman had suffered an injury to her head and completely lost her memory. Her husband was a total stranger to her. She couldn't remember her family or friends. Her past was a mystery to her and she had to start all over." He shoved his hand into his pocket. "I figured that must have happened to you."

But she could remember her past, Nelwina thought. Just not Jocelyn's. Her head started to ache. This man was Jocelyn's husband?

"How long have we been married?"

He glanced away from her, as a blush stained his cheeks. "The trip to England was to have been our honeymoon."

"But—"

"We had a huge argument right after the wedding and you left."

That explains the pain last night, she thought as memories of Adam rushed back. She should be horrified by what she'd done last night, but it had felt so right. She loved Adam. And she'd hoped he might come to return her feelings.

Well, until a few hours ago.

"Jocelyn?"

She focused on Philip. "And you let me go?"

"I thought I'd give you some time to cool down. I know that if I give you your space, things work out."

Nelwina couldn't argue with that. She had no idea what Jocelyn was like or what she'd prefer to do. She knew nothing of the woman whose body she inhabited.

"Listen, I think we should work this out at home. Mr. Dempsey's worried sick about you."

"Who?"

"Your boss, Mr. Dempsey." Philip rubbed his forehead. "This is going to be much more difficult than I thought." He narrowed his eyes. "You do remember where you work and what you do?"

Nelwina shook her head.

"Oh, man. This is bad. Really bad."

A mantle of dread settled heavily upon her shoulders.

"But don't worry. I'm here for you. We'll get you home and have a doctor check you over."

Nelwina rubbed her stomach.

Philip pulled his hand out of his pocket and took her fingers. "Oh, and you left this behind."

He placed a gold band on her left hand. She folded her hand into a fist. The ring felt cold and foreign on her finger.

"Let's get you home, Jocelyn. I think you'll feel better there. Around familiar surroundings and all." Taking her hand, Philip turned them toward the manor. "Oh, and we'll need to stop by a lawyer's office in London. It seems you're an heiress."

Startled, Nelwina looked up at his smiling face. "An heiress?"

"Yes. You received a letter from a London attorney. We have an appointment with him first thing tomorrow morning."

Nelwina stopped and tugged her hand free. "Mr. James, be assured that I will not be going anywhere with you. You are a total stranger to me."

"Aw, now Jocelyn, we'll get all that sorted out back in the States."

"I'm not going to the States with you."

Philip turned away from her and she watched his shoulders rise as he deeply inhaled and then exhaled. He turned back to her. "Okay, fine. We'll do this one step at a time. First things first. We've an appointment with Dudley Titchlark tomorrow. So let's take care of that, and we'll go from there."

An inheritance. Who would be leaving her anything? No, it was Jocelyn who was being left something. But did Nelwina have the responsibility to take possession of it?

And what about Nelwina's other actions? Like last night. If they reverted back to their own bodies, how would Jocelyn feel about Nelwina making love with Adam last night? And what about her marriage? Nelwina had committed adultery with Jocelyn's body.

She put her face in her hands. *Oh my God, what have I done?*

"Jocelyn?"

She looked up at Philip. What was she to do? She wanted to be alone. She wanted to weep.

"I'll tell you what. I'll come by first thing tomorrow morning and we'll meet with the lawyer. Then you can decide where you want to go after that." He patted her shoulder. "We'll just take it one step at a time."

Nelwina nodded, not because she wanted to go to London. Heavens, she'd never been in a large city before. But because she desperately needed to be alone.

Now.

"So you'll go?"

She nodded again.

"Great. I'll pick you up at nine."

Nelwina nodded again and began walking back into the forest.

She stood screened from the road and watched Philip drive off. She found a relatively smooth spot on a large rock jutting out of the ground nearby and sat down.

She'd managed to make a mess of everything. Poor Jocelyn, what would she think if she were to come back now? How would she know what had happened?

And how was Nelwina going to sort it all out and make things right?

Having met Philip, Nelwina knew for a certainty that Jocelyn had a life someplace else. Until a few moments ago, she hadn't really thought about it. Oh, she'd considered the notion, but not in depth. Jocelyn had seemed rather like a figment of her imagination. She snorted. Was she beginning to sound like Jocelyn, what with her new words and such?

The roar of an engine brought her head up and she watched Adam speed off down the road, away from Spenceworth.

Did he look for her? She jumped to her feet and ran out of the woods waving her arms. But his car disappeared around the curve. He hadn't seen her.

She sighed and trudged back to the manor. No doubt he'd be even angrier with her when he got home after searching for her.

Mayhap he wasn't even looking for her, but like Haslett when he was in a rage, Adam went to find solace at the bottom of a bottle.

Of course, Haslett hadn't needed any excuse. 'Twas his pastime.

Nelwina entered Spenceworth through the kitchen. The house was deathly quiet and a chill stole up her arms. Rubbing them, she made her way to the hall. There on the table by the door was a piece of yellow lined paper.

Meeting my lawyer to unravel this mess. Will
return tomorrow.
A

"Aye, you fooled yourself, Nelwina my girl." Her voice echoed around the hall. He was trying to undo the damage she and his mother had caused. She climbed the stairs to her room to wait for Sophia's return.

Guilt was a heavy companion.

Sophia didn't come home. All evening Nelwina started with each creak of the house. Around nine it began to rain. The wind blew and Nelwina crawled into bed, putting her pillow over her head to muffle the noises.

'Twas a huge house to be alone in.

By morning the rain had stopped and when Philip arrived, Nelwina was waiting. During the night she had decided that she'd collect Jocelyn's inheritance and then find Hilda and get things sorted out. If she were to stay here, she would hand whatever inheritance she received to Adam. Mayhap it would be enough to make up for the damage she and Sophia had done.

But everything rested on whether Nelwina could find Hilda and what information the woman gave her.

As Philip pulled up to the front of the manor, Nelwina grabbed her bag and dropped a piece of paper on the table by the door. Sophia still hadn't returned. No doubt Mr. Jefferson consoled her, she thought, and closed and locked the door behind her.

She wasn't certain about Philip, but if Jocelyn had married him, mightn't he be trustworthy? She just didn't know. But the idea of repaying Adam for the loss of income motivated her to take a chance and trust in the stranger before her and the one whose body she inhabited.

Adam unlocked the door. The meeting with his lawyer had been disappointing. The will had been specific as to the charity to receive Spenceworth's funds. He could challenge the will, but that, too, would take money. He supposed they could continue the tours and maybe later include the gardens. But would that be enough to support the manor? He dropped his briefcase beside the door of his study and headed upstairs.

He went to his mother's door and knocked. No answer. He frowned.

There was no answer at Nel's door either.

Damn, where were they? It couldn't take this long for two women to spend eight hundred pounds. Could it?

He went to the old wing and what Nel had referred to as the servants' rooms. He opened the door of the room he'd seen her coming out of once. And he froze. It looked like a museum, he thought.

Nel had brought down an old iron bedstead. A hand-stitched quilt covered the mattress. In front of one of the windows sat an old chair and a small table. Scissors, thread and pins were arranged on top of it.

From a wooden hook on the wall hung an apron Adam recognized as the one Nel wore when she worked in the old kitchen.

Beside the door was a washstand, complete with bowl and pitcher. Braided rag rugs covered the floor in front of the washstand and the bedside.

This is where Nel liked to spend her time? He shook his head. It must be a female thing, he thought.

Curious, he looked in the rest of the rooms. Nel had arranged each one in the same sparse fashion. Servants certainly hadn't lived in the lap of luxury back then, he thought as he opened the last door.

Nel hadn't gotten to this room yet. A jumble of objects filled the room. He waded in, stepping over a footstool with a broken leg, weaving around an empty crate and an old worn chair. He rummaged around, finding an old ball and wondering who had played with it. Stacked against the furthest wall were framed pictures.

He pulled them out, one at a time. There were photographs of his father and uncle when they were boys. In one they stood with their father on the steps of Spenceworth. In another, an older woman sat, with his father standing on one side and his uncle on the other.

He flipped through the rest and leaned them back

against the wall. A wardrobe, its doors sagging on their hinges, took up another wall and Adam made his way to it. Old blankets and linens filled the inside. He reached down to open one of the drawers and found it stuck. Giving it a tug, he heard something drop behind it.

Moving to the side, he saw the gilded edge of a picture frame. He shifted the wardrobe forward enough to pull it out.

Taking a pillowcase from the wardrobe, he dusted the painting off and let out a low whistle.

It was a beautiful portrait. And in pretty good condition, he thought as his gaze scanned the features of a man and woman. It had to be a Warrick ancestor. The same nose, chin and lips that Adam saw every morning were reflected in the portrait. The woman's eyes were gray. The artist had outlined the irises in black.

So that's where his gray eyes came from. He'd wondered about that as a child. Both his mother's and father's eyes were brown. No one could figure out where Adam's gray eyes had come from.

He had no idea of the date of the portrait, but it was old, he knew that. He whistled low. "Quite a bauble she wore around her neck. And matching earrings, too. It's good to know that at some time in our history, Spenceworth wasn't struggling."

He picked the painting up and left the room. Oh, Nel is going to love this, he thought. He'd do a little research and see if he could find out exactly who the people in the painting were.

He returned to his study, leaning the painting up

234

against the wall beside his desk, and started going through the books he'd dragged down from the attic a week or so ago.

He'd sorted through them one day, putting them back in the box in a more orderly fashion. There was everything in the box from books of poetry to estate account journals.

He sorted through the journals. Maybe he could find the entry that paid for the painting. Stewards in the past were quite diligent in their details.

He'd thumbed through several and happened to catch the word "portrait" in one entry.

June 1803. Paid to Vigee Le Brun, the 22nd of June 1803, for his lordship's and the Lady Jocelyn's portrait at length. 100 pounds.

Jocelyn.
The name jumped off the page at Adam. It wasn't a common name back then, was it? He glanced at the portrait. Was that a coincidence? He shook his head. Maybe it was, but it sure as hell made his skin crawl. He wondered what Sophia would think of it. He put a slip of paper in the spot and set the journal aside.

He picked up another journal and thumbed through it, glancing out into the empty hall.

Surely Nel and his mother would return soon. "They probably went out for lunch," he muttered as he pulled out another journal.

This one was earlier than the one he'd set aside. He flipped through the pages. He came across an entry for seeds for the garden. Reading through the list, he found each of the flowers Nel had listed in her drawing of the garden as well as seeds for the kitchen garden.

He flipped through a few more pages and caught an entry for the seamstress.

April 1783. To Mrs. Honeycutt on her two bills for material for 1 fine large muslin cravat and 2 pair of fine muslin cuffs and the making. 15 shillings.

He flipped back a few pages and froze.

March 1783. For fine muslin for a petticoat for Mrs. Honeycutt's daughter who works in the kitchen, brought up from town at my lord's request. 5 shillings.

Nel had told him about that petticoat. Could this be a coincidence? He stared at the entry, as if through sheer force of will it would explain things to him.

"Adam?"

His mother's voice pulled him from the account journal.

"In here, Mother," he called, going back to the journal. "You won't believe what I found."

"Is it safe?" Sophia poked her head around the door, her face a solemn mask.

Adam glanced up. "Yes." He waved her in. "Mother, I've found the old account books."

"That's nice, dear."

"No, Mother, you don't understand."

236

"My, what a beautiful painting." She stood staring at the portrait. "Ancestors?"

"Mother, would you pay attention? I found an entry for a petticoat for the daughter of Mrs. Honeycutt."

"Well, of course you did, Adam. My goodness, don't look so surprised. They did keep exact records back then." She canted her head to the side and looked again at the painting. "Oh, my dear. So that's where your gray eyes came from."

"It doesn't expressly identify Nel as the daughter. I just thought it was a strange coincidence."

"It's no coincidence, Adam dear."

Adam blinked. "You're taking this rather well, don't you think?"

"Of course I am, dear. If only you'd listened to me, your eyes wouldn't look as if they're about to explode from their sockets." She chuckled. "Isn't it marvelous?"

Yes, Sophia had finally done it. She'd finally escorted him right around the bend to total lunacy. This wasn't possible. There had to be a logical explanation for it.

He tried coincidence, but that wouldn't work.

Could Nel have gotten this information someplace else and come here to . . . to what? He ran his hands through his hair.

"Has Nel seen this?" His mother pointed to the painting.

"Of course she hasn't; she's with you." At Sophia's surprised expression, Adam added, "Isn't she?"

He frowned, turning his gaze from his mother to the opened door of his study and back again.

She gave him a blank look. "Was she supposed to be, dear?"

"Didn't you both go shopping?"

Sophia shook her head. "I haven't seen her since we left the garden." She pushed up from her seat. "You mean she isn't here?"

"No."

Heavy knocking on the front door brought Sophia and Adam to the hall. Adam opened the door and found a constable and a man in a black suit standing before the door.

"Yes?" Adam frowned. God, don't let this be bad news.

"Lord Spenceworth?"

"Yes?"

"Sorry to disturb you, sir. I'm Detective Sanders and this is Agent Barker, the legal attaché in England for the FBI. We're looking for an American, a Mr. Philip James."

"James, did you say?" Where had Adam heard that name before?

"Yes." Barker reached into his suit pocket and pulled out a photo. "Do you recognize him?" He handed the picture to Adam.

Adam looked at it. Nothing about the man's image was familiar. "I'm afraid not."

"So you haven't seen him around?"

Adam shook his head.

"May we speak with Jocelyn Tanner? We were told in Ramsgil that she was staying here."

"Who?" Sophia stepped up. "What's this all about?"

"We've a warrant for Mr. James's arrest. We have reason to believe he's come here to find Miss Tanner."

"Who's Miss Tanner?" Sophia reached for the picture Adam held.

"Nel, Mother," Adam murmured to his mother.

"Oh, yes. Of course." She met Adam's gaze and smiled.

"How is Miss Tanner connected to this James man?" Adam turned his attention to the officer.

"They were engaged."

Chapter Sixteen

Sophia gasped and grabbed Adam's arm.

Adam felt the ground drop beneath his feet. Nel was engaged? Was that what she'd been talking about yesterday? Was this other man the reason she couldn't stay?

He shook his head in confusion. She hadn't said anything about another relationship, let alone an engagement.

Philip James.

The memory of a conversation tickled his mind. What had the women from the tour said? Something about James abandoning Jocelyn.

And the detective had used the past tense. *They were engaged.* His relief made him lightheaded.

"But this is the man from the tour."

Adam and the officers turned to Sophia.

"The tour?"

"Yes, Adam, the tour." She held up the picture. "He was on the tour. I believe it was the first day. He lingered behind, but I thought he was just asking Nel a question."

Adam stepped back, motioning for the men to come inside.

"Did you overhear their conversation?"

Sophia turned to the detective. "No, and Nel didn't say." She handed the picture back to him. "But why would he want Nel?"

"Mrs. Warrick, you keep mentioning Nel—is she a guest here?" Agent Barker asked.

"Well, you see . . ."

Adam held his breath. Oh please, Mother, not that nonsense about past lives.

"Nel is Jocelyn," his mother finished. "She preferred to use the name of a servant who worked here in the eighteenth century." She linked her arm with Adam's. "It lent more authenticity to the tours, you see. We just got in the habit of using the name."

Adam sighed. Thank you, God.

"Hmm, I see." Barker rubbed his chin and produced another photo from his pocket. "Is this the woman?"

Sophia looked at the picture and smiled. "Yes, yes. That's our Ne . . . er, Jocelyn."

"May we speak with Miss Tanner?"

Adam looked at his mother. She shook her head. "I'm not sure where she is."

"She's left?" Sanders stepped forward.

"I doubt it. She's probably out for a walk," Adam supplied. "What is James wanted for?"

"Embezzlement."

"But I don't understand. What does Ne . . . I mean, Jocelyn have to do with Mr. James?" Sophia's eyes widened. "You don't think she's involved, do you?"

"Oh, no, Mrs. Warrick. They worked together at the same accounting firm."

"Are you certain she isn't here?" the officer asked.

"No. We've only just realized that she wasn't with either of us." Sophia sent Adam an accusing glare.

The four of them did a quick search of the rooms, but didn't find Nel.

"Can you show us her room?"

"This way." Sophia led the men upstairs to Nel's room.

The men looked around Nel's room and found nothing missing but her purse.

"But how did you know to look for Mr. James here?" Sophia asked as they descended the stairs.

"A couple days ago James called Miss Tanner's boss and told him of her accident. We traced him here." Agent Barker shook his head. "Due to an audit Miss Tanner requested on her accounts, we found proof that James had siphoned funds from one of her larger accounts. A warrant has been issued and extradition papers will be drawn up to take him back to South Carolina."

The detective said, "And you've no idea where Miss Tanner's gone off to?"

"No. I haven't seen her since yesterday." Adam couldn't hide the worry in his voice. Nel had been away from Spenceworth, but never alone. Had she gotten lost? Or was she hurt? He rubbed the bridge of his nose. What had happened to her?

"And you've not seen Mr. James about? Other than the tour, I mean?"

"No. But I went to London yesterday and only just returned."

The officer shook his head.

As they stood at the foot of the stairs, a worried frown creased Sophia's brow.

"Do you think this James person has Nel?" Sophia stood in the foyer, her hands gripped at her waist.

"We don't know, Mrs. Warrick."

"What will you do now? Please, you must find Nel; she's not familiar with . . . with the countryside." Adam recognized the panic creeping into his mother's voice.

"We'll do what we can, ma'am, but we haven't much to work with here."

"Adam?" He heard the tremble in her voice and knew she was close to tears. Worry settled in the pit of his stomach. Anything could happen to Nel.

"Does James know about the warrant?" If Philip James knew the authorities were after him, he could be desperate.

"No, sir, I don't think he does. We've moved pretty fast on this."

As Adam turned to open the door for the officers, he saw a piece of white paper on the table and absently picked it up. The men walked out and stopped. The detective handed Sophia his business card. "If you hear from her, please ring us."

Adam opened the paper, scanning the flowing script. "Officer." His breath caught in his throat and he glanced to his mother. "I believe I know where

Nel has gone and where you can find Philip James."
His hand shook as he handed the note over. Nel, in
the hands of Philip James—he swallowed against the
fear pushing up his throat. She had to be okay.

"Excellent." Carefully reading it, the FBI agent
handed the note to the officer.

"May we use your phone?"

Unfamiliar countryside sped past Nelwina's window
as Philip drove to London. They were on a motorway
where hundreds of cars slipped by them. Philip's face
was a study of concentration. It was evident from his
white knuckles and the beads of perspiration dotting
his forehead that driving among so many other cars
made him as nervous as it did her.

"Damned Brits, why can't they drive on the right
side of the road?"

"Pardon?" What did he mean, the right side? Surely
everyone in England didn't drive on the wrong side
of the road. Did they? What made it the wrong side?

Philip glanced over at Nelwina and gave her a tight
smile. "Nothing, Jocelyn. I'm just not used to driving
on the left-hand side of the road."

"Oh." Biting her lip, she wondered how anyone
could get used to all the cars and the speed with
which they traveled.

Philip glanced at his watch. "If I don't make any
more wrong turns, we should just make our appointment at the bank."

Nelwina looked out her window. Philip had been
nice, asking if she were comfortable, hungry or in
need of a bathroom. Why he thought she needed to

bathe was a mystery to her. She'd taken a shower just this morning.

But despite his kindness, there was something about him that made her uncomfortable.

He wasn't Adam, she thought with a sigh.

Nay, Philip was her husband. She twisted the heavy gold band on her finger and blinked back her tears.

Hopelessness filled her heart. How could she go back to this South Carolina with Philip, when she loved Adam? She slumped. How could she not? She was bound to this stranger.

How would she survive? Never to see Adam again? Never to feel his protective embrace? Or to experience his kiss? Surely she would wither and die.

But she had done enough damage to Jocelyn's life, she thought with a sigh. 'Twas time to make the right choices. But there was one thing she would not be swayed from.

The inheritance. She would attend to that before anything else. She hoped it was something of value that she could give Adam in payment for the damage she'd brought to him. And Jocelyn would simply have to understand.

Nelwina thought about leaving Jocelyn a letter, explaining why she had given Adam the inheritance and her virtue.

'Twas best if Jocelyn knew what had transpired while I occupied her body.

But where would she put such a letter and how would Jocelyn know how to find it?

Nelwina rested her head against the back of her seat, fighting back tears of frustration. There were too many questions and nary an answer to be found.

They drove into London and Nelwina's attention was riveted on the congestion of vehicles. Philip pulled up before a large building and turned off the engine.

Once inside, Philip left her to search for the solicitor. He came back to her.

"Titchlark isn't here yet." He led her to a chair. "We'll wait here for him."

They waited half an hour. When the solicitor still hadn't arrived, Philip asked to use the telephone at the desk near them.

Nelwina still didn't understand how it worked. Sophia had tried to explain it to her, but it made no sense.

She shrugged aside her thoughts and looked at Philip. His face turned a bright shade of red.

"What do you mean he had to cancel? We're here at the bank now." His loud, angry voice unsettled Nelwina. She glanced around the bank and several employees looked away.

"Isn't there anyone else there to take care of this?" Philip's face was a tight mask of anger.

"Damn it all. I don't have time for this."

A moment later, Philip slammed the earpiece down. "She hung up on me." His eyes rounded. "The bitch hung up on me." Striding to Nelwina, he grabbed her wrist and hauled her with him as he left the bank.

Gone was the kind, considerate man of earlier. Fear inched along Nelwina's nerves.

She tried to pull free of Philip's grasp, but he only tightened his grip and glared.

"Mr. James." Despite his claim that they were married, Nelwina refused to be so familiar as to use his given name.

She couldn't imagine anyone having tender feelings for this man. Oh, he was kind and thoughtful on the trip to London. His concern had seemed genuine when he questioned her about her past, trying to get her to recall things that Jocelyn would know, but Nelwina had no knowledge of. He spoke of Jocelyn's job as an accountant, their wedding, how they met and what their plans were for the future.

With each shake of her head when he asked if she remembered, he became more and more distraught.

And as the time of their appointment at the bank had come and gone, she watched his distress change to anger.

Yanking her wrist, he pulled her along to his car.

"We'll come back tomorrow."

Nelwina sighed in relief. She would ask Adam to accompany them tomorrow. She didn't like being alone with Philip, no matter that he was her husband, not after his display of anger. His behavior brought back memories of Haslett and she wondered if she were doomed to repeat her first marital mistake.

Once in the car, Nelwina held tightly to her bag. Though she wasn't very knowledgeable of the operation of cars, Philip barely seemed in control of the conveyance. He pulled out into traffic with a loud roar from the car.

His face was red with anger. "We'll stay at a hotel

tonight and first thing tomorrow morning we'll get that inheritance of yours and then we'll get back home."

Nelwina heard only that he expected her to stay the night with him.

"But aren't we returning to Spenceworth?"

"Are you nuts? I'm not making this trip again."

"But—"

"Listen, Jocelyn, don't push me. I'm on the edge."

The car stopped at an intersection and Nelwina didn't think beyond her fear of Philip.

Clutching her bag, she flung open the door and jumped out.

Philip's shouts followed her until she rounded a corner. Glancing back, she didn't see him behind her, but she wasn't taking any chances. Haslett had foiled her flight to freedom, but she was going to succeed in escaping Philip James.

She went down one street, then up another, rounded a corner and slipped into a shop, all the time checking over her shoulder, certain Philip was somewhere close behind her.

Fear and panic battled as she wandered the streets of London, lost as the sun began to sink behind the buildings.

Nelwina needed help, but she had no idea where to turn for it. Her feet hurt and she was exhausted, both physically and emotionally.

Spying a bench, she made her way over to it and sank down with a sigh. She clutched her bag with both arms, the only security she had. Absently she snapped it closed, hoping nothing had fallen out during her run through the London streets.

Twilight tinted the sky a deep lavender and still she sat on the bench, trying to figure out what she should do, where she should go.

"Why is it you young girls can't seem to stay where you belong?"

Nelwina turned around and nearly dropped her bag as she jumped to her feet.

"Hilda?"

"Lost, are you?"

Nelwina slid back onto the bench. "Yes, and I fear I've made a complete mess of things. I've lost Jocelyn's virtue, committed adultery and caused Adam to lose his stock and Spenceworth." Tears ran down her cheeks and a sob spilled from her lips. "And there's an inheritance, did you know?" She glanced at Hilda. "I was going to get it today and give it to Adam to help with the finances of the manor." She hiccuped. "But it isn't mine to give, is it?"

Nelwina shifted her handbag to the space beside her and looked down at her hands. "I wish I knew what to do. I don't know when or if I'll return to my time. I can't live Jocelyn's life for her." She covered her face with her hands. "Even if I wanted to return, I don't know how."

Hilda plopped down and sighed noisily beside Nelwina. "Stop your weeping. Never solved anything. Won't this time."

Nelwina dropped her hands and met Hilda's gaze. "You want to go back?"

Nelwina gave an uncertain nod of her head.

"All you have to do is sit on the block in Ramsgil." Hilda arched a gray brow. "Same one you fell off." She grinned hugely. "But you have to do it at the same time as the other one in your time." Folding her arms across her chest, Hilda nodded. "That'll do it. Well, you might need a storm, too. Hard to tell."

The older woman scooted off the bench. " 'Tis glad I'll be to have the two of you where you belong."

Grabbing up her handbag, Nelwina followed Hilda through the darkening streets of London. "What did you mean by 'the two of you where you belong'?"

Hilda ignored Nelwina's question.

"You think I'm hovering around, waiting to help you?" Hilda stopped, her hand on Nelwina's arm. "I've a lot to do. You're not the only one having problems, you see. I'm a very busy person." She turned and started down the street.

Nelwina caught up with the old woman. "But how do I get to Ramsgil?"

Hilda just glared at her and kept walking. " 'Tis getting dark, we best get you settled for the night. Tomorrow morning you can take the bus to Ramsgil."

"Niles, I'm so terribly glad you've come." Sophia opened the door at his knock. He stepped inside, concern furrowing his brow.

"What is it, Sophia?" She clutched his arm, guiding him to the salon.

"I don't know what to do. The police told Adam to remain here at Spenceworth and they would notify him once they found Nel and Philip James."

"Slow down, Sophia. I don't understand anything

250

you're saying. Who is Philip James and why would Nel be with him? And what have the police to do with all this?"

She took a deep breath and dabbed at her tears with her hanky before launching into an explanation of the events of this morning.

When she finished, Sophia twisted her hanky. "But Adam wouldn't have any of it. Said he'd find her." She dabbed at her eyes. "The police said that he's an embezzler. Our poor, dear Nel is with him." Sophia turned to Niles, sitting beside her on the settee in the salon. "Oh, Niles, I pray Nel is okay; that Mr. James hasn't harmed her."

"He's an embezzler, Sophia, not a murderer."

Sophia inhaled sharply. "Niles," she gasped.

"Now, now, Sophia. Between the police and Adam, I'm sure everything will work out."

"I hope you're right, Niles. Adam has come to care deeply for Nel."

He picked up her hand and patted it. "As we all have, my dear."

Chapter Seventeen

Adam tossed his keys on the coffee table in his London flat. They slid off the surface and landed on the floor. He sat down in a chair, cradling his head in his hands.

Where the bloody hell had they gone?

The authorities had arrived too late. They'd missed Philip and Nel and now no one knew where they were.

The police had checked the nearby hotels, believing that they would stay the night in London because of the early appointment in the morning. But their search had turned up nothing so far. Either Philip had used an alias or the police had yet to find the correct hotel.

Adam rubbed his face. Where was Nel? Had Philip James hurt her?

A bank employee had told the police that Philip became enraged after speaking with Mr. Titchlark's secretary by phone and forced Nel to leave the bank with him. But other than the general direction they'd taken from the bank, the police didn't have any other information to go on.

Adam was worried about Nel. The woman had said that Nel looked frightened and had tried to get free of Philip's hold.

So where were they now?

All in all it had been a botched job. He leaned back in his chair. Tomorrow morning, first thing, he was going to call Titchlark and confirm the meeting set for ten. And then he was going to be the first one at the bank.

"Oh, Nel, why did you go with Philip?" His tired voice echoed in the empty room.

He pulled her note from his pocket.

Adam,
I've an appointment with Mr. Titchlark, London solicitor. I pray that you will forgive me for causing such trouble for you. I will endeavor to make restitution.
Nelwina Honeycutt

He glanced at the word "restitution" and guilt gnawed at his stomach. He'd been pretty rough on his mother and Nel. But not without good reason, he assured himself.

He was certain it had been his angry words that had sent Nel off with Philip James. Maybe if he'd stayed at Spenceworth instead of rushing to London and his attorney, Nel would still be safe.

He didn't need Nel's inheritance. He'd find a way to manage.

He needed Nel.

He pulled the officer's business card from his pocket and punched in the number.

"This is Adam Warrick," he said when Detective Sanders answered.

"Lord Spenceworth. Have you heard from Miss Tanner?"

"No, I was hoping you'd have some news."

"Sorry, sir. Nothing yet, but we've still quite a few hotels to check. Mr. James might have checked into one of the bed and breakfast places, which will make it harder to find him."

"So we just wait until tomorrow morning?"

"Yes, well, I don't see that we have much choice."

"Do you think she's safe with him?"

There was a long pause on the other end of the line. Adam's nerves stretched tighter. "As Agent Barker said, he doesn't know we're looking for him, so there's no reason for him to harm Miss Tanner. We spoke with Mr. Dempsey. Mr. James seems to think that bringing Miss Tanner home will solve his immediate problem. I think she's safe until tomorrow."

After saying good-bye, Adam hung up.

What the officer said made sense. Still, Adam didn't like the idea of Nel being with Philip. He'd recovered from the initial shock of hearing of the engagement. In an earlier conversation, the constable confirmed Adam's conclusion. There was no engagement now. Philip had left Nel at the altar.

He got up and went to the kitchen. Pouring himself a glass of scotch, he went back to the living room.

The ringing of the phone interrupted his thoughts.

"Hello?"

"Adam. How is Nel?"

"I don't know, Mother."

"She's not there with you?"

"No." Adam took a sip of his drink, savoring the warm smoothness that slid down his throat and settled in his stomach.

"Where is she?"

"I wish I knew, Mother."

"Adam, will you please tell me what in the world is going on? I've been waiting by the phone since you left. I thought the police were going to apprehend that Philip James person."

"They were, but they got to the bank too late. Philip and Nel had already left."

"Well then, where are they?"

"We don't know. The police have searched the hotels near the bank, but they haven't found them. They're still looking, but I doubt they'll find them before tomorrow."

"But tomorrow could be too late. Nel is in danger now." He heard panic rise in her voice. "Adam, I think you should get out there and find Nel. I don't have a very good feeling about this."

"Neither do I, Mother. I've been out looking for them, but I haven't had any more luck than the police." Adam took another sip of his drink. "Nel and Philip are to meet Titchlark at the bank tomorrow morning at ten. The police and I will be there to greet them."

"And you'll bring Nel home directly?"

"That will be up to her, Mother. She may well wash her hands of me and return home."

"Oh, pish posh. Anyone with eyes can see you have captured her affections."

Hope flickered in his heart, but he tamped it down. "Then why would she go with him?" Until he heard it from her lips, he'd best put aside his feelings.

"For her inheritance, silly. If you'd been just a bit more understanding and appreciative of our efforts." Sophia sniffled. "If you hadn't been so unreasonable and shouted so, Nel would be safe at home where she belongs."

He heard Sophia blow her nose.

"It's all your fault, Adam. And I expect you to apologize to her and beg her forgiveness. And you'd best call me in the morning when you've found her."

The phone went silent.

He looked at the receiver. Had his mother completely lost her mind? He couldn't force Nel to return to Spenceworth.

And he would apologize. He shouldn't have shouted as he had, but Sophia and Nel had put Spenceworth in jeopardy—albeit unwittingly. How else was he to react?

But no amount of justifying his actions could lift the guilt from his shoulders. He was the one who'd started the whole series of events that had led up to this.

He tossed back the rest of his drink. He might as well try to get some sleep.

* * *

Nelwina boarded the tour bus late the next morning. The sky was overcast and she was tired. The inheritance was lost to her. No doubt Philip had secured it this morning. She would never be able to help Adam keep Spenceworth. Regret tore at her heart.

She would follow Hilda's directions when she reached Ramsgil. She would sit on the block of wood until she found herself back in her own time. How long that would take, she couldn't say.

Guilt gnawed at her stomach. She'd bungled things pretty badly here. What right did she have to return to her own time, leaving Jocelyn to deal with the problems?

What else could she do? She didn't have the knowledge to handle anything like this.

She'd spent the night writing Jocelyn a letter, to explain what she'd done and apologize.

After careful thought, she decided to place the note beneath her as she sat on the block of wood later today. It was the best she could do.

Nelwina reviewed her plans one more time, checked her bag again for the letter and settled back in her seat, finding the openness of the bus much better than the close confines of a car.

In her missive to Jocelyn she'd included a report of Philip's actions. The poor woman should know what kind of man she was married to, if she didn't already.

Mayhap she would wish to divorce Philip.

On one of their trips to Ramsgil, she and Sophia had overheard a conversation between two women in a shop. One's daughter had just obtained a divorce from her husband. And far from being scandalized, the women were pleased, stating that the girl was much better off without him.

Confused, Nelwina had questioned Sophia.

"Oh, my dear, divorce is quite commonplace these days. More's the pity. But in some instances, I think it's wonderful that the stigma is gone."

Though she cringed at the thought of divorce, contemplating life with Philip made it seem the lesser of two evils. Mayhap Jocelyn would feel the same.

She gripped the sides of her seat. What would she find when she returned to her own time? What had happened to Haslett? Who would she find she was married to?

Nelwina swallowed against the fear climbing up her throat. She deserved no better than what she was leaving Jocelyn. She would deal with whatever she found when she returned.

How long would she have to sit on the block? she wondered. It seemed a lot to expect that Jocelyn would sit in the same spot at the same time, but that's what Hilda had said must happen.

Nelwina blinked back the tears burning her eyes. She was hopelessly confused and prayed she was doing the right thing.

"This is Philip James. I need to reschedule the appointment with Titchlark."

"But Mr. James, Mr. Titchlark is at the bank waiting for you."

"Jocelyn is feeling a bit under the weather. Can we make it for this afternoon? I'm sure she'll feel better in a few hours." That didn't give him much time, but he should be able to find Jocelyn by then. He'd just make a trip to Spenceworth, and if he had to drag her kicking and screaming from the pile of stones, he would.

"Could you hold a moment, sir?"

Before James could reply, he heard a click and then an occasional blip.

"Mr. James?" The receptionist came back on the line.

"Yes?"

"Perhaps you could meet Mr. Titchlark. He might be able to help expedite the transfer of the inheritance."

"Excellent." He hung up the phone and picked up Jocelyn's passport from the bureau in his room. Maybe they could do this without Jocelyn being there. And if that didn't work, then he'd explain about Jocelyn being ill.

Damn, he didn't have much more time. Mr. Dempsey had been pleased to hear that he'd found Jocelyn, but worried over her injury. What Dempsey hadn't said was whether the audit was going forward. But then, he didn't know that Philip knew about it.

Damn. He needed to get Jocelyn back to the States. He'd covered his tracks, he knew that, but he couldn't take any chances an audit would expose his creative accounting.

Philip stepped through the tall glass doors of the building and glanced around. How would he know the man? he wondered. He went up to a bank employee.

"Excuse me, I was to meet Mr. Titchlark here."

"Oh, yes sir." She smiled, glancing around the bank. "Uhm, this way, if you will."

He followed the woman, wondering at her nervousness. She showed him into a small office devoid of windows. "If you'll wait here, Mr. Titchlark will be with you in a moment."

The door closed and a moment later three men entered; a uniformed officer, a man of medium height in a black suit and another tall, well-built man. He wondered which one carried the ludicrous name of Dudley Titchlark. Neither one of the civilians appeared likely candidates.

Glancing from the officer to the other two men, a surge of excitement raced through Philip. Swallowing a grin, he resisted the urge to rub his hands together. Must be a huge inheritance to need security like this, he thought.

Meeting the disapproving gaze of the taller of the two civilians, Philip turned to the officer and the hairs on the back of his neck rose. His palms began to sweat.

Something wasn't right here.

"Where the bloody hell is she?" Adam rushed Philip, grabbing him by the shirtfront. "If you've done anything to her—"

"Lord Spenceworth." The officer pulled him off Philip. "Mr. Philip James?"

"What's this all about?" Philip straightened his

shoulders, straightening the collar of his shirt. "I want to press charges against this man."

"Mr. James." The man flashed him a badge. "You're under arrest."

"For what?"

"Embezzlement."

Adam glanced at the black-suited man, who then whipped out a pair of handcuffs and slapped them on Philip's wrists.

"Where is Nel?" Adam fisted his hands.

"Nel?"

Adam shook his head. "Where's Jocelyn? If you've harmed her—"

"I don't know where she is. She took off yesterday afternoon and I haven't seen her since."

Agent Barker riffled through Philip's pockets, pulling out two passports.

"Here's her passport." He handed it to Adam.

Flipping it open, he looked into Nel's eyes. "Where did she leave you?"

"How the hell would I know? We were going to a hotel and she jumped out of the car at a stoplight. I don't know where."

Barker escorted Philip out of the office and the detective stayed behind.

"Lord Spenceworth, we'll get right on this. We'll find Miss Tanner. You might want to call Spenceworth and see if she's returned there."

"Right. Good idea." Adam stared after Philip as he flipped open his cell phone.

Philip James was taken care of; now he had to find Nel. He punched the number to the manor.

"Mother?"

"Oh, Adam, you've found her, then?"

"No. But Philip is in custody and the police will be searching for her." Adam glanced at the officer and the man nodded. "I'll keep in touch, Mother. If Nel comes home, call me on my cell, would you?"

"Of course, dear. And Adam?"

"Yes."

"Bring her home safe. I miss her so."

"So do I, Mother. So do I."

He left the bank. Rather than get in his car and drive around London, he decided to walk, taking the direction Philip had gone the day before.

If Nel had jumped out of the car and run off, she probably went in directions Philip couldn't, going down one-way streets and crossing alleys.

It was nearing lunchtime when Adam sat on a bench. He'd checked with every bed and breakfast, tavern and hotel, showing Nel's passport picture, but no one recalled having seen her. She could be anywhere, he thought. How was he going to find her?

"Lost something, laddie?" A jangle of metal and he glanced up from Nel's picture.

"Where did you come from?" Adam stared in surprise at the old woman from the tour. The one who claimed to be a medical professional.

"So you lost her, did you?"

"Nel?" He stood up. "Have you seen her?"

"Well, now, I just might have."

"Where is she?"

"And what's happened to the other gent?"

"What? Philip?"

262

She nodded.

"He's been arrested." Adam clenched his hands. "Do you know where Nel is or not?"

"Aye, that I do." She rocked back on her heels, a grin splitting her wrinkled face. "Hilda knows a lot of things." She cackled gleefully. "Ah, the things I know." And the cackling commenced again.

Adam waited until her fit had passed. "And where did you say Nel was?"

"What?" She wiped at the tears running down her cheeks, a snaggle-tooth smile on her lips. "Ah, my." She sighed. "You're wanting Nelwina's direction, are you?"

"Yes." Damn, but the woman was mad, he thought. He bit his tongue and folded his arms across his chest to keep from saying or doing something to prevent him from getting the information from Hilda.

"Right, then. Well . . ." She paused, looking up and down the street. "She's gone back." She smiled and started to walk away.

Panic hit Adam straight on. "Back? You mean she's gone back to the States?" No, it couldn't be. There were things he needed to tell her. He had to apologize and he wanted to show her the portrait.

And he had to tell her he loved her.

"What was that?" She stopped and turned around. "She's where she belongs."

"And where the bloody hell is that?"

"Tch, tch. Temper, temper." Hilda waggled a bony finger at him. "She's returning to Spenceworth."

Hilda turned around and tottered off, disappearing around a corner.

"Spenceworth? She's gone to Spenceworth." He muttered to himself as he pulled his cell phone from his pocket.

"Mother?"

"You've found her?"

"I haven't caught up with her yet, but I know she's going back to the manor. If she gets there before me, call me, will you?"

"Of course, dear."

Adam flagged a taxi and returned to his car. Once he found Nel, he'd make damned sure she never left again. His heart was in her hands and by damn, he'd see she married him or know the reason why.

Chapter Eighteen

Lightning flashed overhead, followed by a rumble of thunder, as Nelwina left the bus. Making her way to the green, she found a crowd of strangers milling around. Pushing through the people, she headed for the block of wood situated in the center.

A woman dressed in clothing of Nelwina's time stood atop the block, a man beside her.

"I've a bid of two shillings."

Nelwina froze. *No!* She struggled through the throng of people; *she* was the one who needed to go back to her time. The woman had to get off the block before something happened.

"Nel?"

She glanced up to meet Adam's worried frown.

"Thank God." He took Nelwina in his arms, giving her a quick kiss. "I was so worried about you, love. Come on, let's go home."

Stepping out of his arms, she said, "No, Adam, I must do this." She looked at him. "I have to get that woman off the block before it happens to her."

"Nel, please, it's going to rain."

"But you don't understand." Urgency filled her voice as Adam's hand closed over hers. "I have to stop it."

A burst of applause filled the air and the crowd began to disperse.

Nelwina turned to see the woman walk away from the block, smiling and chatting with a few other women. She didn't look or act any different. Nelwina rubbed her forehead.

Adam touched her arm. "Nel?"

"It didn't happen." She frowned. When she saw the woman on the block she had thought . . . Nelwina shook her head, confused.

With the green nearly empty of people, Nelwina went to the block. Adam followed behind her. She rummaged in her bag, pulling out the letter. Placing it on top of the wood, she sat down. Mayhap it was only her that it happened to, she thought, glancing up at Adam as he hovered beside her.

He frowned, his gray eyes darkening with confusion.

"Nel, what are you doing?"

She sighed. "I have to go back." She blinked back tears. "I've made such a mess of things here."

"No, Nel, you haven't done anything. I shouldn't have lost my temper. I said things I didn't mean."

Nelwina glanced away from Adam, misery weighing her shoulders down. "You don't understand; I have to return."

"Yes, to Spenceworth." He offered his hand. "And I'll take you there straightaway."

Nelwina shook her head, lacing her fingers together in her lap to keep from taking the hand he offered. "No, I have to stay here until it happens."

"Until what happens?"

She gazed up at him. "Until I return."

Adam scratched his head, but then with a shrug he said, "Won't you come back to the manor and say good-bye?"

Nelwina shook her head. She didn't know if she could bear to spend more time with Adam or face Sophia again. 'Twould be that much harder to leave.

"Sophia will be very hurt if you leave without a word, you know."

The wind whipped up, blowing strands of Nelwina's brown hair across her face. She pushed them aside as the first drops of rain fell.

"Come, Nel, you'll catch cold if you sit in the rain."

"But I must." She glanced up at Adam, the pain of her leaving doubled upon seeing the confusion and concern on his face.

"No, Nel, you don't have to. Please, come home with me. Mother is worried sick about you and told me not to come home without you." The lopsided grin he gave her tugged at her heart.

The rain blew in her face as Adam gently took her arm and pulled her to her feet. She really didn't want to leave him, but didn't she have a responsibility to Jocelyn to make things right?

She glanced back at the block, seeing the rain-dampened envelope, its ink beginning to run. Pulling her arm from Adam's gentle grasp, she retrieved the letter, stuffing it inside her handbag.

He waited, holding his hand out to her. Wordlessly, they walked to his car. The silence held during the drive back to the manor.

Hilda had told her to sit on the block in a storm and it would happen. But it hadn't. Did this mean that Jocelyn didn't wish to return? Hope tickled the edges of her heart, but Nelwina pushed it aside. Surely there would be a sign if that were the case, else how would she know? Would she have to come to Ramsgil each day and sit upon the block until it did happen?

She glanced over at Adam's profile. Had she the strength of will to do it again and again? She loved him, and leaving him would be the hardest thing she ever did. But she'd made such a shambles of his life, costing him his home and disrupting his life. And there was Jocelyn to consider, too.

Her head began to ache and she leaned against the cool window of the car, fighting against the tears threatening to overtake her.

Adam glanced at Nel. She looked so miserable, he thought. Her damp hair hung around her face, her shoulders were slumped and her eyes were red and watery.

He would have broken the silence and told her that James was in custody, but she seemed so fragile just now. He didn't want to do anything that would shatter the control she clung to.

What was she trying to accomplish by revisiting the wife sale? He didn't understand why she kept saying she had to go back. It just didn't make any sense. He worried what her experience with Philip James had done to her mind. She was more confused now than ever before.

He pulled up to the manor, but before he could get out to help her, Nel had opened her door and climbed the stairs.

His mother must have been watching for them, because the door opened and she folded Nel in her arms.

"Oh, Nel, I'm so relieved you're home." She held Nel out at arm's length. "I'm so glad they caught the criminal."

And Nel's control finally broke. Pushing past his mother, she ran up the stairs. He could hear her sobs as she made her way to the old wing.

"Adam, what happened? Did he hurt her?"

"Physically, it doesn't appear that he did. But I'm not sure what happened to Nel emotionally." He glanced in the direction Nel had taken and frowned. "I found her sitting on the block on the green in Ramsgil. She kept saying something about going back."

"She's been through a lot in the last day, Adam. She's just confused is all." Sophia started to climb the stairs, but turned back to him. "Did she collect her inheritance?"

"No." He ran a hand through his hair. "I guess I'll have to make another appointment with Titchlark."

"Dear, why don't you ask him if he could bring it here. I don't think Nel will be willing to go to London anytime soon."

Adam sighed. "Yes, I suppose you're right. I'll give

him a call. Would you check on her for me?"

Sophia smiled. "Of course, dear."

Adam hung up from setting an appointment for to-morrow with Mr. Titchlark and put his head in his hands. He was afraid this whole episode had made Nel's confusion even worse. And it was high time he consulted a neurologist. A country doctor was fine for bumps and bruises, but something like this needed specialized attention.

He should have done it sooner, he thought. But other than believing she was from another time, Nel had seemed fine.

He snorted. As if her belief were ordinary. His mother was starting to affect him. Maybe he should make that doctor's appointment for all three of them.

"Nel, dear?"

Nel looked up from her place on the old bed as Sophia pushed open the door. Clutching the lumpy pillow, wet from her tears, against her chest, she drew her legs up beneath her.

"Oh, Nel." Sophia sat beside her, brushing Nel's hair away from her face. "You mustn't cry now. Everything has worked out fine."

"Nay, my lady. Nothing has worked out."

"Oh, now that's a bit dramatic, don't you think?" Sophia scooted up on the bed, resting her back against the wall. "They've Philip in custody, Nel, and he'll return to America."

" 'Tis good news. But what of the inheritance? What did Philip do with it?"

"Oh no, dear, there's no way he could take possession of it. You'll have to sign for it and go through all the legal mumbo jumbo."

"Truly?"

Sophia nodded, a smile lighting her face.

"But then, mayhap I can make things right before I leave." Nelwina sighed in relief. She only hoped whoever bequeathed something to Jocelyn had a generous heart. She was determined to at least make this right with Adam before she left. Staying a few days longer to get things arranged would make it more difficult to leave, but there was nothing for it.

Sophia's smile faded. "Leave? But Nel, you can't leave."

"But my lady, I don't belong here. I—"

"Oh, pish posh." Sophia frowned and waved her hand. "You belong here more than anyone I know."

Nel started to answer, but Sophia held up her hand. "No, I won't listen to another word. You were meant to be here, Nel, and there's no mistake about that."

Sophia moved to the edge of the bed and then stood. "Now, I'm going to let you rest for a while. Can I get you anything? Are you hungry?"

"Nay, my lady." Nel sighed. She'd come to love Sophia like a mother and she knew it was fruitless to argue with her over leaving. Besides, Nel was too tired both emotionally and physically to do anything more than sleep.

Adam met his mother as she came down the stairs.

"How is she?"

"Exhausted, I think. I left her to sleep in her room in the old wing."

Adam started for the stairs, but Sophia's hand on his arm stopped him.

"Let her rest, Adam. She's been through so much."

He glanced up the stairs and then back to his mother. "I suppose you're right." He pushed his hands through his hair and sighed. "I found her sitting on the block in Ramsgil. She kept saying something about going back." He shook his head. "Do you know of a good neurologist?"

"A neurologist? For heaven's sake, what for?"

"Nel."

Sophia reached up and touched Adam's cheek. "A doctor won't help her work through her problems, son. Only time will do that."

"But she's even more confused now than before."

"Well, so much has happened to her." She patted his arm. "Just give her a little more time to deal with the situation." She smiled. "Did you reach Mr. Titchlark?"

"Yes, he'll be out tomorrow afternoon."

"Excellent." Turning back to the stairs, she said, "I could use a bracing cup of tea. What about you?"

"Coffee." And he followed Sophia to the upstairs kitchen. "Oh, and Niles called. He's on his way here."

Sophia glanced over her shoulder, a girlish smile on her lips, and her eyes twinkled. "Oh, my. Then I should make myself presentable, shouldn't I? And make enough tea for two."

Adam chuckled. Niles had apologized profusely for his part in the tours and Adam had absolved him of all fault. He knew how persistent and stubborn his mother could be. She would have gone ahead with her plans with or without Niles's help.

Besides, how could a man deny anything to the woman who held his affections? And Sophia definitely held Niles's, from what he could tell.

As evening fell and Nel hadn't appeared, Adam began to worry. In the kitchen he made a sandwich and cup of tea. Placing them on a tray along with a lit candle, he headed to the old wing.

Balancing the tray on one hand, he knocked on the door. "Nel?"

Adam pushed the door open and held the candle up, the light from its flame casting a warm glow over her sleeping form. Approaching the bed quietly, he set the candle and tray on the small table and carefully sat on the bed.

She lay curled on her side, her hands folded beneath her tearstained cheeks. His heart thumped erratically in his chest.

He smoothed back her hair, his heart stopping as his fingers made contact with her soft, warm skin.

"Nel, love?"

Her eyes fluttered open and she gave him a lazy smile.

"How do you feel?"

She raised her arms above her head and stretched. "My eyes are stiff." A moment later, her smile vanished and a frown knit her brow.

"Are you hungry?"

Nel shook her head, wrapping her arms around herself.

"Well, you have to eat or you'll get sick." He

smiled. "I brought you a sandwich and some tea." He hated to see the sad look in her eyes and her lips drawn down in a frown.

He reached out and tucked a few strands of her hair behind her ear. "Eat something, and then you can go back to sleep if you like."

Adam was rewarded by her nod. He stood up and she slid to the edge of the bed. Placing the tray in her lap, he stepped away.

He didn't say anything while she ate her food; he simply watched her.

Finished, Nelwina placed the tray back on the table.

"You know, you'd probably be more comfortable in your other room."

She nodded and he held his hand out to her. He curled his fingers around her delicate hand and a protectiveness welled within him.

He gave her the candle, picked up the tray and led her out. They made their way to the new wing without talking. Adam tried to find something to say to relieve the silence, but he couldn't think of anything that would put her at ease.

He let go of her hand and opened her door.

"Nel?" Nelwina brought her gaze up to meet his and he reached out to take her hand again. Mayhap he'd forgotten about the tours and the loss of the mysterious stock. He didn't seem angry now.

"Yes?" Tremors of heat raced up her arms, lodging in her heart and low in her belly at his touch.

"Promise me something?"

"Aye?" Nelwina shifted from one foot to the other and glanced down at her toes.

"You'll be here in the morning."

She brought her head up, surprised at his request. She wasn't certain what she'd expected, but that wasn't it.

"We've a few things to settle between us."

The warmth in her heart chilled. Mayhap he hadn't forgotten about the tours and the calamity that followed.

Adam tugged gently on her hand, pulling her closer to him. Canting his head, he lowered his mouth to hers and Nelwina forgot to breathe.

It started as a gentle exploration, but soon built to a passionate embrace that left them both breathless.

He broke the kiss off, leaning his forehead against hers.

"Oh, Nel." His arms tightened around her. "I was so scared when I couldn't find you. Promise you'll never leave me again. I don't think I could bear to go through that again." His breath fanned her face. "I love you." His whisper held the power to weaken her knees. Tears pricked her eyes.

"And I love you." She whispered her heart's words and tore away from his grasp, closing the door even as her heart broke.

Chapter Nineteen

Nelwina leaned her back against the door. What had she done? Why had she told Adam of her love? 'Twould only make it harder to leave.

He'd said he loved her, but Nelwina didn't know if he loved Nelwina Honeycutt or Jocelyn Tanner. Her head began to ache anew.

She was so confused and didn't know what to do or think. Should she go back to Ramsgil in the morning and try again. Would it work tomorrow? Or was Hilda wrong? She caught her breath with that thought.

She pushed away from the door, hitting the switch and flooding the room with light.

And what about the woman yesterday? She didn't seem any different after the sale. Nothing seemed to have happened to her.

Would it only happen to Nelwina?

The panicked need to return to her time had lessened. There was no way to change the loss of Jocelyn's virtue and Nelwina hadn't even known about Philip James when she'd shared Adam's bed.

All that was in the letter to Jocelyn, the one stashed in her bag, a little more tattered from yesterday's rain. She found her handbag and pulled out the letter. Slipping the sheet from the envelope, she smoothed out the paper, rereading it. Would Jocelyn understand?

Adam stood there and stared at the closed door, a smile stretched his lips. "By damn, she loves me." He hadn't meant to say those words just yet; it had just slipped out.

With a grin on his face, he walked down the hall and went into his room.

Maybe he shouldn't have said anything; it could confuse her even more. But the words were out before he could stop them.

Even though his mother told him to give her more time, Adam had scheduled an appointment for next week with a specialist in London. The way he saw it, he would do whatever he had to in order to help Nel recover from the injury her fall had caused. He'd speak with his mother and try to get her not to encourage Nel's belief in past lives. It couldn't be good for her recovery.

A tendril of guilt curled around his conscience. Though he hadn't encouraged Nel, neither had he discouraged her from believing this past-life nonsense. No, he simply cut her off when she started down that road. But what else could he do? Direct confrontation only agitated her and served no purpose.

He'd just taken off his shirt when there was a knock on his door and his mother came in.

"How is Nel, Adam?"

"She's had something to eat and is in her room."
Sophia started to back out of the room. "Oh,
Mother?"

"Yes, dear?" She stepped up beside his bed.

"Do you think I should wait to ask Nel to marry
me until after she's seen a specialist?"

"But you've already asked her. My word, that's
why she's here." She sent him a calculating look. "So,
you're finally going to give her a ring, are you?"

"A ring?"

"Yes, dear, you know one of those sparkly things
a woman wears on her finger?" She gave him a be-
nevolent smile. "Don't have one, do you?" She
reached out and patted his hand. "I've the perfect
thing, a Warrick heirloom. I had a feeling I should
bring it with me when I came to the manor." Sophia
hustled to the door. "I'll just pop into my room and
get it for you, shall I?"

The door closed and Adam stared at it. How did
his mother do it? He closed his eyes and shook his
head. Did she ever listen to him?

But she'd planted an idea in his head. A ring for
Nel. The thought brought a smile to his lips. He loved
her; it was the next logical step. He glanced at his
bed, remembering the night they'd shared. She was a
blend of passion and innocence, of old-fashioned and
modern. She found joy in simple things. There was
nothing artificial about Nel.

And he loved her.

He stretched out on his bed, waiting for Sophia to
return. He recalled seeing his mother wearing a beautiful diamond and emerald ring on special occasions.

Through their hard times after his father died, she'd refused to sell it, saying it was for Adam's wife.

He must have dozed off because when he opened his eyes, a green velvet box was on the table beside his bed. Picking it up, his hands shook as he opened it. Inside, nestled in the velvet, was a marquise-cut diamond with emerald baguettes on either side.

It was perfect for Nel.

He finished getting ready for bed and slipped between the sheets. Sleep was long in coming though. He was busy searching for the perfect way to ask Nel to marry him.

Adam woke the next morning and, after taking a quick shower, he supervised the delivery of the flowers and shrubs. The men and their lorry left and Adam gazed at the garden. The pots had been placed higgledy-piggledy, creating a confusion of beautiful color along the paths.

Nel would love it, he thought.

In a flash of inspiration, he found the white wrought iron table and chairs and arranged them on the flagstone patio.

Smiling, he left the garden. He had a few things to do before he went in search of Nel.

A little later, Adam led Nel, her hands covering her eyes, to the garden. He positioned her facing the white table, which displayed a tray holding afternoon tea and a linen serviette draped over a plate of cookies in the center.

He draped his arm around her shoulders. "Okay, you can open your eyes."

She brought her hands down and blinked. She turned to him, a smile lifting her lips.

"Oh, Adam, 'tis just as I remember it."

Adam returned her smile. Must run in the family, he thought, this propensity to fall in love with women a bubble off of plumb. His father had done it when he married Sophia and from all accounts the two had been deliriously happy.

"Did you make the tea?"

Adam nodded. Only love would send him to the kitchen on a mission to make a pot of tea.

"Will you do the honors?" He pulled a chair out for her.

"Oh, Adam, you'd think I was a lady of quality." Nelwina giggled.

The smile left Adam's lips. "Nel, you are. Quality has nothing to do with your lineage." He sat in the other chair. "Now, I like my tea with cream and three sugars."

"Three?" Nel's eyebrows climbed to her hairline.

"And for sustenance . . ." He uncovered the plate of Mallows with a flourish. "Mallows."

Nel's eyes sparkled. "My favorite." She grinned. "Shall I cut them in half?"

He chuckled, watching as she served his tea and poured a cup for herself. Adam hated tea, but when he watched pleasure light Nel's face as she looked around the garden, the tea didn't taste bad at all.

Nel turned around. "Oh, and the statue as well?" She touched Adam's hand and he took the opportunity to fold her hand in his. " 'Tis perfect." She smiled up at him and Adam knew Nel was the perfect woman for him.

His nerves sprang to life and made his hands shake as he ran his thumb over the pulse point of her wrist.

He took a deep breath and met Nel's inquiring gaze.

"What is it, Adam? Are you feeling unwell? You've gone a peculiar shade of pink."

"Shh, Nel. Just let me do this." Adam dropped to his knee beside Nel's chair. He squeezed her hand in his. "Nel, love, I know we haven't known each other long, though to me it seems I've known you all my life." Nel nodded, tilting her head to the side. A little frown puckered her forehead.

"And, well, would you do me the prodigious honor of becoming my wife?" He produced the green velvet box and flipped open the lid to reveal a beautiful diamond and emerald ring.

"Oh, Adam." Tears sparkled in Nel's eyes and she squeezed his hand. "I would so love to be your wife, but . . ."

"But?"

She started crying. Adam set the ring aside and took her in his arms, rubbing her back. "Tell me, Nel. What is it?"

" 'Tis Philip."

He pulled back, holding her shoulders, and looked into her face. "Nel, I promise you, I won't desert you at the altar like he did. I would never break your heart so."

"But how did you . . ."

"Know?" Adam smiled. "The police told me."

"Philip . . . deserted?"

"Don't you remember?" Adam frowned. "He left you at the altar. You were never married to him."

They were never married. Philip had lied to Nelwina.

Her world righted itself. She hadn't committed adultery.

And Adam loved her.

Then the promise Adam had tried to extract from her last night came crashing down. He had requested that she vow not to leave him again. How could she make such a promise? She had no control over her life right now. She wondered if she ever would. Would she live like this for years, wondering when she'd find herself back in the eighteenth century? She still didn't know if sitting on the block was the only way to return. Hilda had been so vague.

"Adam." Nelwina scooted out of Adam's arms and stood up. " 'Twould be my honor if I could wed you, but I don't know if I'll be here in five minutes or five years." A sob broke from her throat and she fled the gardens.

"What the bloody hell does that mean, Nel?"

Adam's shouted words followed her as she sought refuge in the servants' room she'd shared with her mother.

"Adam?" Sophia's voice stopped him as he headed to the stairs. "What is it, dear? Where's Nel?"

"Up there." He nodded to the stairs, running a hand through his hair.

"What is it? Are you feeling ill?"

"No, Mother. Just confused."

Sophia canted her head. "About what?"

"About why Nel can't marry me. She said something about not knowing where she would be in five minutes or five years." He searched his mother's gaze. "Do you understand what she was talking about?"

"Adam, the poor thing has been through so much the last couple days. She just needs a little time to get her feet back on the ground." Sophia patted his cheek. "Would you like me to talk to her?"

Adam shook his head. "Maybe you're right. Things have been difficult for her." He kissed Sophia's cheek. "Let's give her a little time."

The morning seeped away and Nelwina sat before the window, forcing all her confusing emotions aside, trying to keep her mind empty to avoid the pain brought by thoughts of a life without Adam.

The door creaked. "Nel, dear?"

Nelwina roused herself from the chair she'd placed in front of the window and glanced over her shoulder.

Sophia poked her head inside. "There you are." She stepped inside, closing the door behind her. "I've been looking all over for you."

"Sophia, Adam asked me to marry him, formally."

"Yes?"

"Oh, Sophia." Nelwina slid from the chair and went to Sophia. " 'Twould make me the happiest of women to be Adam's wife. But . . ."

"But what, Nel? What holds you back?"

"I can't tell how long I'll be here. I could end up back where I belong tomorrow."

Sophia put her arms around Nelwina and patted her

back. "There now, Nel. Don't go on so. We must live in the moment, for none of us knows what tomorrow will bring."

Nelwina pulled out of Sophia's arms. "But—"

"No buts, dear." Sophia produced a hanky from her pocket and dried Nelwina's tears. "Do you love my son?"

"Aye, my lady, with all my heart."

"And he loves you. So I really don't see the problem. You must learn to recognize those things you can control and those you can't. You and only you can decide to marry Adam. But you can't control how long you're on this earth. Plain and simple."

Nelwina opened her mouth to speak, but Sophia put her finger against Nelwina's lips. "Just think about what I said, Nel. Take the plunge, dear. You'll see that I'm right."

Sophia was right, Nelwina conceded. Even though what Sophia was talking about was very different from what Nelwina was, the principle still applied. She could live her life waiting for a moment that might never come. Or she could grasp the happiness Adam offered her and pray it would all work out.

Sophia stood at the door. "Oh, dear, I almost forgot, Mr. Titchlark is waiting for you in the salon. The police took your passport from Philip and gave it to Adam. And he's given it to the solicitor."

Sophia must have read the confusion on Nelwina's face because she said, "It's part of the legal nonsense—they need identification."

Sophia left her then and Nelwina went along to her other room. After splashing cold water on her face and brushing her hair, she went downstairs.

"Miss Tanner, it's a pleasure to finally meet you." Dudley Titchlark shook Nelwina's hand and smiled. "Dreadful happenings yesterday. I trust you've fully recovered, then?"

"Yes, Mr. Titchlark, I'm fine." Though her insides shook, Nelwina returned his smile. She wished Sophia were with her.

"I must apologize for the delay in notifying you."

Nelwina glanced at the solicitor. "Oh?"

"Yes, you, see, my uncle passed away a few months back—"

"My condolences, sir."

He waved a hand in the air. "Quite all right, quite all right. He was in his nineties and so it wasn't unexpected. But he was a bit of a pack rat and it fell to me to clean out his office. I found Lady Spenceworth's will, or rather a portion of it, beneath the drawer of his desk."

Nelwina frowned.

"It had fallen behind the drawer, you see."

Nelwina nodded. "Yes, of course." Though she wasn't certain she understood at all.

"As a solicitor, I felt it incumbent upon me to take care of the details. So I started searching for you."

"But how did Lady Spenceworth know of me?"

"I thought that strange as well. I could find no connection between the Tanners and the Spenceworth name. Rather strange, don't you think?"

Nelwina cocked her head. Everything was strange to her; she couldn't point to any one thing being more odd than another.

Mr. Titchlark shrugged and flipped through some papers. "Now, if you'll simply sign here and here."

Nelwina took the pen he offered and started to write her name, but the print beneath the line caught her attention. Lord, she was to sign Jocelyn's name, not hers.

Sophia had mentioned the signing of documents yesterday, but Nelwina had been so distraught, she'd completely forgotten about it.

Her head started to ache.

Their signatures wouldn't match, and then what would happen? Would she be returned to America, a place totally foreign to her? Or put in prison for forgery?

And then she recalled why she was doing this. It was for Adam and Spenceworth. She just hoped it was something of value she'd inherited.

Jocelyn's passport lay open on the table. Canting her head as if she were reading the document before her, she glanced at Jocelyn's strange handwriting. One could barely make out her name.

A strange twittering sound emanating from the solicitor's pocket startled Nelwina. She glanced up as he pulled what she now knew was a cell phone from his pocket.

"Excuse me, Miss Tanner." And he turned his back, taking a few steps away from her.

Nelwina looked back down at the passport. Concentrating on the first letter of Jocelyn's name, she did her best to copy the signature. She was to sign another page as well, and she thumbed through the papers until she located a line with Jocelyn's name printed below it.

Mr. Titchlark hung up. "Sorry for the interruption." He picked up the papers, glanced at them and handed Nelwina the passport and one set of the papers. "This copy is for your files. Now." He handed her a key and, from a box, took out a wooden casket. "Here's your inheritance. Would you like to open it now?"

The cool metal key lay in the palm of Nelwina's hand as she stared at the polished wooden box. Her hand started to shake, the hairs on the back of her neck rose.

"I'm not sure." Her voice was shaky.

"I understand, Miss Tanner. You're free to open it in private if you like. But I must caution you that should the contents be of value, it would be wise to deposit it with the bank."

"Thank you for the advice, Mr. Titchlark."

"Very good, miss." He took the casket and put it back in the box and held it out to Nelwina. "If there's ever anything I can do, please don't hesitate to call on me."

Nelwina followed the solicitor out the salon door. "Thank you, sir; I shall remember that."

Nelwina carried the box to her room. Placing it on the table beside her bed, she sat down and stared at it. She should open it, she thought, but couldn't force herself to reach for the box. Her bravado of earlier deserted her.

"Nel?"

Nelwina recognized Sophia's voice and she left the box to open her door.

"Did everything go well?"

"Aye." Nelwina stepped back, allowing Sophia into the room.

"Well, dear, don't keep me in suspense. What did you inherit?"

"I haven't opened it yet."

"Well, then, why don't you bring it down to the salon. Niles and I are fairly champing at the bit."

'Tis best to get it done, Nelwina thought as she picked up the box and key. Sophia looped her arm though Nelwina's and together they went downstairs to the salon.

They entered the salon to find Niles and Adam sitting, talking quietly. Both men looked up when Sophia and Nelwina came in.

Adam gave Nelwina a tentative smile, but she read the sadness in his gray gaze. She'd hurt him terribly with the scene in the garden.

Mayhap after she discovered what was in the casket, she and Adam could have a private talk. On the way downstairs, she'd decided that she would take the plunge, as Sophia recommended. She loved Adam and the thought of life without him . . . well, it wasn't something she looked forward to.

Nelwina stood in front of the table, setting the box in the middle. She removed the wooden casket. As she inserted the key into the lock, the hairs on her arms rose and a shiver rattled up her spine.

Taking a deep breath, she turned the key and the lock opened.

She lifted the lid to expose the black velvet-lined

interior. Two black satin drawstring sacks lay in the bottom.

"What is it, my dear?" Sophia's voice came from beside Nelwina.

"I'm not certain." Her voice wavered and she cleared her throat as she lifted the smaller of the two sacks.

She pulled open the strings and shook the contents into her palm.

A pair of emerald and diamond earrings filled her hand. The pear-shaped emeralds glowed warmly in the light, while the diamonds winked happily back at her.

"My stars." The words escaped her lips on a rush of air. She looked up from the earrings and met Sophia's gaze. " 'Tis the most beautiful thing I've ever seen."

She held one up and Sophia gasped. "My goodness, Nel, they're gorgeous."

Nelwina turned to Adam.

"They're lovely, Nel." He failed to meet her gaze and Nelwina's heart squeezed against the pain she'd caused him.

Carefully, she placed the jewelry back in the sack and picked up the other one.

This one was heavier than the first. And when she pulled out an emerald pendant, she gasped again.

"My gracious." Sophia touched Nelwina's arm.

Nelwina met her shocked gaze and watched as Sophia looked at Adam.

Adam came over and stood beside Nelwina.

"They're beautiful, Nel." He frowned. "But haven't

I seen those before? They look very familiar."

Nelwina picked up the small bag and shoved both into Adam's hands. "I would like you to have them. Mayhap now you won't need those stocks to finance Spenceworth."

Adam looked at the jewels in his hands and his mouth fell open. "Nel, I can't take these."

"Yes, you can and you must. You can't lose the manor."

"But Nel—"

"No, they belong to you."

Adam shook his head. "No, they were bequeathed to you and you should keep them." He tried to hand the pendant and earrings back to her, but she stepped away.

" 'Tis because of the tours—"

"Nel, I'll find a way to support Spenceworth." He glanced at his mother, then back to Nelwina and smiled. "You two made a success of the tours, I'm sure . . ." He glanced down at the jewels in his hand and frowned, not finishing his sentence. "I know I've seen these before." He placed them back in their sacks and laid them in the box. With a distracted nod, he went to the door. "I could swear I've seen them somewhere."

Chapter Twenty

Nelwina turned from watching Adam leave and encountered Sophia's worried gaze. The older woman opened her mouth and stepped forward, but Niles touched her arm and when she glanced at him, he shook his head.

"They need to work this out, Sophia." Though he spoke in a low tone, Nelwina heard him just the same.

Niles took Sophia's elbow and escorted her from the salon, leaving Nelwina alone with the jewels and her thoughts.

She reached inside the box and emptied the sacks into the velvet interior. The emeralds let off a warm, comforting glow and Nelwina wondered why the lady of Spenceworth would bequeath something of such value to Jocelyn? Was Jocelyn a descendant? As she gazed at the jewels, she realized that though she'd wanted to give them to Adam, she couldn't. They weren't even hers. They were Jocelyn's.

But who, exactly, was this woman? Nelwina's

thoughts circled around again. And why the inheritance?

Something niggled at her mind. Teasing her. There was something she wasn't seeing here and she felt it was the key to understanding everything.

She placed the emeralds back in their sacks. As she put the smallest bag in the box, she saw a bit of ribbon peeking from between the side and the bottom.

Curious, she pulled on it and a small loop of ribbon appeared. She pulled again and the bottom came up, exposing the wooden base of the box and a folded piece of paper.

Nelwina removed the paper and smoothed it out.

Dear Nelwina,

I wonder how you're faring in my time? Has your adjustment been as difficult for you as mine was for me? Hilda told me that I was having an easier time than you were and after thinking about it, I must agree. I had the benefit of prior knowledge. You, poor thing, have been tossed into a world of the unknown. I do hope you're managing okay.

Nelwina sat down in the chair beside the table, her mind tumbling over the beginning of the letter. A letter addressed to her.

I'd better get to the explanation of the jewelry. I realized that you might find yourself in financially difficult times; you probably wouldn't be able to take over my job in America. These em-

*eralds are to ensure your financial independence
as I mean to stay here in the eighteenth century.
It was a difficult decision, I tried to take into
consideration how it would affect you, but in the
end my heart decided.*

Please find happiness, Nelwina, as I have.

Love,

Jocelyn Tanner

Countess of Spenceworth

(don't you just love it, a countess!)

*P.S. I'm enclosing the information on my bank
accounts. The money is there for you to use at
your discretion.*

Nelwina read the letter over several times before
her mind could grasp it all.

She laughed and, jumping to her feet, she spun in
a circle in the middle of the room. She clutched the
letter in her hand and stopped.

She had to show Jocelyn's letter to Adam. She had
to tell him she loved him, that she would never leave
him.

Adam sat down in his chair and stared morosely
around the study, glancing down at the stack of journals on his desk.

He wasn't certain what the journal entries really
meant, other than the fact that Nel had known about
a servant's child.

But how? Maybe he should give this past-life belief
a bit more consideration.

He snorted. He'd become as daft as his mother.

His gaze landed on the back of the picture he'd brought down from the attic. He'd meant to show it to Nel and ask where she thought it should hang. But with everything that had happened, he'd completely forgotten about it.

Adam got up and went to the picture, turning it around.

Bloody hell.

The emeralds adorning the woman's neck and ears were the same as the ones Nel had in the box.

Now he knew where he'd seen them before.

Damn, but what did it all mean? How was Nel connected to Lady Spenceworth?

Maybe Nel could answer that question. He left his study.

Nelwina rushed from the salon and nearly knocked Adam down as she flew around the corner.

"Adam—"

"Nel, I've got to show—"

"Look." She waved Jocelyn's letter in his face. "You must read this, Adam."

"Later, Nel. Right now, you've got to see what I found in one of the servants' rooms."

He grabbed her wrist and pulled her toward his study.

She tugged on his arm. "But Adam, you must read this letter."

"In a minute, Nel." He opened the study door. "Look at this."

They stood before a portrait and Nel gasped.

"See? Amazing, isn't it?"

"That's . . . that's . . . m—me." The room started to

spin and Nelwina clutched Adam's arm. "Oh, my God." She blinked at the painting, her eyes burning with unshed tears. "Adam, that is my body." She enunciated the words slowly, carefully. "The gray eyes. Those are my gray eyes."

Adam looked from Nel to the woman in the portrait and shook his head, frustration tightening his jaw.

"No, Nel. I mean, look at the emeralds around her neck."

Nelwina moved her focus from the familiar gray eyes staring back at her to the necklace hanging about the woman's neck. It was the same.

She smiled as she gazed into Jocelyn's eyes. Scanning the picture, she noted that the woman in the painting was thinner than Nelwina remembered her body being. Obviously she didn't have a taste for food, Nelwina thought. But it was Jocelyn's body now and she was welcome to do with it as she wished.

Nelwina's smile widened. As she had done with Jocelyn's body. She ran a hand over her hips and laughed.

What was wrong with Nel? Adam wondered as he watched her changing facial expressions. She'd gone from shock to happiness to total insanity. And now she was laughing. He glanced between the picture and Nel. She shoved the paper at him.

"You must read this." The words came out in gasps, her laughter rolling around the room.

Absently he took the paper, his gaze on Nel. Was she okay?

He glanced down at the paper, his eyes scanning the writing. He reached the bottom.

Jocelyn Tanner Warrick, Duchess of Spenceworth.

His gaze flew to Nel's face, her lips stretched in a silly grin. She rocked back on her heels, giggles erupting from her throat.

He turned back to the paper and this time he read it thoroughly. With each word his amazement grew.

"Do you know what this means?" Adam looked up from the letter, his voice barely a croak.

Nel nodded, her brown hair bouncing with the movement, her face alight with joy.

"Oh, my God." He rubbed his face. "You actually . . ." He couldn't put it into words. It was just too fantastic.

"Aye. I really did switch times and bodies with Jocelyn Tanner."

Adam shook his head.

"Aye. I truly did live at Spenceworth, in another life." She giggled again, clapping her hands. " 'Tis wondrous, isn't it, Adam? And now I know," she said, glancing at the picture, "I'll be staying in this time."

Adam needed to sit down, but before he could act on his need, his mother flew into the study. Niles followed at a more sedate pace.

"What is going on, Adam?" She looked from him to Nel. "Nel?"

"Oh, my lady, just look." She pointed to the painting. " 'Tis Jocelyn." She tugged the letter from Adam's fingers. "And she wrote me a letter, my lady." She handed it to Sophia.

Adam's mother scanned the letter and smiled benignly as she handed it back to Nelwina.

"Mother, I don't think you realize the full extent of it."

"Oh, pish posh, dear."

Nelwina touched Adam's arm. "Now your financial worries are over."

Adam looked at Nel, frowning. "What do you mean?"

"You can use these to take care of the manor."

"You most certainly will not, Adam Warrick. I will not see those jewels leave this family."

"Mother, I would never take Nel's inheritance or sell family jewels."

"Good." Sophia nodded. "Besides, you won't need it."

"Oh?" Adam raised his eyebrows and then he remembered the tours. "I think the tours will at least support the manor. Maybe I'll take a loan out to make the necessary repairs."

"You won't need a loan. As soon as my flat sells, you'll have what you need. Or at least a good start."

"Your flat sells? Mother, I won't take your money."

"Well, it isn't my money, Adam. I made the payments using the money you've sent me over the years." She glanced at Niles and he nodded to her. "So, you see, it was your money that bought the flat, therefore it will be your money when I sell it."

"But where will you live?" A sudden thought hit him. His mother was planning to move to Spenceworth. This was too much.

Niles cleared his throat, drawing Adam's attention. "Lord Spenceworth, I had hoped Sophia would live with me. I've a small house just outside of Ramsgil."

Shock rattled through Adam's body. His mother living with a man? His eyes rounded as he looked from Niles to his mother.

Sophia stepped back beside Niles and looped her arm with his and beamed at Adam. "Don't look so shocked, Adam. Niles and I are engaged."

"Oh, Sophia." Nel rushed to his mother's side. "Felicitations to you both." She hugged Sophia and then Niles.

It was more than Adam could handle. He ran his hands through his hair and shook his head. Didn't anyone realize how extraordinary Nel's presence was?

He glanced at his mother's beaming face and smiled. Later he'd ponder all this. For now, he'd enjoy his mother's happiness.

"Congratulations, Mother." He hugged her, kissing her cheek. "And Niles." He stuck out his hand and the older man gave him a firm shake. "I hope you know what you're in for."

Niles grinned and nodded. "Yes, I believe I do." He took Sophia's hand. "Now, Sophia, let's leave these two alone." He gave Adam a conspiratorial wink. "They've some things to work out, I suspect."

"Of course, Niles." She grinned at Adam. "Birdie Higginbotham will never find me now. I'll be free of the old bird at last." She laughed as Niles led her out the door.

With the exit of the older couple, Adam's study was silent. He stared at the closed door. His mother's engagement didn't come as a surprise to him. Niles had been attentive and understanding, not to mention tolerant of her crazy ways. And they'd work out the sale of her flat.

What amazed him was his mother's lack of reaction to Nel's letter. She was taking this all in stride and he wondered at her sanity. But if he questioned hers, he'd have to question his own. Because he believed it all. What else could he do when presented with all the evidence?

He turned to meet Nel's smiling face.

"I'm so happy for them. They're perfect together, don't you think?" She canted her head.

"Yes." He smiled, glancing at the closed door. "I don't recall seeing my mother glow like that."

He turned to Nel, the smile dropping from his lips. In light of all this, he could understand, at least a bit, why Nel had dashed from the garden earlier. Dare he ask her again?

Stupid question, he thought. If he had to ask her every day for the rest of his life, it would be worth it.

Taking her hand, he led her to a chair. She sat down, a puzzled frown on her face.

"What is it, Adam?"

He reached across his desk and picked up the velvet box and for the second time that day, went down on one knee before her.

Tears sparkled in her eyes and she nibbled on her lower lip.

"And for the second time today, Nelwina Honeycutt, I ask you, will you marry me?"

Nel blessed him with a tender smile.

"Yes." She hugged his neck. "Yes, 'twould be *my*

honor to wed with you, Lord Spenceworth."

Their lips met in a tender kiss, filled with the promise of love forever.

He took the ring from the box and placed it on her finger. "You were meant to be my bride, my Spenceworth bride."

The
Very Virile Viking
SANDRA HILL

Magnus Ericsson is a simple man. He loves the smell of fresh-turned dirt after springtime plowing. He loves the heft of a good sword in his fighting arm. But, Holy Thor, what he does not relish is the bothersome brood of children he's been saddled with. Or the mysterious happenstance that strands him and his longship full of maddening offspring in a strange new land—the kingdom of *Holly Wood*. Here is a place where the blazing sun seems to bake his already befuddled brain, where the folks think he is an act-whore (whatever that is), and the woman of his dreams fails to accept that he is her soul mate . . . a man of exceptional talents, not to mention a very virile Viking.

DOMINION
MELANIE JACKSON

When the Great One gifts Domitien with love, it is not simply for a lifetime. Yet in his first incarnation, his wife and unborn child are murdered, and Dom swears never again to feel such pain. When Death comes, he goes willingly. The Creator sends him back to Earth, to learn love in another body. Yet life after life, Dom refuses. Whatever body she wears, he vows to have his true love back. He will explain why her dreams are haunted by glimpses of his face, aching remembrances of his lips. He will protect her from the enemy he failed to destroy so many years before. And he will chase her through the ages to do so. This time, their love will rule.

NIGHT VISITOR

MELANIE JACKSON

All self-respecting Scots know of the massacre and of the brave piper who gave his life so that some of its defenders might live. But few see his face in their sleep, his sad gray eyes touching their souls, his warm hands caressing them like a lover's. And Tafaline is willing to wager that none have heard his sweet voice. But he was slain so long ago. How is it possible that he now haunts her dreams? Are they true, those fairy tales that claim a woman of MacLeod blood can save a man from even death? Is it true that when she touched his bones, she bound herself to his soul? Yes, it is Malcolm "the piper" who calls to her insistently, across the winds of night and time . . . and looking into her heart, Taffy knows there is naught to do but go to him.

___52423-6 $5.50 US/$6.50 CAN

Embers of Time

Eugenia Riley

In the aftermath of the second great war, two lonely people are destined to meet in the splendor of Charleston, South Carolina. He is a handsome RAF pilot; she is a beautiful young army nurse. Each has known the horror of war and both have experienced devastating loss, the death of a beloved child in a recent, tragic fire.

But are the children really lost? Even as Adrian and Vickie forge a deep bond, both are haunted by poignant glimpses of the children's ghosts in the Charleston streets, visions that soon lead the couple back to search for the children in an earlier time. There, they discover a city as grand and mysterious as time itself, and a miracle that will heal their wounded hearts.

___52408-2 $5.99 US/$6.99 CAN

Dorchester Publishing Co., Inc.
P.O. Box 6640
Wayne, PA 19087-8640

Please add $2.50 for shipping and handling for the first book and $.75 for each book thereafter. NY, and PA residents, please add appropriate sales tax. No cash, stamps, or C.O.D.s. All orders shipped within 6 weeks via postal service book rate.

Canadian orders require $2.00 extra postage and must be paid in U.S. dollars through a U.S. banking facility.

Name _____
Address _____
City_____ State_____ Zip_____
I have enclosed $_____ in payment for the checked book(s).
Payment <u>must</u> accompany all orders. ☐ Please send a free catalog.
CHECK OUT OUR WEBSITE! www.dorchesterpub.com

THE PLEASURE MASTER

NINA BANGS

Stranded by the side of a New York highway on Christmas Eve, hairdresser Kathy Bartlett wishes herself somewhere warm and peaceful with a subservient male at her side. She finds herself transported all right, but to Scotland in 1542 with the last man she would have chosen.

With the face of a dark god or a fallen angel, and the reputation of being able to seduce any woman, Ian Ross is the kind of sexual expert Kathy avoids like the plague. So when she learns that the men in his family are competing to prove their prowess, she sprays hair mousse on his brothers' "love guns" and swears she will never succumb to the explosive attraction she feels for Ian. But as the competition heats up, neither Kathy nor Ian reckon the most powerful aphrodisiac of all: love.

___52445-7 $5.50 US/$6.50 CAN

VIRTUAL WARRIOR
ANN LAWRENCE

Where does reality end and fantasy begin? With a computerized game that leads to another world? At the fingertips of a bedraggled old man who claims he can perform magic? Or in the amber gaze of an ice princess in dire need of rescuing? As the four moons of Tolemac rise upon a harsh land vastly different from his own, hard-headed pragmatist Neil Scott discovers a life worth struggling for, principles worth fighting for. But only one woman can convince him that love is worth dying for, that he must make the leap of faith to become a virtual warrior.

Dorchester Publishing Co., Inc.
P.O. Box 6640
Wayne, PA 19087-8640

_52492-9
$5.99 US/$7.99 CAN

Name: _____

Address: _____

City: _____ State: _____ Zip: _____

E-mail: _____

I have enclosed $_____ in payment for the checked book(s).

For more information on these books, check out our website at www.dorchesterpub.com.
_____ _Please send me a free catalog._

Ann Lawrence

Lord Of The Mist

As he kneels in the darkened chapel by his wife's lifeless body, he knows the babe she has birthed cannot be his. Then the scent of spring—blossoms, wet leaves, damp earth—precedes an alluring woman into the chapel. As she honors his dead wife with garlands, she seems to bring him fresh hope, just as she nourishes the little girl his wife has left behind.

Even though this woman is not his, can it be wrong to reach out for life, for love? He cannot deny his longing for her lush kiss, cannot ignore her urge to turn away from yesterday's sorrows and embrace tomorrow's sweetness.

___52443-0 $5.99 US/$6.99 CAN

TESS MALLORY
HIGHLAND DREAM

When Jix Ferguson's dream reveals that her best friend is making a terrible mistake and marrying the wrong guy, she tricks Samantha into flying to Scotland. There the two women met the man Jix is convinced her friend should marry—Jamie MacGregor. He is handsome, smart, perfect . . . the only problem is, Jix falls for him, too. Then a slight scuffle involving the Scot's ancestral sword sends all three back to the start of the seventeenth century—where MacGregors are outlaws and hunted. All Jix has to do is marry Griffin Campbell, steal Jamie's sword back from their captor, and find a way to return herself and her friends to their own time. Oh yeah, and she has to fall in love. It isn't going to be easy, but in this matter of the heart, Jix knows she'll laugh last.

___52444-9 $5.50 US/$6.50 CAN

Susan Plunkett

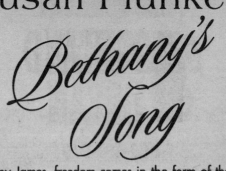

Bethany's Song

For Bethany James, freedom comes in the form of the River of Time, sweeping her away from her old life to 1895. But on awakening in Juneau, Alaska, Bethany discovers a whole new batch of problems. For one thing, she has been separated from her sisters—the only ones with whom she shares perfect harmony. And the widowed mine-owner who finds her—Matthew Gray—is hardly someone with whom she expects to connect. Yet struggling to survive, drawing on every skill she possesses, the violet-eyed beauty finds herself growing into a stronger person. She is learning to trust, learning to love. And in helping Matt do the same, Bethany realizes the laments of the past are only too soon made the sweet strains of happiness.

___52463-5 $5.50 US/$6.50 CAN

Dorchester Publishing Co., Inc.
P.O. Box 6640
Wayne, PA 19087-8640

Please add $2.50 for shipping and handling for the first book and $.75 for each book thereafter. NY and PA residents, please add appropriate sales tax. No cash, stamps, or C.O.D.s. All orders shipped within 6 weeks via postal service book rate.
Canadian orders require $2.00 extra postage and must be paid in U.S. dollars through a U.S. banking facility.

Name_____
Address_____
City_____ State_____ Zip_____
I have enclosed $_____in payment for the checked book(s).
Payment <u>must</u> accompany all orders. ☐Please send a free catalog.
CHECK OUT OUR WEBSITE! www.dorchesterpub.com